A Just Cause

Howard S. Ford

Auburn, NY

Cover Painting:
'Writing the Declaration of Independence, 1776'
Jean Leon Gerome Ferris (1863-1930)

For information on this title contact:
Downtown Books Publishing
66 Genesee Street
Auburn, NY 13021
(315) 515-3411
www.downtownbooksandcoffee.com

ISBN: 978-0-615-92907-1

INTRODUCTION

WHEN THE AMERICAN Colonists first heard of the battles at Lexington and Concord, they were vitally disturbed because this was the first bloodletting both sides suffered over the clashes regarding the mercantile hold Britain had over them. America was bountiful with products, such as iron ore, timber, codfish, grain, and other goods which the Navigation Acts forced them to sell to Britain exclusively, and they had to be exported to the mother country in British ships.

Since the prices were established by agents, producers were paid with a credit balance rather than cash, giving the sellers of English manufactured goods a monopoly on subsequent sales. It followed that the colonists were bound to sell at prices fixed by the buyer and to buy what they were not allowed to manufacture, at the seller's high price thus using the credit. They could have done much better if the British middleman was out of the cycle.

That was the crux of the argument: that sort of unfair arrangement is what generates wars; whether they are branded under the mask of religious, racial, or pure aggressive instincts, the politics are almost always economic.

The British government had spent an enormous amount in the so-called Seven Years War, (the French and Indian War here). The last of them was world-wide in which Britain obtained Canada and interests in India. But there were four such wars extending back to 1689, and suddenly, the government insisted that Americans pay a large share of this total because a significant amount of the fighting and expenses occurred in North America.

Up to the coronation of George the third, the ministry had practiced "Silent Neglect," and now the new young, untried king wanted to place a high tax on the colonists. The ministry thought, "why not?" The total taxes imposed on them were only one twenty-sixth of what the average English taxpayer paid.

At first, a tax on playing cards, pamphlets, diplomas, and legal documents was imposed and it had to be paid in specie, or hard money, requiring many to wipe out their cash because they bartered or used paper currency and had to convert it to specie to pay the tax—a cost in itself—the government intentionally didn't mint enough specie, especially for the colonial economy. The Stamp Tax was repealed due to economic forces, but it was followed by a set of taxes on paints, glass, lead, paper, and tea. It was repealed for the same reasons, except for the tea, to emphasize government's right to tax. In all cases whatsoever was the rule; the strict phrase was used over and over. As some of the taxes were used to pay the governor's salary, this was resented because, for years, the colonists had worked to control him by paying it themselves.

The inspection of ships, warehouses, even barns, for contraband and resulting import duties were made more thorough and penalties for non-payment were more severe. John Hancock, the wealthy importer and merchant, allegedly owed the government over £100,000 sterling, but they couldn't legally catch him even though one of his ships was held hostage. Finally, the Sons of Liberty organized its most notable outrage by dumping numerous casks of tea overboard in Boston Harbor in December of 1773. Other port cities repeated this action. Parliament threw the book at Boston by closing the port and shutting down its legislature. The attorney general, judges, sheriffs and justices of the peace had to be approved by the General Gage, the newly appointed governor, and town meetings and their agendas also had to be accepted by him.

Of course, the military sent several more regiments to control British interests. While those in control of the government thought resentment was merely local in New England, other colonies sent food and welcome necessities to the beleaguered residents of the seaport. They reasoned that if the government could treat Boston harshly, it could do the same to them.

General Gage sent a thousand troops marching to close-by villages to find stored military supplies and to arrest and bring in Sam

Adams and John Hancock, but the armaments and the two "rabble rousers" had been hidden out of harm's way. That's when the populace from a wide radius rose up and confounded the redcoats at Lexington and later that day at Concord. The musketry of the minutemen was so deadly that reinforcements had to buttress the British battalion and they realized that the "bumpkins" had the spirit to embarrass the professional soldiers.

At that point in our history, Americans had to decide which side they were on, and the four main characters in my novel, "Some Call it Treason" chose to be rebellionists, even though three were English visitors. It was one of the most serious decisions that we made and many Americans thought and argued their way to be heroes or fought to immortality.

The second novel of the trilogy is a sequel to the first called "In all Cases Whatsoever," the phrase coined by Parliament to show their arrogance and firm belief in their rectitude compared to that of the rebels. We were at war against the strongest nation in the world and we weren't named the United States yet; we had no organized army or navy, no armaments, and no taxing powers to pay for them. General Washington's staunch defense during the first six months of fighting dismayed many fervent rebels but his strategy at Trenton and Princeton at Christmas time of '76 raised our hopes and dampened General Howe's.

Resentment against the British army for plundering the farms in New Jersey for forage and valued items persuaded even Tories so that one couldn't guess that skirmishes between redcoats and rebels would require as many as a thousand men on each side rather than just a few. The Howe brother's conciliatory efforts backfired and their difficult-to-replace soldiers were killed, wounded, or captured. So numerous were these skirmishes that the total number of casualties were as large as full-sized battles, and these continued during the winter when European military protocol called for cessation of armed conflict.

The larger battles like Saratoga, Brandywine (the loss of Philadelphia) including the fiasco at Germantown, were headline stories. Please notice that the British lost an entire army at Saratoga, and eight months later, abandoned Philadelphia as they decided it had no military value. The British retired to New York, were harassed at the Monmouth battle on the way, and with all their pomp and bluster, were back where they started two years before with only New York City under their control. These battles are covered in these pages.

My friends, Crispin, Trevor Shaw, and Chief Honeoye, and I were at Saratoga, and we were shelled for three weeks at the siege of Fort Stanwix before the Tories, redcoats and Iroquois gave up and dissolved back into the north woods. Most of the balance of Revolutionary battles took place in the South so that we only read about the 'to and fro' desolation in the Carolinas and the final artillery duel at Yorktown that spelled the end of the English Empire as it affected the United States.

Our exploits at home and in the field, from the end of the fore mentioned siege, Saratoga, and decimating the Iroquois in 1779, are the contents of this chronicle. I hope that you approve and enjoy reading about what we did.

A Just Cause

CHAPTER ONE

BOOM! BANG! BOOM! Each cannonade was close enough to blow my ears out; they were hammering our stockade walls, getting closer, and persisted for three weeks. Just as it was beginning to break through, the barrage stopped unaccountably, and the enemy swarm gave up the siege of Fort Stanwix. At first the Indians, then the redcoats and Tories fled in disarray through the woods back towards the eastern shore of Oneida Lake.

Several days later we received our first mail in several months and both my letters were from Chatham. The first was from Olivia, my bride of twenty months:

Dear Jamie,

    This is to tell you that loves' labor is not lost---I am pregnant and the baby is due in March. Doctor Iverson kindly examined me and said that all is well, I am healthy and well able to give birth, I could have told him that! I hope that by March, this war is over and that you will be home and able to conduct yourself as a father.
    The population of Chatham and Morristown has diminished quickly since Washington and his army have gone south to Pennsylvania, having finally located General Howe off the Virginia Capes, and most recently at the Head of Elk in Chesapeake Bay. Howe's destination is Philadelphia and the armies are gathering thirty miles west of that city to do battle. The papers are excited about the coming collision and especially about a coterie of young

1

Frenchmen, the leader of whom is a nobleman and friend of King Louis, known as the Marquis of Lafayette, who has joined General Washington's forces. Congress has scattered to Lancaster and I read that the Liberty Bell has been sequestered else-where for safekeeping. The latest we have heard is that Burgoyne has easily taken Ticonderoga and is on his way soon to reach the Hudson with Albany and New England as his targets.

Fort Stanwix is under siege by the British, Tories, and Indians, but their cannons are not powerful enough to breach the walls of the fort. You probably are aware of all this. It seems that events of great importance are on the brink of completion with the lives of our countrymen at stake. I pray for the wisdom and safety of General Washington, General Schuyler, your commander, Colonel Gansevoort and Colonel Marinus Willett. With men like this, how can we fail?

Arabella is knocking on my door to go shopping in Morristown—I'd better go now. You know how prompt she feels everyone must be.

> *Love,*
> *Your Olivia*

The other letter was from John Hawkins:

Dear Jamie,

I must chance sending this information to you. I have found out the names of the two men who killed my father and younger brother and plundered our farm. They are Robert Trainor and Bartholomew "Bart" Dickson. They are in the New Jersey militia and are ordered to Albany in defense of the area against General Burgoyne. They should arrive during the first week in September. I may be transferred there, too. If so, I will look you up and proceed accordingly.

Trainor is tall, blonde, has a mean face and a cleft chin. Dickson is dark-haired, short, humming most of the time, and well educated. They are friends and together most of the time.

Keep your eyes opened for them. Sic semper tyrannis!

Your friend,
John Hawkins

So, I was to be a father soon. I know nothing about taking care of babies or spanking-new mothers. My brother Jonathan was born when I was only three. The only thing I learned then was that I was jealous of the attention my parents lavished on him.

Olivia seems to be pleased and able to look forward to the birth and having a baby for company. I hope it's a boy. This war isn't going to last forever and when I finally get home again it will be fun introducing a son, or a daughter, to the arts and intrigues of the world.

I damned well ought to get home. I've been lucky so far. And now we have survived yet another scrape with the enemy; this time, it's with Indians along with the British and Tories.

For my friends and I, the remarkable fact was that we all came through the siege safe, successful, and satisfied. As Doctor Honeoye (also known as Chief Honeoye) suspected from his snooping at the Indian's encampment, Joseph Brant and his Indians would abandon the siege and General St. Leger had no alternative but to withdraw his regulars and Loyalists back to their boats at the beach on Oneida Lake. Indeed, if the general hadn't withdrawn, he would have been the only combatant remaining, as his men were fleeing with their former Indian comrades in arms. As we watched from the ramparts, it had become every man for himself.

Colonel Willet had been sent to Stillwater on the Hudson to request reinforcements from General Schuyler. General Benedict Arnold volunteered to lead this brigade and was on the way up the Mohawk Valley to relieve the fort. Surprisingly, he was delayed by a military trial at Fort Dayton.

The reason for this was that a few Tories had gone to German Flats to enlist more recruits for an uprising but were captured in the act and indicted. One of them, Hon Yost, a young white man who dressed and lived as an Indian, was weak-minded but claimed to receive messages from birds, trees, rocks, and the Great Spirit himself. We had been introduced to him in the woods by Thomas Spencer, an Oneida scout, before the siege began and Yost seemed distracted, but harmless.

I talked with Sergeant David Campbell, who was one of Arnold's soldiers on the scene. Though he was at Fort Dayton and Fort Stanwix only briefly, he described what happened: "The Tories were tried as spies, and the ringleaders were to be sent to Albany for their sentences to be carried out. Hon Yost's mother and brother pleaded for clemency for him with some success. Arnold concocted a hoax using this muddled-minded young man to run into the Indian camp, as if escaping from confinement, to report that Arnold was coming soon with a vast army, "as many as the leaves on the trees" and with new, deadly weapons. No quarter was to be given, and the news was spread that Burgoyne had already surrendered.

"To make the threat more credible, some Oneidas volunteered to follow him with the same story, and shot holes in their clothing to suggest their hairbreadth escape and the necessary haste to flee. The success of this gambit would free Hon Yost and his brother who was held hostage."

Spencer had told us about Hon Yost, but the story of the Indian's gullibility was incredible."You mean to say that the Indians abandoned a three-week effort that was important to them based on the frenzied statements of one man, a man who was considered weak-minded?" I asked.

Campbell explained, "Yeah. What made the hoax possible is that Indians are superstitious and believe such revelations from the mentally ill. They put the same faith in dreams even if it demands that they hazard death. The hoax worked so well that our brigade didn't even have to engage the enemy to end what began here. Evidently, they were so despondent because of their losses at Oriskany, their lack of prized possessions due to Willett's raid, the lack of sleep with no blankets, and they resented St. Leger talking them into joining the British and staging the ambush. They lost a lot of warriors and can't afford this kind of drain on their resources."

The Indians abandoned the siege which, according to Chief Honeoye's spying, we thought they were about to do anyway, and the regulars and Tories followed.

Days later, Arnold marched his troops, including some of ours, back to the Hudson where they could best be used to hamstring Burgoyne's invasion.

Charles Chipping's body lay only a hundred feet from the gate. He was tomahawked and scalped when he ran out to single-handedly challenge the enemy to attack us (Chipping was a British army major who had deserted and fled to the fort when St. Leger's vanguard first appeared. He had been frustrated by his inability to find and take vengeance on Trevor.) But no one felt the need to recover his remains.

That the siege of the last three weeks was finally over and the constant artillery barrage had ceased were the most important concerns of all of us at the fort. It was so abrupt a change after the long impasse that Colonel Gansevoort warned everyone that it might be a strategic trick and to be cautious.

After only a few hours he allowed the main gate to be opened and Trevor and Crispin were sent out with detachments to the west and north for signs of lingering braves. They returned having seen nothing except the trash left by angst-ridden besiegers. Scouts sent south and east reported the same conditions.

Daphne, Chipping's widow, cried after seeing the brutal evidence that her estranged husband had finally brought about his own death. She insisted that Gansevoort send a detail to bring him in so that Christian rites could be performed, and the sight of his mutilated remains could be purged from her memory. Trevor and Crispin, Chief Honeoye and I, as well as Daphne and the colonel, who officiated, were the only ones attending the brief ceremony.

Cleanup of the fort and surroundings after the siege took two weeks, including the time to finish burying our garrison's dead, of whom there were forty; perhaps more. Captain Gregg, who had been scalped, still survives after already enduring more than thirty days of convalescence. Others in the infirmary had mortar-shell wounds, burns, dysentery, and there was one case of scurvy.

Surprisingly, the Indians had not destroyed our corn, squash, pumpkins, peas, or cabbage so that edibles were gathered from the garden and brought in. Forage for our horses was almost gone and farmers went out to save as much of the trampled hay as could be recovered. They reseeded fields in the hope that the remaining season would be benign enough to grow another crop to last the coming winter.

Crews that had felled trees, but had been interrupted by roving Indians just before the siege began, went out to finish their work. Timbers were sawn and stacked in the wagons and brought in. Early September nights were disarmingly chilly despite the warmth of the autumn sun.

Trevor, Chief Honeoye, Crispin, and I were again sent out in a larger sweep to round up any lingering Indians or Tories, but there were none; the siege was definitely over. St. Leger's regulars had left the scene almost as fast as the tribes, and garrison duty returned to tedium for the few remaining days of a wet summer.

Colonel Gansevoort had stood up to the arrogant and threatening enemy but his main concern now was that Chief Brant might seek vengeance on the Oneidas for scouting and fighting on our side. If he raided their nearby villages would he make another attack on Fort Stanwix? He wondered.

We made our report. "Our Oneida scouts said that their main castle, fifteen miles to the southwest, had been raided and burned but few Oneidas were killed and most of the village could easily be rebuilt before winter. General Schuyler has offered them pine boards from his mill and it appears that Brant has refrained from more mischief; they say he's returned to his longhouse at Oquaga."

With this concern removed, the Colonel took leave on board a Durham boat for Albany where his fiancée, daughter of the socially prominent Van Schaik family, was awaiting his arrival. Colonel Willett was in charge of the garrison until Gansevoort returned.

A combination of events had brought about the dissolution of the invading army, some planned, some due to the incompetence of a Hessian detachment of Burgoyne's army a hundred miles east, and some a result of the Indian mindset.

The first of these was the attempt by the Tryon County militia under General Herkimer to reinforce the garrison of the fort. I spoke with one of the survivors who hesitated to speak of the disaster, he felt so guilty by surviving when many of his friends and neighbors did not.

"Word got to Joseph Brant that our force of eight hundred men and boys was on the way from Fort Dayton and would cross the Mohawk River at Deerfield and follow a wagon road near the small Indian village of Oriska. On the fifth day of the siege, Brant and his collection of savages, army regulars, Sir John Johnson's Greens and Butler's Rangers, set out from their siege line to take concealed positions about six miles from the fort near where the road descends a small defile, to ambush our column.

"Herkimer wanted to proceed cautiously and be certain that his messengers got word to Colonel Gansevoort that help was on the way. Three cannon shots from the fort were to be a positive answer. But some of his officers wanted to move the mile-long column at a faster pace and even accused Herkimer of cowardice because of his cautionary stance. We were slowed by four hundred ox carts of supplies in the middle of the column but, even so, his officers expected a more spirited approach.

"After days of such abuse and against his better judgment, the general discarded his caution and we stumbled into the ambush the next day. We were attacked when the column was beginning to leave the low point of the defile, and it caught us off guard and was a complete surprise. It was well planned and executed: their braves were so well concealed that our sixty Oneida scouts failed to detect them waiting to pounce."

My informant adjusted the blood-stained sling supporting his arm before he continued. "At about ten in the morning, the enemy fired at us from close range and secure cover with terrible effect. Unlike their standard practice, the British and Loyalists fought Indian style, aiming at individuals and firing at will rather than only when and where an officer ordered. Much of the fighting was hand-to-hand and father against son, neighbor versus neighbor; the hatred was that bad.

"After an hour of intense mayhem, a thunderstorm drenched everyone and wet the priming of both sides. The fighting ceased for almost an hour and when it stopped raining, we resumed firing, but it was sporadic and finally slacked off entirely.

"Early on, General Herkimer had been wounded in the leg and tumbled from his horse which had also been shot. His aids propped him astride his saddle on a slight rise under a beech tree where he calmly smoked his pipe and gave directions to the men protecting him in a defensive circle."

I interrupted here. "That morning, August sixth, all four of Herkimer's runner's appeared at the fort and told us that supplies and help were on the way. They said they had been delayed by having to evade Indians in the woods the night before. We fired the gun shots to show that we were ready to collaborate with the militia. You probably never heard the shots because of the commotion."

"No we didn't, there was too much going on to notice anything else." he said.

"The ambush also explained the enemy's shortened siege line, so Colonel Willett led a two-hundred fifty man sortie to fire on and plunder the camps of the Indians and the British. We had with us a field piece, and three wagons which we filled several times with packs of blankets, food, camping utensils, clothes, medicine bundles and other good-luck charms. We also came away with Sir John Johnson's private and official papers, firearms, and camp equipment; twenty-one wagon loads in all! We returned six times with the wagons before not daring to press our luck any further. Not a man of Willett's force was even injured!"

My informant listened politely to my account of that day, despite his fatigue, before falling back to sleep sprawled on the cot in the infirmary.

The ambush had important military consequences: the tribes lost far more warriors than they could afford, many of them were chiefs and sachems who could direct them in war and guide them at sacred ceremonies. Since Indians preferred fighting free of most clothing, they'd left their usual garb at camp. Those and their blankets were part of the booty plundered on the raid; they severely missed these during the cool nights. The loss deprived them of sleep, and dampened morale. Honeoye's snooping revealed this, Crispin said.

Instead of piling up plunder from the fort and the valley, as they had been promised by St. Leger, the braves lost valuable possessions, the lives of fellow warriors, confidence in their military prowess diminished, and with the Oneidas fighting on our side, their more than two-hundred-year-old confederacy showed signs that it was beginning to disintegrate.

General Burgoyne had problems, too. He had started out from Montreal with almost eight thousand men, including his regulars, Loyalists, Hessians, a few Canadians, and as many as a thousand Indians, mostly from the Upper Lakes. He had easily taken Fort

Ticonderoga by threatening to bombard the fort from a nearby mountain top, a danger that was an acknowledged possibility but ignored by successive rebel commanders. General St. Clair knew of the danger but had little time to forestall it in the brief period he was commander before Burgoyne's confrontation. Rather than lose his army, he chose to abandon the fortress. It was the better decision but he and General Schuyler were blamed for the loss of the important fort. Burgoyne had been told that the area was saturated with Loyalists, especially around Skenesboro at the head of Lake Champlain. Allegedly they were lusting to serve His Majesty and some had pursued rebel troops fleeing from Ticonderoga. But few materialized or made any significant effort.

By the end of July, Burgoyne was only fifty miles from Albany where he was to link up with General Howe who was thought to be coming up the Hudson. Burgoyne became more confident and it was later revealed that he had made a bet in London the previous winter that he would be in Albany by the coming Christmas.

He began to have trouble with his Indians who were led by St. Luc la Corne, a half-breed who for the better part of his sixty-six years had directed bloody raids and campaigns against the British in the French Wars. Burgoyne had given a speech to his Indians at Cumberland Head on Lake Champlain directing them to not scalp non-combatants such as women, the elderly, and children unless they were found dead.

In the same speech he warned the colonists that if they didn't lay down their arms, he would "give stretch" to the Indians and presented a schedule of cash bounties to be paid for scalps. Even London papers scorned such pompous hypocrisy. Of course, the Indians were confused by these opposing directions and ignored the general's naive expectations.

After Ticonderoga, the hardest part of his campaign was getting from the southern tip of Lake Champlain at Skenesboro through twenty-two miles of a swampy, forested area to Fort Edward on the Hudson. Burgoyne could have taken the easier Lake George route, which had been used on most forays by the English and French in the past. But he reasoned that it would appear that he was backtracking to his troops, because he would have to go north before again going south, an operation which he thought would lower morale. And he would still have nine miles more to get to the Hudson by that way.

Philip Skene, a Tory and large landowner whose mansion Burgoyne used as his headquarters, encouraged the general to cut a road through the shorter, more direct distance to Fort Edward via Fort Anne. Short as it was, the path was through a swamp and virgin forest. The road would also be convenient to develop Skene's large acreage after the war, and some cynics think that's what motivated Skene's suggestion.

General Philip Schuyler soon heard of Burgoyne's plans, and to slow his progress and gain time for preparing defenses, he directed many axe men to destroy bridges and causeways and to fell myriads of trees so that they fell and interlocked in place. It took Burgoyne's troops twenty-two days to clear and progress the twenty-two miles, allowing more time to fortify the ground where the definitive battles would likely be fought.

Jane McCrea, twenty-three year old winsome lass with long auburn hair was living with a portly cousin, Mrs. McNeil, near Fort Edward, a poorly defended post. In the last week of July, some Indians had raided the fort and killed a few of the small garrison. They then went to Mrs. McNeil's house, seized the two women and some horses but had to neglect the older lady when she couldn't mount her horse.

The two Indians left for Burgoyne's camp with Jane McCrea but they got into an argument over the girl and one went berserk, and shot and scalped her in his rage. Jane McCrea's tresses were recognized hanging from the belt of the murderer while he was returning to camp by her fiancé, a Tory officer in Burgoyne's army.

Burgoyne wanted to hang the savage but St. Luc informed him that the Indians would desert in large numbers if he carried out the sentence and would probably murder many whites, rebel or British, on their way home. Burgoyne backed down but the Indians began to desert him anyway, depriving him of an advanced scouting guard but relieving him of their unreliability.

There were many occasions in which the red men were uncontrollable and loyalists, as well as rebels, were scalped, murdered, or taken prisoner without political distinction.

General Gates, directed by Congress to replace General Schuyler as commander of the Northern Department, made the most of the

McCrea atrocity to induce locals to leave their chimney corners to enlist and defend their families. It worked, and many New Englanders and men from the upper Hudson and lower Mohawk valleys joined Gates' army. At the same time Gates' army was expanding, Burgoyne was losing troops because of casualties, desertions, and illness.

Other problems ensued. Burgoyne's Hessian dragoons had not acquired enough horses when they departed Montreal, forcing the horse soldiers to plod the distance in their clumsy, hip-high jack boots. They had heard that herds of horses were in the upper Connecticut River Valley and that other supplies could be had for the taking by raiding a rebel military depot in Bennington, not too far off the path to Albany. Mounting the dragoons would speed Burgoyne's sweep south, he thought.

Lieutenant Colonel Baum and his Brunswick dragoon regiment was ordered to leave the main army, commit the necessary raids and return before the army crossed to the west side of the Hudson. It was now mid-July and a fortunate coincidence that Colonel John Stark was available to intercept them. He had quit the Continental Army rather than take orders from junior officers though he had served as a favorite of Major Robert Rogers' Rangers in the French war, with distinction at Bunker Hill, the Quebec campaign, and battles up to and including Trenton.

Like Arnold, he was one of those generals who had been passed over for promotion by Congress that spring despite an inspiring military record. He attracted men to his command and knew how to lead stubborn Yankees with fixed ideas.

As concerned New England leaders realized, Burgoyne could turn his forces east in their direction instead of south to Albany, and they were not prepared for such a turn. Stark was approached by them to lead a battalion. He let his strong opinions be known but agreed to accept the command as general of the New Hampshire militia and within two weeks he had enlisted twenty five companies totaling almost fifteen hundred men! On the way to engage with Burgoyne's forces he discovered that Baum and his Germans had been detached from Burgoyne's main force and were on the way to raid the depot at nearby Bennington, a crossroads of a few log cabins in hilly and wooded country.

While Stark had insisted on an unusual level of latitude in his commission, General Lincoln of the Continental army was wise enough in dealing with crusty officers to cooperate with his type of stubbornness because he knew of General Stark's capabilities. Stark's aim was to harass and badger Burgoyne's forces on his flank and rear in the area known as the Hampshire Grants, soon to be re-named Vermont.

Colonel Baum's Germans, some eight hundred of them, were bogged down with heavy equipment and poorly-made supply carts, and slowly marched as if on a parade ground, halting as many as ten times an hour to form up and adjust their lines. Besides this, many were dragoons wearing the hard-to-walk-in jack boots and trudged muddy roads through heavy rains so that they averaged only a half mile per hour!

Nor were they aware that Stark and his battalion were in the neighborhood. They were told that the region harbored many Tories who were eager to rise up and resist the rebels, a persistently incorrect bit of intelligence favored by Lord Germain, head of the ministry directing the war from London. Burgoyne had been so informed, not only by Germain, but by Philip Skene, his headquarters host, the leading local Loyalist, and a former British Army officer.

When Baum was attacked by Stark's battalion, he sent a request for reinforcements to Burgoyne but failed to reveal the serious predicament in which he found himself. He spread his forces out over an area where, because of the many hills and deep streams, made it difficult for his units to fight cohesively and easier to subdue. By the time Colonel Breyman arrived with another regiment of Hessians, many of Baum's detachment had been killed or wounded, including Baum who suffered a mortal wound. Tories that actually did join the Hessians did not speak German so there was little communication with them and their efforts were useless.

And Breyman's men were mauled as well. They were running out of ammunition when the last ammunition cart blew up and when their supporting Indians were confronted with Stark's artillery, they deserted and fled into the woods. This culminated August the sixteenth, and Burgoyne's good luck during the first months of his campaign had changed.

He lost well over eight hundred regulars and Germans to capture and casualties at Bennington and with the lack of men necessary to garrison Ticonderoga and other supply posts, as well as men lost through illness and desertions, he had an effective army of only about forty-three hundred fighting men remaining by the first of September. Nor did he gain the coveted supplies and horses.

As for Stark and his militia, having thoroughly trounced Burgoyne's Hessians and saved the supplies from confiscation, and despite Gates' desperate need for men, they went home. They had enlisted for only two months, their time was almost up, and the harvest needed to be garnered.

At this time, Burgoyne must have heard from St. Leger at Fort Stanwix about his near "victory" because of Oriskany and his plans to link up with his commander at Albany. Several weeks later, Burgoyne learned of St. Leger's defeat and inability to support Burgoyne at Albany. St. Leger then planned to retrace his way to Lake Ontario, down the St. Lawrence and follow Burgoyne's path on Lake Champlain. But Burgoyne knew he could no longer expect help from that direction or St. Leger.

It was now early September. Crispin, Trevor, Chief Honeoye, and I were ordered to pack our gear and travel to Stillwater on the Hudson, where the enemy had pushed our army; there, we we'd receive further orders. That's all he said. It was most mysterious, especially since we were not sent as a group but separately, even though it was obvious when we compared our orders that we were to function together.

Horses at the fort were quite weak due to the lack of forage so it was suggested that we do without. Thank goodness that the fleet of Durham boats had resumed service. We gathered at the rebuilt lower landing for the most recent arrivals to unload, and it was our good luck that we would again sail with Captain George who had brought us here only two months ago. So much had happened since then that it had seemed like six months.

"When are you planning to go downstream?" I asked the captain.

"You're here at just the right time. We're leaving tomorrow morning at daybreak, which is at seven o'clock. Well boys, you did right well against Chief Brant and his savages, Where are you off for now, eh?"

"We're on our way to take Burgoyne now that we've put St. Leger in his proper place, Captain. We're off to Stillwater to get orders from Gates."

"He's moved up river, the Hudson that is, boys. They suspect Burgoyne will cross the Hudson to the western side soon. It will be much more difficult for him if he waits and does it farther south. That is, if he gets farther south. Gates has now moved north about five miles to a wide place in the road--Bemis Heights, named after a tavern there; the rebels are building some fortifications on the bluffs nearby.

"If I were you, I would get off at Amsterdam and go cross country to Ballston Spa and then to Bemis Heights. There's a decent road and you won't have to maneuver among crowded army regiments on the way."

With the season being very wet, the Mohawk flowed full and rapidly and we didn't have the laborious and time-consuming portages at the rifts as we had two months earlier when coming upstream. We took Captain George's advice and, at dusk the same day, we were able to disembark at Amsterdam, a small town that resembled hamlets of the New Netherlands. The gables were stepped, the front porches were built of a slab of white stone and fronted close to the street, and everything was tidy and neat. We had a good opinion of Amsterdam.

CHAPTER TWO

WE WERE STARVING when we left the captain and his boats, having eaten all the snacks we brought along by the time we glided past German Flats. Amsterdam, small as it is, had a cafe where we sat at a small counter and ordered a full menu of corn on the cob, lamb chops, summer squash, and cantaloupe. After dinner, we went a little farther to where we saw an immense barn and asked the farmer if we could rent space for the four of us overnight. He asked where we were going and fixed us up for free when he found we were on our way to fight Burgoyne.

The next morning he brought us four mugs, a kettle of coffee and asked if we liked bacon and eggs to eat in his kitchen. People in the valley were nice that way.

He had lost a son to the Quebec campaign, he told us as he prepared breakfast for us at his fireside. He pointed to the road to Ballston Spa and said we had only thirty or so miles to Bemis Heights on the Hudson, and then wished us well.

This land was well groomed and the crops had been harvested. Wheat, buckwheat, oats, alfalfa and beef and dairy cattle were the main crops that we could see, along with orchards ripe with pippins gracing the rolling hillsides. We stopped to buy apples from a stand, but the owner, upon learning our destination, gave them for free if we would pick him a bushel apiece, which we were happy to do.

The fragrance of the fresh fruit and the tang of the overripe apples on the ground brought back memories of almost two years ago in the West Country of England. My younger brother Jonathan and I had brought our older brother, Dordy, a regular in the British army, home from Plymouth to recuperate from his shot-away ankle suffered at Bunker Hill.

Dordy has since retired and married Sally Bushnell and they have a son now. "This makes me an uncle," I blurted out from my reverie to my comrades.

"Jamie! Wake up, you must be day dreaming." Crispin shook my shoulder. "You just said that Dordy has made you an uncle. Are you getting a spell of home sickness at this late date?"

"No. But here we are, marching to a place we've never heard of to fight against Englishmen, some of whom might be our brothers, school chums, or relatives. I don't want to wound, or much less kill any one of them, but to change governments and do away with unjust and unfair laws, we must."

"I hope that you're not backing out of the fight. Are you?" Crispin said.

"No. Nothing like that. It's a nasty thing we must do, but it's essential. Nothing would make me happier than to stop Burgoyne and his troop of redcoats and Indians and send them packing. I was merely remembering when life was simpler."

Trevor spoke up. "You know, when I had my store in New York, many of my customers were regulars in the British army, and some were high-level officers. Most were friendly, once I got to know them and they to know me. I enjoyed their company. But, aside from this pleasing aspect of running the store, there was an underlying purpose in making these connections. I was subtly coaxing them to reveal sensitive information regarding British plans and policy. In other words, I was spying on them and if caught at it I would have been subjected to the supreme penalty.

"I had no musket, no sword, bayonet, or pistol. But I was waging war just the same. And I'd do it again if it became opportune.

"Those fellows, friendly as they were, do the bidding of our real enemies, the very ones who wish to impose unfair burdens on us and our progeny. So we must not forget the unhappy connection and our reason for opposing it with our lives."

Chief Honeoye then pointed ahead two hundred yards to two men sitting on a stone bridge over a small stream. "Perhaps they're on their way to join General Gates, too. Let's be careful though, they could be Loyalists going to join Burgoyne."

16

As we came closer, they seemed to acquire a defensive stance. Honeoye, who has very keen sight, said they had moved their muskets within arm's reach. Trevor hailed them first.

"Good day gentlemen. Are you hunting or are you on your way to the Hudson for greater sport?"

"Good day to you! We've heard about the redcoats and the Indians killing defenseless women and decided we should do something about it. At first we thought that the British, being related in a way, would be somewhat reasonable. But they've proven to be as vicious as some said they were. It was bad enough defending the Grants against thieving Yankees, but the Brits want your land and your life, too."

"So, you live nearby and are on your way to join Gates?" Trevor stated.

"No. We're from Newark, New Jersey. We're in the New Jersey militia although you'd never know it since we haven't uniforms. What about you?"

To Trevor and the rest of us, this seemed a poor answer. It seemed rehearsed and the stranger didn't really declare what side they were on. Trevor decided to reveal as little as possible to these reticent soldiers, if they were soldiers.

"We just left Fort Stanwix which withstood the siege. We're going to the Hudson where we think they can use our services. What's going on in New Jersey?"

The tallest of them spat his quid of tobacco, as if to establish his credentials, "Washington left his camp at Bound Brook when he found that Howe was going to Philadelphia by way of the Chesapeake. Just the same, we were ordered to come up here. We take it that this is the more important battle."

Trevor nodded, "That's what we think." After a few minutes of meaningless palaver, Trevor turned to us and said, "Let's fill our canteens and be on our way, boys, we still have twenty or so miles to go. So long, gents and good luck to you."

After we had walked about two hundred yards, Trevor said, "Did you happen to notice that both of their canteens were British. I think they're local Loyalists on their way to join Burgoyne."

"If they are really from New Jersey, why would he appear to be bitter about the Hampshire Grants? And telling us about Washington going to Pennsylvania to fight Howe told us nothing. Everybody knows about that," I chimed in.

Crispin added his opinion. "They didn't speak like they were from New Jersey, they were more nasal and spoke with a broad a. I think they're local and are afraid we may be rebels bent on attacking Loyalists. Trevor, do you have that small telescope with you? Perhaps we should scan our trail in case they follow us. They looked scruffy enough to be freebooters. They may be afraid because they think we may do to them what they're thinking of doing to us. Take a look. If they're still by the brook, there may be more of them."

We stopped momentarily so Trevor could check. "The two of them are still there. I see no others." Trevor turned and squinted forward at the road ahead. "No one ahead of us either," he said as he sheathed the scope. He added, "I think it best that we make sure our muskets are primed at the next bend in the road."

I could no longer withhold the information contained in Hawkin's letter. "Crispin, do you remember John Hawkins, the British deserter we caught last February? I got a letter from him just before we left Stanwix. He said he found out who his families' murderers are and described them. The two of 'em were from New Jersey and had just been ordered to report to Gates. As soon as I saw these two at the brook, I thought of them.

"But the description doesn't fit. One is tall, blond, and has a cleft chin. Hawkins said his face is mean-looking. The other is shorter, dark-haired, and well educated--- and he hums all the time--sounds kind of weird."

"They're together most of the time, the letter said. The blonds' name is Robert Trainor and the other's Bart Dickson. They're supposed to arrive here the first week of September. I don't expect to spot them so easily, like we did those two at the brook, but we'll keep our eyes open for the pair of 'em."

At the next bend, we stopped and primed the pans of our muskets. Trevor took a few steps back to the edge of the trees and scanned the road behind us with the glass. "They're gone," he said, and turned forward to look ahead. "There is a big sign that says "Lots for Sale, Kayaderosseras Patent, first house on the left." He said the name again, but this time slowly.

In a half mile, we saw the cabin at the edge of the woods. It was the only house but the surrounding ground was staked out for others.

Smoke rose out the chimney and a middle-aged man stepped out, anxious to shake hands.

"Howdy! Welcome to Kayaderosseras Patent. I guess you fellas have heard about Jennie McCrea and are on the way to the Hudson to fight alongside General Gates, eh? Where ye from?"

"We're from all over, but lastly from Fort Stanwix," said the Chief. "Yes, were almost to Bemis Heights, we think, where we're told Gates has his headquarters. But who is Jennie McCrea?" The Chief acted dumb.

"She was a young lass minding her own business when two of Burgoyne's Indians seized her near Fort Edward to take her prisoner to Burgoyne's camp. The Indians were drunk, as usual, and got into an argument. One of them was enraged about something and shot poor Jane off her horse and then scalped her and threw her corpse into the bushes.

"When the two Indians arrived at the British camp, her fiancé, who happened to be a Loyalist officer, recognized her long, auburn tresses hanging from the Indian's belt! They were to be married soon.

"Word travelled fast and soon everyone around here, and as far as Albany and Springfield, heard about the atrocity. They remembered General Burgoyne's speech to the Indians, which the pompous general had had printed and distributed to the countryside, warning us that he would "give stretch" to the Indians if we didn't lay down our arms. In the same speech he directed the Indians to not scalp women and children unless they were already dead, and then presented them with a schedule of cash bounties the British would pay for scalps. So that's who Jennie McCrea was. But welcome to the Hudson Valley."

Chief Honeoye became solemn as the story unfolded. At the end he said, "We've had similar tragedies happen. One was three young girls being attacked while picking raspberries within a quarter mile of Fort Stanwix. Two died. We don't know if the third will survive, but this happened before the siege began. Two officers were also tomahawked the same week. One was killed on the spot. The other was scalped but still survives. And of course, there was the bloody and tragic ambush at Oriskany but you've probably heard about that."

"Yes, we heard and so did General Schuyler. He shocked many of us when he was willing to detach a battalion from his already undermanned army to relieve the fort, but now that he was successful and Arnold and his troops are back here, we realize it was a difficult but necessary decision for Schuyler to make."

"Is this patent the same as Ballston Spa?"

"Yes. No one wants to have to say Kayaderosseras all the time, so we've named the town after Mr. Ephilet Ball. He's from the same family as Washington's mother, Mary Ball. Though the patent goes back to Queen Ann's time, it was surveyed into lots only a few years ago.

"And we do have wonderful mineral springs. Some think they are therapeutic. The Mohawks introduced Sir William Johnson to the spring to help him to recover from his wound suffered at Lake George. They are refreshing to swim in and some drink it as an elixir. Down the road at Saratoga Springs there are several other springs but many of them taste and smell like rotten eggs, or worse."

I noticed that Chief Honeoye's ears perked up when he mentioned elixir. Selling Seneca Oil, or snake oil, was how the Chief had made his living.

"You fellows must be tired. One of our other founders has improved a beach for swimming at our spa. I'm sure he will welcome you for a swim. Just stay on the road, it's only a mile to his bath house. If you need anything, he has a store handy."

We all thought this a good idea as we still felt grungy from the month-long siege. It had been an unusually warm day and the prospect of relaxing, in a spa no less, aroused our curiosity so we hiked in a more spirited manner even though we had already trudged about fifteen miles by early afternoon.

The owner of the spa had done his best to add amenities for his patrons. The board and batten bathhouse could accommodate perhaps as many as a dozen people to change into rented bathing clothes and one could check valuables and muskets in his office. If you wanted a drink, you could get it from a spigot coming out of a rock.

The water was refreshingly cool to the palate and washed not only our bodies, but our concerns and apprehension of the coming days fell away.

There were two other men swimming and they ceased their conversation when we strode into the small pond. It was awkward, so Crispin introduced us. They shook hands but were reluctant to give their names or information about themselves. Undaunted, Crispin thought to start a conversation; "We just came from Fort Stanwix and the siege. Now we're going to join Gates and, hopefully give our good luck to him." He expected a laugh, but the two men looked askance at such lack of reticence.

The older of the two spoke as if he were still in the uniform of a ranking officer, "Soldier, you are talking to us about military matters as if we were friends, or at least acquaintances. You don't know whether we are rebels or Loyalists and so put yourselves at risk needlessly. If we were Loyalists, we could act friendly but dress and arm ourselves and capture the lot of you, or worse."

Crispin was in the habit of open friendliness with most everyone and was correspondingly flabbergasted at being so rudely put down. But he recognized the harsh style as being that of a military man from his encounters with armies.

"Yes sir! You're right. But I saw your uniform in the bathhouse and knew you must be an officer on our side—the Continental Army." Crispin had the wit to nail the officer for chastising him for the same incaution the officer himself was guilty of, but wisely refrained from rubbing it in. He could tell that the officer recognized the impropriety of his own comments and Crispin's discrete courtesy in return.

An awkward moment elapsed and then the officer unbent and made introductions. "I am Colonel John Brown and this is my friend, Captain Allen Johns. We are pleased to meet you gentlemen. It seems providential that we should meet here. It saves you going to Bemis Heights to appear before General Gates and then having to search me out. We came from Pawlet where General Lincoln and two other commanders are making plans to attack various fortifications at Ticonderoga.

"Colonel Willett told me of your talents and I requested your assistance in an important mission that could vitally affect General Burgoynes's campaign.

"I'm under General Lincoln and am charged with harassing and interfering with Burgoyne's supply line and to take Ticonderoga, if possible. You men are to be part of this mission. When we finish here we'll be on our way to the environs of the fort. It's about seventy miles of no-man's land from here, with Loyalists, rebels, Indians and freebooters rampant in the area, and no way to tell them

21

apart until it's too late. So it's well that we met and can join forces for better security on the trip. If you have questions or suggestions, speak up."

The sudden encounter with these officers left us breathless and barren of ideas although I was sure that Chief Honeoye or Trevor, especially, would come up with both questions and ideas. I wondered how many men were involved in this mission, where were we to camp, how to feed us, how many British were garrisoned at Fort Ti and where were the other posts on "Gentleman Johnnie's" supply route.

Our next week or so promised to be exciting and hair-raising. No, that's an inappropriate term to use in Indian country.

CHAPTER THREE

WE KNEW THE British were not far, but our army didn't know their exact location and they seemed to not know ours. Our group, since enlarged by Colonel Brown and Captain Johns, was separate from both armies and inland from the Hudson River a few miles. Our therapeutic swim refreshed us so that we hustled north along the road to Saratoga Springs and Fort George with stops at the edge of safe meadows or ridge tops. It was mid-September and the dark green leaves of the season were occasionally turning bright red, yellow or orange. Stands of maple, oak, hickory, chestnut, and black gum were soon to be at their most splendid. What a region for residence and industry, we marveled.

These woods and Morgan's riflemen, ordered here by Washington from Pennsylvania with their Kentucky rifles, were largely responsible for what we thought was our advantage over the redcoats. And Arnold's return from Fort Stanwix with two thousand troops improved the odds, too. The British still favored fighting European style, which are lines of men shooting at the mass of the enemy rather than aiming at individuals. Offsetting this, the British use three lines of men who, when ordered, fire their muskets sequentially and then charge with the bayonet, often overwhelming and causing severe damage to our troops, who by then, have discharged their muskets and are hurrying to reload.

We use sharpshooters to pick off their officers in the hopes of causing chaos. They have well-trained personnel to march, follow orders, and shoot in the enemy's general direction, but only when directed. Their soldiers are automatons unlike our self-assured and resourceful men.

Since our small group was going north, away from Saratoga, to join General Lincoln, we saw troops only from a distance when thick woods and the terrain permitted. When we topped a ridge, we could see the British army beginning to cross the Hudson on a bridge built of boats about a quarter of a mile north of where the Battenkill enters the river. It was impressive but frightening at the same time. It was the thirteenth of September and we realized that Burgoyne had made an important and irrevocable decision.

Soon, our army would have to make a stand but not until Burgoyne advanced south a few miles more to near Bemis Heights where our fortifications had been built. More importantly, our general morale had improved to the point where we could talk about winning this contest between armies.

Colonel Brown proved to be much friendlier than his dour first impression. He told us of his adventures on the Quebec campaign and he spoke highly of General Montgomery, who was killed in a blizzard on New Year's Eve assaulting a British redoubt at the edge of the city. But he had a low opinion of General Arnold who was severely wounded the same evening attacking another redoubt nearby.

He had a copy of the New York paper which printed Burgoyne's letter to Gates complaining of Gates' men allegedly refusing to give quarter to prisoners. This was followed by General Gates' reply, denying the charge, and castigating Burgoyne for hiring Indians and paying them handsome bounties for scalps which resulted in many atrocities such as the Jane McCrea affair. Burgoyne admitted the brutality of the McCrea incident but declared that it was the only such instance and defended his backing down when he declined to hang the Indian murderer. It would avoid mayhem on both their regulars and our men, he had said.

Everyone knew that saying the McCrea attack was the only atrocity was a lie. The woods were rife with savage murderers of men, women, and children throughout the region. When the public became more aware of "Gentleman Johnnie's" way of making war, our militia materialized in great numbers to swell the army.

We hiked for two hours and arrived in Saratoga Springs where Colonel Brown knew of a fine tavern. Business was slow and so we had the entire occupancy of one of their private rooms. Both the colonel and Captain Johns were convivial after a drink or two so that they could relax with the four of us, whom they no longer considered strangers.

Brown turned the conversation to the battleground. "That was a fine exhibition of bridge construction and his army crossing the river. Burgoyne must be proud of his troops. It was so well organized on both sides of the river; he didn't have to fend off our troops when he was most vulnerable."

Chief Honeoye said. "I understand that he goes easy with the lash and shows concern for his men's welfare, an unusual officer in that army."

I added my knowledge of the man. "He's been a member of Parliament for years before the war and always voted in favor of the colony's position on the ministry's oppression. Strange, the same is true of the Howe brothers, both the admiral and General Howe. The pressure put on them to lead an army against us must have been overwhelming, but the honor of the King's appointment and the apparent ease of winning against us must have been attractive."

Not to be outdone, Trevor added, "The Howe brothers lost an older brother right around here, near Fort Ticonderoga. He was second in command to General Abercromby in the infamous Fort Carillon campaign in '58, but, in actuality, he was the brains of the operation. He was also well-liked by rank and file. But in one of the first skirmishes of the campaign, his unit encountered a French and Indian patrol and he was mortally wounded. From then on, the campaign foundered.

"Abercromby didn't use his artillery which had been brought all the way from Albany. Instead, he insisted on driving his men to advance against a deadly abatis several times when a cannonade would have breached the fort's wall. His men were invariably caught in the abatis tangle and shot with horrendous results. Though his successive attacks failed and suffered many casualties, his count of men still outnumbered the French three to one, but he withdrew his forces leaving the French and their fort intact. During none of that time was Abercromby in the thick of it; he commanded the fighting from the safety behind his own lines where the unused artillery was. He also abandoned to the enemy a large amount of his provisions.

"The only good thing about the affair, as well as the Braddock massacre, a few years before, was that our people realized that our faith in the reputation of the British army, supposedly the best trained in the world, was severely misplaced. It emboldened our leaders to rebuke the mother country's arrogance and to challenge British authority.

"In honor of the senior Viscount Howe, Massachusetts raised funds for a memorial crypt in Westminster Abbey. This simple, thoughtful act has softened the heart (and some say the minds) of the viscount's younger brothers who, as joint heads of a peace commission, have tried to negotiate with Benjamin Franklin and John Adams. The Doctor and Adams refused to withdraw our Declaration of Independence, so the Howe Commission was stalemated by the hard stance taken by Lord Germain and the King." Trevor finished.

"Thoughtful and brave men on both sides have been stymied by those two hard-headed men, and the lives of many thousands are dependent on their whims." gravely said Colonel Brown.

We were impressed by Trevor's stories and hoped he would continue.

Brown explained his earlier pronouncement. "I say Burgoyne has made an irrevocable and critical decision by crossing the river because he has committed his army to the western shore of the river which has terrain unfavorable to their European fighting style. High bluffs close to the shore crowd the only road going south and the bluffs are covered with dense woods alternating with a few cultivated fields overgrown with brambles. There are deep ravines every few hundred yards. They'll have to spread out but bring their baggage, artillery and supplies along the road or the river, exposed to our artillery fire from the bluffs.

"He'll probably have two more battalions, one on the far western flank and passing through thick woods---that's where Morgan's sharpshooters and their Kentucky rifles will shine--- and a battalion in the middle where Burgoyne will most likely oversee, as much as possible, the other two to coordinate the whole.

"I say irrevocable because it will now be very difficult to get back to the eastern side if he finds that he must withdraw to Ticonderoga for the winter. He has a long and vulnerable supply line and, even if he doesn't run out of supplies, there are no places between here and there where he can reasonably camp his army. His army could either starve or freeze to death. "Locals have practiced a scorched-earth policy, and north of here on this side, there are few farms to find forage for man or beast. Mrs. Schuyler, the wife of the general, has even set the torch to their wheat field. It is critical for Burgoyne to have enough supplies to make it to Albany, which means he may have to cut rations.

"In short, he has now placed himself in an unfortunate predicament. It'll be interesting to see how it plays out." He paused briefly to catch his breath before suggesting, "Let's order another drink."

I had listened closely to Brown's discourse. "You say Burgoyne, being in such a desperate situation, should be thinking of retreating. It seems to me that he should be thinking of advancing. He has travelled the longest and most difficult part of his campaign so far. I would think that the remaining fifty miles would be easier for him to sweep his way to Albany where, presumably, he will be met by General Howe."

Brown had listened to my statement as if he expected and welcomed such disagreement. He must have been planning to give a long-winded answer since he lifted his mug of rum for a long draught before responding.

"Yes, what you say is creditable except for several considerations: You forget that Howe is miles west of Philadelphia and about to fight Washington for possession of that city. So Burgoyne has no hope of help from him. We have intercepted messengers from both Burgoyne and General Clinton in New York. Burgoyne is desperately hinting that he could use a diversion to be created by Clinton, and Clinton has yet to commit himself or others to provide relief to the beleaguered Burgoyne.

"Soon it will too late for Clinton to decide to come north and make it in time. Though it's just the beginning of fall, winter comes early up here. Sometimes they get snow as early as mid-October, as our people know. But the British look at the world as if God is on their side and will accommodate them with favorable European open fields and warm weather. Let them, but they could be in for a surprise.

"As for easier prospects for Burgoyne, our army is gaining in size while Burgoyne's is waning. The British belief that a sizeable army of Loyalists is ready to rise up and supplant their losses has continually been overly optimistic. While our militia has been disappointing at times, it has also surprised us and the enemy, with valor, gallantry, and success when they're fighting to defend their homes and farms.

And that's exactly what's going to be the case during the next month or so.

"And don't forget that Morgan's sharpshooters have long range and accurate Kentucky rifles, most of them made in Pennsylvania, by the way. They'll oppose Burgoyne's right flank which will be in the woods. Except for a few overgrown and neglected farms, the rest of the ground where Burgoyne will be boxed up is deep ravines covered by brambles and second growth vegetation. So I'm very optimistic."

Chapter Four

After the tavern keeper, a Mr. Davenport, finished serving another round of Madeira and left the room, Colonel Brown continued. "Our mission will be to frustrate the delivery of supplies to Burgoyne by attacking convoys, destroying food and munitions, and reducing the number of their personnel involved as well as attacking Fort Ti and freeing American prisoners. General Lincoln directed us to not be surprised if Ticonderoga is unassailable. It's well garrisoned despite Burgoyne's need to be stingy by leaving of a rear guard there. However an escaped sergeant said that their Indians have deserted them and that the fort is poorly manned. If it appears that this is not true and there is no way that we can take the fort, Lincoln said we should not risk the loss of troops—our main mission is not to take territory or fortifications but to reduce or eliminate the delivery of supplies to Burgoyne.

"We are told by a number of deserters that Burgoyne has cut rations so they are already feeling the unpleasant pinch of difficult logistics. In con-junction with General Lincoln's forces, we will first free the prisoners who are in a building on the Lake George outlet. Then we will attack the old stone fort and the other posts.

"Of course, it'll take us several days to reach Ticonderoga from here but you can be thinking of ideas or questions on the way. Crispin, I have some surveying instruments with me. We want you to survey our route and the terrain of the western side of Lake George as well as the complex at Ticonderoga. The maps we have are inadequate."

At that moment, Mr. Davenport hurriedly came into the room and whispered to Brown that it might be better if Brown and our group reserve rooms at his tavern as the other inn at the springs was occupied by British officers. The Colonel quickly reserved two rooms assuring us of a good night's rest compared to the barn and farm animals the night before. We were not concerned by any hostile moves by British officers—there seemed to be a tacit agreement that there was an armistice on such inadvertent occasions. But these few instances were uncomfortable and awkward for both sides. After a delicious breakfast of eggs, bacon, hash fries, and lots of well-buttered toast at the tavern, courtesy of Colonel Brown, we followed the forest road due north to the Hudson. The woods were quiet except for the squawking of blue jays and crows and the wind sighing in the upper branches of the pines. Nor did we encounter anyone. A morning fog enveloped our trail. We did see signs of atrocities perpetrated at some time before. It was the remains of a corpse tied to a tree, with several arrows shot through the body and the skull had been crushed. Wolves had probably come down out of the Adirondacks to rip and tear the body and the skeleton was clean. We shivered to think that an English gentleman, such as Burgoyne, had wished such a death on anyone.

We made a wide circuitous detour around Fort George, one of Burgoyne's supply posts, and then started a long slog climbing a hill north of there. We must have gone five miles before we topped the ridge and rested where it was noticeably cooler.

"The climate here is cooler winter and summer than the surrounding area, but there's no poison ivy or rattle snakes in the higher elevations. At least, I've never seen any," Brown explained.

"Offsetting this, the woods are usually thick with gnats, mosquitoes and black flies in the summertime. In the fall, they disappear. The best way to avoid them is to apply bear grease or to sit on the smoky side of a campfire made of green wood."

As we resumed our hike, the sound of splashing rapids came to our ears and soon we came to a large stream. Brown kept us informed while we rested. "This is the Hudson River, boys. When you remember how wide the Hudson is downstream, especially at New York, it doesn't seem so vast anymore." We emptied the stale content of our canteens and scooped the cool water to replace it. Chief Honeoye walked along the shore while Crispin set up his tripod to sight a boulder a quarter mile due north by his compass. It would make a convenient benchmark, he said.

The Chief reflected that "the Hudson was named by a Dutchman after himself and that most of the rivers and streams west of here were named for Indian tribes or Indian places. The Mohawk, Schoharie Creek, the Susquehanna, the Seneca, and the Onondaga and the Oswego and Genesee Rivers—you could almost determine the advance of white settlement of the land by knowing their names.

"Up north the Black River drains the western Adirondacks into Lake Ontario and the Oswegatchie, the Grass and Raquette drain the central mountains into the Saint Lawrence. If we went north past Ticonderoga we would encounter the rushing tea-colored water in the chasm of the Ausable on its way to Lake Champlain."

The woods were dense and very slow to move through unless you found an Indian trail going the same direction and, even then, windfalls slowed the pace.

In this hilly country where it rained frequently, moss covered the north side of trees, stumps and boulders and the other side was often in shade long enough each day to grow lichens which appeared as light green coating on sunny, dry days and dark green during wet stretches. Fungus was all over. Trees that had fallen years before, because of windstorms or of old age, were rotted through and covered by a mantle of moist moss, and if you made the mistake of resting on one, you could count on having a wet seat of the pants. Brown was right—we had not encountered mosquitoes or gnats the whole trek since we arrived in the foothills. In clearings, we saw busy dragon flies hurriedly gathering something as if cold weather was soon to cut short their harvest.

We came to a fork in the trail where a narrow path wound northwestward. Brown stopped and dismounted here. "You fellows continue on, I want to see an old friend and mentor who has chosen to be a recluse in the woods. I'll catch up to you. There's a stream up the way about a mile and next to it, there's a good place to camp or at least to make a fire for dinner. Take my horse with you. I don't want her to manure the trail to my friend's place. I'll be maybe a half hour." He turned down the trail and quickly disappeared into the brush.

Chief Honeoye now led the horse and assumed the role of senior woodsman in Brown's absence. As we were getting closer to Ticonderoga, he scanned the path and brush for signs of a picket, recent travelers, or ground where it would be favorable for someone to jump us or warn of our presence.

We soon came to the stream Brown mentioned and examined the place while we waited for him to catch up. Next to the stream there were two hip-high ridges of rock intersecting. Thirty feet away, at the other end, a boulder closed the three sides into a triangle, with a grassy swath in the middle. It made a perfect spot to fort-up and place our bed rolls. A smoke-darkened cleft in the rocks revealed prior parties had thought so, too.

Chief Honeoye appointed me and Trevor to scout for enemy pickets even though we were probably still twenty miles from the Lake George outlet. Trevor went upstream and I crisscrossed in the opposite direction, not only looking for signs of activity, but sniffing for wood or tobacco smoke as well. It was surprising how far you could smell someone smoking, like hearing sound coming across calm waters.

All was clear. The information that the Indians had abandoned General Powell, the commander at Ticonderoga, must have been true. Even so, the Chief decided we should have a cold camp. He wanted no surprises.

As the sun began to settle in the west, the woods became death-dumb-quiet, as if an intruder had alerted the wild life. Indeed, within a few minutes Colonel Brown appeared. He approved our campsite and lack of a fire, but gnawed on a piece of smoked beef.

"I'm glad I went to see my old friend and professor. He taught some of my law classes at Yale and we talked of the many conversations we had over the tables at the local bar." Brown coughed and cleared his throat. "He says the fort has been lax and that the absence of discipline has allowed the troops to be sloppy guarding the outlet and the building where the prisoners are kept. He says we should have no trouble freeing them. The old fort is something else again, he said as I left him."

The next noon, the bulk of Brown's regiments began to emerge from the woods. They had had what passed for breakfast and left their camp at first light. Like most of us, they wore no uniforms, just buckskins and homespun suitable for the season. "They might not look daunting or glorious if they were parading in the streets of Philadelphia, but they've proved to be good shots and brave, and up to the coming challenge." Brown boasted.

After making a brief welcoming speech, Brown repeated the schedule of battle he had delivered to the four of us the night before, and within minutes the entire battalion was off on several routes to the Lake George outlet.

We knew that we would spy out the complex before taking any action and so withheld our questions. We worked our way to vantage points to view the activity at both the gray stone fortress and the newer fortification as well as at the outlet. What a lovely sight! A traveler would welcome spending a summer there if the tents were marquees, and the whole scene was reminiscent of pictures of a chateau on the Loire.

Brown had some advantage as he had accompanied Arnold and Allen in their famous takeover of the fort the first time over two years ago. He broke silence. "Ah, I remember this place. This is not likely to be as easy as that lark was," he predicted.

The enemy commander of the complex was Brigadier General Powell, who was either very nonchalant regarding our presence or unaware of it. After two days of surveillance we estimated his force at about nine hundred regulars, half of whom were Hessians and Canadians who largely were stationed at Mount Independence, a small hill at the tip end of the lake stockade and fortified by our troops after its first capture. Two-thirds of the other half were guarding the old stone fort west of Lake Champlain with the balance at the old French lines, a half mile north.

Each of our officers had been assigned so that he knew what was expected of him and all of us were anxious for action.

As the fog was lifting on the morning of September eighteenth, Brown gathered us at the edge of a clearing and spread the old map against the trunk of an aging pine. He pointed with a stick, "Here's the scheme of our attack as worked out at Pawlet: We have two thousand men which have been divided into four sections of five hundred each; General Lincoln with five hundred will remain at Pawlet, prepared to provide troops where needed; Colonel Woodridge is proceeding from Pawlet to Skenesboro, which the British have already abandoned, and then will move on Fort Edward via Fort Ann; Colonel Johnson is supposed to distract the enemy by making an attack on Mount Independence, the hill-fort I mentioned earlier, which is a short distance from the main bastion, but east of the southern tip of Lake Champlain." He traced their positions for all to see.

"Johnson's feint is to draw enemy fire away from us while we overwhelm the building on the Lake George outlet housing the rebel prisoners. We are to destroy a depot containing a large quantity of munitions and stores, and a blockhouse guarding some sawmills there. Leave the sawmills alone unless their troops are firing from them. Shoot back but don't torch them. We want to spare the mills for future use and they have no immediate strategic value to the enemy or to us," he said.

"General Lincoln ordered us to attack the old French stone fort if we think it is possible to overwhelm it without incurring undue casualties. He delegated us to use our discretion. If we are seen attacking the old fort with any degree of success, Johnson is to be more aggressive in his assault of Mount Independence to continue drawing enemy fire.

"After we finish here, we'll launch their boats beached at the Lake George landing, and sail twenty-five miles up the lake to Diamond Island to destroy supplies there and then to do the same at Fort George at the head of the lake. Any questions?"

"Some prisoners may need help. Do we have surgeons or nurses to tend them?"

"Good point. I have assigned Sergeant Henderson and his aides to that detail. If you see that they need help in getting out the lame, get it from the able prisoners."

"Shouldn't a detail be charged with guarding the boats?' another asked.

"I've ordered Corporal Bean to do that. When we release the prisoners, Bean will be guarding the boats and with the help of able prisoners." Brown answered. He looked as if he were open to more questions, but the ranks were silent. They were anxious for action. You could feel it in the air.

"All right, boys, when I wave a white handkerchief, we begin. Remember; be as quiet as you can! We want to get the prisoners out and away before any firing."

As the fog was lifting on the morning of September eighteenth, we broke from the bushes and charged the Lake George landing and made for the building housing the American prisoners. It was all done quietly as if the remaining fog was absorbing what little noise we made. The first man to reach the door used a bayonet to pry an opening, and rounded up the prisoners to evacuate the building with as little fuss as possible. Most of the prisoners had been there since early July when Burgoyne forced surrender. Some had been wounded, but most were able and followed our directions without hesitation. We had caught the redcoats sleeping and not a shot had been fired.

Then we set fire to the stored supplies, passed by the two sawmills, and rushed the blockhouse garrison which quickly surrendered. A guard platoon on top of Mount Defiance, the key British strategy to the taking of the old fort by Burgoyne, was challenged and became a threat no more. All this happened without a hitch. But Colonel Brown had his eye on taking the main fort. What a feather in his cap if he did!

"Where the hell is Johnson? He's supposed to be attacking Mount Independence on the other side of the lake," he wailed. He stood on a stump to get a better view. This gave an enemy marksman a better view of Brown. He missed, but Brown learned to keep his head down as enemy fire increased.

As General Lincoln had surmised, the old and massive stone fort was impregnable, and the enemy fire of grapeshot from the ramparts above us was more murderous than we expected. Then Johnson and his men came out of the woods on the other side of the lake and let loose their passion and musket balls at the enemy. At the same time the enemy's Lake Champlain flotilla began to bombard us and the cannon on the fort joined in. Then the stored munitions blew up. The boats were probably the boats General Arnold had challenged the previous fall when he delayed Carleton's invasion.

Brown urged us forward. "Get closer. Make your shots count!" He yelled. But the redcoats knew they were relatively safe firing from the fort's walls and, with impunity, continued their return fire despite our improved shooting from our advanced position. Occasionally, I could see Honeoye, Trevor; or Crispin crouched behind a boulder, taking a shot, or running forward, but only briefly.

With the one hundred freed prisoners we now numbered a fighting force of six- hundred, but we were burdened with about three hundred British and Canadian prisoners with few captured provisions to feed them. A small detail was detached to march the enemy prisoners away to Skenesboro.

Volleys of artillery from both sides continued for several hours but with little effect. Colonel Brown knew his demand for surrender would be recognized by Powell as a bluff but he tried any way, and was promptly refused by a curt, "The garrison entrusted to my care I shall defend it to the last." It was as if Powell had used Colonel Gansevoort's refusal of surrender at Stanwix as a pattern.

For the next four days we traded artillery shots with the garrison at Mount Independence to no one's advantage. The only noteworthy action was the cannonading of a movement in the bushes surrounding Mount Independence. Despite round after round, from us and from the fort, the scoundrels kept on the move. A lull in the firing revealed that our "enemy" in the bushes was nothing more than a grazing cow. The oblivious creature survived the marksmanship of both sides. We all got a laugh out of that!

Finally, we realized that we were just wasting time and munitions and that we still had to organize our foray down Lake George to wipe out, or at least, damage the supplies on Diamond Island. The enemy boats had been built for rough service under stormy conditions—they were the size of whaleboats and most of them had a platform in the bow for a small cannon. These were probably remnants from the fleet rowed by Burgoyne's men up Champlain in July.

We had hoped to sail but the wind was strong and right out of the south so we had to row the twenty-five miles against ocean-sized waves and weather. It took all that day just to reach Sabbath Day Point, a low, flat shore halfway up the lake.

Early the next morning, the wind still persisted. It had taken so long to approach the island that we lost the advantage of surprise; they began cannonading us as soon as we came within range. Brown did his best to counter their fire by maneuvering our flotilla so that we were directly downwind of and aimed straight at the island to present the narrowest targets to the enemy and, at the same time, to reduce the effect of the wind.

To catch the attention of our flotilla, he had the men in our and nearby boats raise their oars. He stood up on the bow and called, albeit feebly against the blast, "Follow me and duplicate my maneuvers. Face the island to cut the wind and reduce your profile." Finding only a few nearby who had done so, he called again and asked those who had heard to call the others. Remarkably, this time they heard well enough so that all positioned themselves as directed and so that they were not so close together that an enemy miss would endanger a neighboring boat.

The redcoats sent volley after volley from heavy artillery with disastrous results. We lost several boats to direct hits. Our men opened fire with our three and four pounders but had no better results than collapsing a few tents because the enemy made good use of the island's natural cover. It seemed like a repeat of the poor marksmanship at Mount Independence, but without the comedy of the cow.

After a few hours had passed, Brown called off the barrage and we made for the eastern shore of the lake where we burned our "borrowed" boats in a sheltered cove. Before moving off overland he stepped up onto a stump and spoke to the men, "We have accomplished what we set out to do. Expecting any more than that would be ludicrous. Consider yourselves heroes."

CHAPTER FIVE

WE PAUSED TO eat after having no nourishment for twenty-four hours, and then moved on back to Pawlet where General Lincoln had already withdrawn Johnson's detachment. In turn, General Gates had ordered all of Lincoln's troops to Bemis Heights. On the march, I wondered why we hadn't done what Burgoyne had, that is, intimidate the entire Ticonderoga complex with a barrage from the cannons on Mount Defiance. Of course, further reflection reasoned that the assault on the old French fort was not to gain the fort but to destroy Burgoyne's provisions, release the prisoners, and cause him to divert some of his diminishing army to mind his rear.

Indeed, we were happy to inform Gates that, as of the twentieth of September, Burgoyne had only four week's rations. As Brown had declared, and Gates had agreed, our mission had been accomplished. We even merited a thirteen-gun salute from Gates' entire army when we returned.

Another question arose: the boat we were in had a casement built into the center of the hull. In the case was a large metal plate suspended on a forward through-bolt, probably a pivot, and by a lanyard which could lower or crank up the plate. Because of our perilous passage up the lake I did not try to lower the plate for fear it might cause some difficulty. But, I was curious of its purpose.

I found out later that an inventive British naval officer, a Lieutenant Schank, came up with this idea. Last year, when General Carleton was transferring part of his river fleet from the St. Lawrence to Lake Champlain, he couldn't move sailing boats with deep keels up part of the Richelieu River because the keels dragged the bottom.

His officer experimented with a pivoting board, in lieu of a fixed keel which made possible the transfer of even large boats without having to disassemble each boat to pass the shallows and then reassemble it, as they did with two large sloops. Of course, this so-called center board allowed them to sail up wind and helped defeat Arnold's dramatic attempt to block them. In effect, Arnold did block, or delay them, because Carleton decided to advance no farther because of the late season, and the British invasion was postponed a year until Burgoyne picked up the baton.

When we reported to General Gates, we found that a significant battle had taken place on the plateau known as Bemis Heights ten days earlier. At first it was called the First Battle of Saratoga and later the Battle of Freemans Farm. At any rate, it decimated many of Burgoyne's choice legions.

As I was told, newly arrived Colonels Dan Morgan and Henry Dearborn and their backwoods riflemen, with Kentucky rifles, had much to do with the winning of this battle. General Arnold displayed his bravery, riding ahead of his troops and bolstering them to pick off the British artillery crews. They even captured some of the British field pieces and turned them on the enemy. What a gallant day it must have been! Our casualties were only half of what we thought the British lost. And many of their wounded or killed were officers which left their ranks in a state of chaos. Burgoyne pulled his forces back to lick his wounds and to await help from New York.

Our people in the Highlands had captured a messenger from General Clinton in New York, who was so concerned with defending the city, that he was hesitant to send support to Burgoyne. This inference was gleaned from the carrier who refused to give over his message, which was contained in a capsule he swallowed, until they forced him to down an emetic which soon disgorged the capsule and Clinton's half-hearted promise of help. So we assumed that Burgoyne was biding his time and resting his troops in the hopes that help in the form of, at least a diversion, would materialize.

Our army was grateful for the chance to rest, too. Gates seemed happy enough that his army, including militia, had performed so well. Strategically, the peaceful interval would cause the British to use up part of their dwindling rations with no military gain to show for it. The armies were about three-quarters of a mile apart and every night one of our regiments sent out a patrol to harass an already shattered enemy. We found from deserters that their morale was low—they had assumed that they were invincible, especially against "poltroons," as they had referred to us, but the reality of our troop's strength and courage dashed their arrogance.

My friends and I were grateful that we could stay together and remain in one place for a while instead of marching here and there to battle in distant regions. We were mustered with a New Jersey regiment of militia in which I thought I would recognize some of our Chatham-Morristown friends, but the new men were different and strangers to me.

General Washington had deployed men on the eastern seaboard to spot Howe's flotilla of two hundred sail, carrying his army of fourteen thousand men, and horses, artillery, and enough supplies to last a campaign. Howe had departed New York in late July and had not been seen since he appeared in Delaware Bay three weeks later. He must have decided that the Delaware was too risky a path to Philadelphia for he disappeared again for a week.

Washington was perplexed: his quarry could sail up the Hudson to consolidate with Burgoyne's army; attack Boston from the sea; move against Philadelphia as he had tried several times in the spring; or even go as far as Charleston, the strongest and wealthiest city in the south, but a wrong decision by the commander in chief could be disastrous. To hedge his bet, Washington sent us two Continental regiments up the Hudson from Peekskill, and Daniel Morgan's regiment of expert riflemen from Trenton. He decided, with the help of a council of his officers, and even Congressional deliberation, to camp near Philadelphia, the correct choice as it turned out.

Finally, Howe was spotted in the upper reaches of Chesapeake Bay on August twenty-second, the same day that the siege of Fort Stanwix happened to end. Being cramped at sea below decks for a month of the hottest days in August wilted Howe's men, devastated their cavalry contingent, and required a week of limbering up before his troops could advance northeast. Howe was now as close to Philadelphia as he was in Elizabethtown before he started.

Having heard of a likely confrontation between Howe and Washington, the suspense was over when we received news of Washington's defeat and the loss of Philadelphia. This time the armies were well matched in terms of numbers but evidently American knowledge of the creek fords was inaccurate and

41

confusing, and not until the British had forded the Brandywine did our officers know that our forces were about to be boxed in.

As usual, the British committed atrocities, the most notable of which was at Paoli Tavern, a place twenty miles west of Philadelphia. General Anthony Wayne, originally from that region, had his regiment bivouacked for the evening when a detachment of redcoats crept up on the unsuspecting troops and bayoneted them in their sleep. Only a few escaped unscathed. This only infuriated our side, both troops and civilians, as the act had no strategic value but the loss of over a hundred men. This was typical of the British: they preached Christian virtues but practiced barbarity.

A few weeks later, Washington and his army tried to redeem themselves by assaulting the British encampment at Germantown. The plan was clever, but too complicated in its timing and coordination, especially when a fog made it impossible to know at whom one was shooting. Also, many of our men became casualties when they insisted on clearing a mansion of British marksmen instead of bypassing it and advancing along the main road.

Despite the loss and confusion due to the fog, many thought Washington's army performed as veterans, and even better than at Trenton and Princeton. Not until the end of the siege were we aware of this drama that had taken place for the capture of a city that had questionable military value.

As it had in New Jersey the previous year, Howe's army plundered the countryside of the recently harvested crops in towns like Kennett Meeting, Media, and Paoli. It encountered Washington's army when it reached Chadd's Ford on Brandywine Creek. It was a desperate battle lasting the whole day, but a violent rainstorm wet the powder in his army's muskets causing a rapid retreat. In the end, Washington was overwhelmed and outflanked at one of the creek crossings and the British overran the outlying towns of Philadelphia.

This was the occasion when the Marquis of Lafayette joined Washington's forces. He and his coterie of noblemen had just arrived from France to prove their belief in our nation's cause. The young Lafayette and Washington struck it off together; it was as if Washington finally had a son of his own. In his enthusiasm, Lafayette suffered a leg wound and was sent off to a Bethlehem hospital to recover.

Ironically, a British officer later revealed that in the heat of battle he had a high-level American officer in his sights. Due to the brilliance of his uniform and the manner in which he rode his horse and managed troops, the officer thought it was Washington. But he didn't pull the trigger for some reason he failed to explain. The facts of time and place later revealed that indeed it was Washington. The British officer was Major Patrick Ferguson, the inventor of the famous Ferguson rifle.

With the war reaching Philadelphia, I was reminded of our meeting John Bartram and his fabulous gardens on the banks of the Schuylkill a year and a half ago. I remember distinctly his saying that while the French and Indian War was fought largely in the wilderness, the war with Britain would probably be fought more in the cities. I was saddened to read in a letter from Olivia that Bartram had died just as the British occupied Philadelphia. I hoped that the death of this interesting and gentle man was not due to violence or shock. What a desperate time for his wife Ann.

Our new encampment was just off the road up the hill from the Bemis Tavern. My friends and I sequestered ourselves behind a huge growth of brambles to protect us from the chill north winds and any random British patrol. We dragged some fallen trees to enclose our retreat even more, so that, when we were done, it was a comfortable hut though open to the skies. In this manner, we thought we were blocked off from the chaos of camp life and the constant traffic day and night.

Trevor had unrolled his bedding at the entrance of our new nest and after a while he observed, "This is the perfect place to view our new camp mates. It seems we have located our place of repose right next to the path to the latrine." He laughed in irony, and added, "Maybe your friend Hawkins, and his quarries will come by. If you still have his letter, please re-read the villains' description so we can spot the pair of them."

We all gathered close together so that we could hear, but wouldn't be overheard. I read Hawkins' letter so we could better imagine the scoundrels and then they asked me what Hawkins looked like.

"Hawkins is shorter than me, probably by an inch and he has black, shiny hair. His face is roundish, something like Crispin's only his nose is straight and longer, and his eyebrows are dark and bushy.

He is intelligent and looks like he is, and is usually, in a serious manner, although he has a good sense of humor.

"Since he is a fourth-generation citizen of New Jersey, he talks like one from the northern part of the state, like those we knew around Chatham and Morristown. Oh, and he has a pear-shaped birthmark on his right cheek. That description should set him off from anyone else around here." I was surprised that I could reel off Hawkins' features in such detail.

Crispin was a little miffed. "I didn't know I had a round face. I don't look at a mirror all the time but I thought I looked better than that. And so does Annie."

Trevor interrupted, "Read the letter again about the two villains."

I dug the letter out of my pack a second time and skipped the irrelevant sentences, but read the rest:"They are Robert Trainor and Bartholomew Bart" Dickson. They are in the New Jersey militia and are ordered to the Albany area in defense against General Burgoyne. They should arrive during the first week in September. I may be transferred there, too. If so, I will look you up and proceed accordingly.

"Trainor is tall, blonde, has a mean face and a cleft chin. Dickson is dark-haired, short, humming most of the time, and well educated. They are friends and together most of the time.

"Keep your eyes opened for them. Sic semper tyrannis! Signed John."

"What do you mean, "a roundish" face, like Crispin's? I thought we were friends!"

"We are friends, Crispin, good friends and for a long time. I'm sorry if I offended you. I was only trying to describe Hawkins so you all could spot him and we could learn more about the brigands. I should have chosen a more discrete word."

This didn't mollify Crispin and he wanted to get back at me.

"I've never said anything like that to you. I could have called you a stuffed shirt, but I didn't. You didn't help my wooing Annie when you referred to me as macaroni. I think you owe me an apology."

"I already apologized, Crispin, but I'll gladly do it again. I had no idea that saying you were well dressed diminished Annie's regard for you, or that you were offended. I'm sorry."

"Well you ought to be. I remember..."

Trevor broke in, "Come on, Crispin, simmer down. Jamie apologized to you twice and explained what he meant, which was not demeaning in my opinion. Don't let an innocent remark taint a long friendship."

The words "simmer down" had a remarkable effect and Crispin made no more comments, but he was petulant and pouted a bit.

Chief Honeoye thought to change the subject. "Since we've been here, I've heard so much hero worship of Arnold; I'm beginning to wonder what the truth about this man is. Colonel Brown doesn't like or respect him from his experience on the Quebec campaign and even published a pamphlet saying, "money is this man's God, and to get enough of it he would sacrifice his country." You've got to dislike someone quite a bit to go to the trouble of printing and handing out a statement like that. I'm surprised that a proud and vain man like Arnold didn't challenge Brown to a duel."

I felt the same way. "You've got to be sick to hate a man so violently that you say such a thing. Maybe that's what Brown was trying to do, to provoke Arnold to challenge him and then choose his favorite weapon to shoot the man. It legitimizes murder and happens all the time, you know."

Crispin rejoined the conversation. "We know Brown well enough. Remember his temper back at the Ballston Spa when we went swimming in the pond? We were strangers yet he treated us as lowly privates with no provocation on our part. He's also acted as a know-it-all, as if he never made a mistake in his life. Brown may be the one at fault, not General Arnold."

Trevor jumped on this statement. "It sounds to me like someone is taking the young wonder boy, Wilkinson's revelations too seriously. He's only nineteen, yet he's General Gates' aid and confidant, and he'll say anything against Arnold to make his boss appear better. Far be it from us to make judgments on hearsay, however high the source. And if the generals want to argue incessantly, that's up to them."

A head thrust itself into our company. "Are you taking bets on the Arnold-Gates fracas?" It was Elkanah Pierson, the blacksmith's son in Vaux Hall who befriended me when I first arrived at my uncle's farm. "I knew I had heard that voice somewhere and here is the lot of you. It's good to see you all in one piece," said Elkanah.

"Elkanah! It's good to see you—just when we need an old friend. Let me introduce you to Trevor Shaw who used to operate a general store in New York, and Dan Reitenhaus, one of the best snake oil salesmen. But we call him Chief Honeoye since he was raised by the Oneidas. I think you already know Crispin Johnson."

After the shaking of hands and brief blather, Elk asked how wagon making and my springs were working out. I told him about being transferred to Fort Stanwix with Trevor and Crispin, repairing wagons there, and briefly about the siege. I also mentioned our part in the raid on Ticonderoga.

"So you were in on that? My brother was one of the prisoners you released. He said it was a neatly organized and executed enterprise. I've been here only a few weeks—just in time to get volunteered in the latest squabble with the redcoats, and now you guys are here for the next fight, which should break out any time.

"I'm on my way to see General Maxwell, so I have to rush. But let's have dinner tonight, say at the Bemis Tavern at six," he said, and was gone.

The next skirmish took a long time coming and the army seemed to have more and more anxiety each day the main action was delayed. After we had been there for a week, news came from downriver that on October third their General Clinton had commanded three thousand men and gone upriver from New York. It was a diversion probably suggested by Burgoyne, to relieve his predicament.

Clinton was foxy in that he landed at Tarrytown, and the next day he landed again a few miles south of Peekskill on the east side of the river and flaked the rebels out of a twelve pounder and that part of the Hudson shore where he camped. But his real strategy was to have his men cross the river and hike around the rear shoulder of Dunderberg, Bear Mountain, and attack both Fort Montgomery and then Fort Clinton on the western side.

The forts were still in the construction stage and located on high rocky shelves on either side of a small stream that enters the Hudson. Most of the defenders were militia mixed in with a few Continentals, and commanded by General James Clinton at Fort Clinton and his brother, Governor George Clinton at Fort Montgomery.

It was like Bunker Hill all over again, with our Sunday soldiers firing down at the British assault party and taking a terrible toll on the ever-pressing British. But in the end, both forts were overwhelmed as well as Fort Constitution, a small, undermanned post on an island opposite West Point.

From here, all the way to Albany, the British under their General Clinton had clear sailing. But Clinton had no intention of taking anymore risk. His officers later burned Esopus (Kingston), the new capital of the state, and Clermont, the main estate of the prominent Livingston clan, before returning to New York. So, as destructive as Clinton's sortie from New York was, we didn't have to worry about a diversion or any other reinforcements for Burgoyne.

Crispin decided to make the time we languished pass quicker. "I'll bet the lot of you that Burgoyne makes his move by the tenth of October. How about it, Jamie? My five dollars against your five."

"I have no reason to think he will or won't. Besides, you know I don't gamble."

"You must have some idea. We know he's running low on rations, and he's the aggressor. We also know he likes to gamble. He can't just sit there with his mistress while his troops are getting restive. He's got to break out of his lethargy, and soon."

"Everything you said makes sense, but whether it's the ninth, tenth, or eleventh, I have no idea when he will go into action again. And I see no sense in venturing money on it."

"Well, it's only..."

Trevor cut in, "I'll take you on for five dollars, Crispin. I'm betting that Burgoyne doesn't initiate a move on the tenth. He may on any other day, just not the tenth. Agreed? And by a move we mean an offensive with his entire army, not just a patrol. For that matter, let's make it a ten dollar bet—I can use the money."

Crispin knew he was being put down for his persistent desire to bet me, but he accepted the larger wager and its precisely defined terms. Trevor hadn't dealt with lawyers for years without learning to be precise in wagers and contracts. Crispin said no more, but again began to pout.

That evening, the four of us had dinner with Elk Pierson at the Bemis Tavern. If Colonel Brown needed us in an emergency, the army knew where we could be reached. The place was noisy and raucous as tired arrays of troops came and went to ease their travails. Our paper money was losing value and they had few opportunities to spend what little they had. But Elk said that this was his treat.

He was a cornucopia of news. "After the Cornwallis move at Bound Brook, there was little attempt by the British to advance across Jersey. Their foraging and our raids on their foraging parties continued as spring advanced but there was no full-fledged battle plan until June when Howe tried one last time to cross the state to Philadelphia. No one of us knew why he was so insistent to occupy that city except maybe he wanted to scatter Congress with which desire many could agree.

"I've happened to see Olivia at Chapman's. Congratulations! She looks fine and in no way does she show any signs of inconvenience. Your uncle Arther has assumed the position Squire Lamsden had before he joined the army, so disgruntled farmers are still under control.

"Did you know the Eccles family? They have a farm at the edge of the Great Swamp."

"Well, the son joined the Continental Army while the father remains a staunch Tory, but he's respected enough to not be mobbed by the crowd. The son may even be up here to fight Burgoyne's redcoats."

I asked Elk if he knew John Hawkins and was he up here. He didn't, until I described him and then mentioned his being called down by Colonel Cheyne. "Oh yes, he's here, and so is Cheyne, to Hawkins's sorrow. I think everybody has Cheyne on their shit list. One of these days we'll find Cheyne shot, not heroically from the front by the enemy, but in the back. That will be a victory everyone can applaud. But it seems that every regiment has to have someone like Cheyne."

Trevor told him about Hawkins' search for the men who murdered his brother and father. Elk didn't recognize them, but said they had a few who still plundered civilians when the chance arose and they thought they could get away with it.

"How is your father? I suppose he's in the army, too."

"Yes. He's with Washington in Pennsylvania—came through the Battle of Brandywine all right but the fighting lingers, I've read in the Philadelphia papers. Both Dad and my brother enlisted last February when the Continentals were hard up for men. My brother said that he felt like a veteran now that he had some fighting experience."

Elk continued. "I guess you never did get a chance to finish your wagon-springs experiments. I got to thinking about some of your ideas and banged out a set of springs for my father's wagon. What a difference that made! Too bad that I decided to join the army after Dad and my brother did. Running the forge was too much work without them"

Just then a commotion erupted in the barroom of the tavern. A vicious argument had turned into a fight, and chairs had been smashed as well as glassware. I recognized a bullying voice. "I can hear that Cheyne is right here and that someone is not putting up with his torment. Let's see what's going on," I said.

We had pretty much finished our meal but brought our drinks with us to the crowded scene in the bar. There was Cheyne being braced by two younger enlisted men who seemed to know more about brawling than he did. I had never seen these two, but something about them made them seem familiar.

Crispin, who has an eye for detail, whispered, "They look like the description Hawkins gave in his letter; just like wolves ganging up on a sick doe. Maybe Hawkins is in this crowd, too."

It wasn't likely, but all four of us looked around at the crowd for Hawkins' presence. I asked Elkanah if he knew who Cheyne's antagonists were. He said he didn't, but would ask around. Finally, we were honing in on Hawkins' quarry.

CHAPTER SIX

BEFORE WE LEFT the tavern, Elk had found that the brawlers were indeed Robert Trainor and Burt Dickson, notable for their obstinate disruption of the regiment and occasional thievery. Now, all we had to do was to locate John Hawkins.

As we walked up the hill to our hut, the dampness of the night began to cloy along with the cold nip of the air as the season affirmed its settling in. Surely, there was going to be a killing frost tonight. We lit a small fire in the center of our humble home, made a place for Henry, and continued our conversation.

"Crispin's right: Burgoyne does have to make a move soon. As they say, 'he has to fish or cut bait.'" This from Chief Honeoye. "He's losing men through desertions and disease as well as casualties on the field. He'll lose the morale and enthusiasm of his troops if he continues to ponder whether to advance or retreat to Ticonderoga. But the season and his men's appetites are working against him. He might even resume operations tomorrow."

Sure enough, the next morning, October seventh, Burgoyne fired his signal gun to announce the beginning of his great thrust from the site of the first battle of Saratoga, already being called Freeman's Farm by some. As Colonel Brown had predicted, Burgoyne divided his legions into three main sections, with General Riedesel and his Germans on his left and British grenadiers under Major Acland farther off to the right. General Fraser was on the far right, and Burgoyne commanded in the middle with Brigadier Hamilton. They gravitated to the west where there was some open ground that best accommodated the European style of fighting, but not so far as to be easy targets for Morgan's riflemen just inside the woods.

This was remarkable in that it left only two regiments to guard Burgoyne's supplies and boats for their transport, the loss of which would have settled the conflict then and there. I thought that they must be especially good troops to be trusted with such valuables.

General Gates sent out Colonels Morgan and Dearborn to our left where there were dense woods punctuated with occasional clearings. To their right Generals Learned and Poor held sway, supported by New Hampshire Continentals under Cilley, Hale, and Scammell, and Van Cortlandts and Livingston's New York militia and the Connecticut militia of Cook and Lattimer.

As in the First Battle of Saratoga, General Gates directed our forces from his behind-the-lines headquarters, not once venturing to the field, but entirely dependent on messengers to keep him informed and to direct his officers. While he and General Arnold collaborated well previously, they had furious disagreements at Saratoga to the point where Gates had relieved Arnold of his command.

Arnold was outraged by this man whom he thought shouldn't outrank him, and was all set to leave the vicinity when a coterie of officers convinced him of the necessity of his attendance. His name alone would have a military value, they said, and most felt that Gates' allowing him to leave the field would be like shooting yourself in the foot. Arnold changed his mind and stayed within Gates' presence, but simmered while the battle raged without him. As the afternoon wore on and he heard the messages coming in and the orders going out, he resolved to join in the fray and jumped on his large brown mare.

With this information and his practiced eye, Arnold knew where to go and what to do. When the troops saw him on the field, their morale and resolve surged and they followed where he led them. We were aware of this when we heard the troops roar their approval over the booming of cannon and the clickety bursts of musketry but the smoke of the enemy artillery and other commotion, as well as the trees, obscured our view. General Gates had a fit and sent Major Armstrong to recall Arnold but Arnold had been so rambunctious that the aid didn't catch up with him until it was too late.

From where I was, it was impossible to see the glorious moment that Arnold had created but we heard the hurrahs shouted by the participants. Arnold had been aware of the prominent officer successfully leading the other side; he was a threat to all he'd accomplished so far, and Arnold asked Morgan to select one of his sharpshooters to dispose of General Simon Fraser, one of Burgoyne's more aggressive generals. On the third try Tim Murphy placed his shot in Fraser's midriff which proved to be fatal the following morning.

Only a few moments later, Arnold's horse was shot from under him, and Arnold took a bullet in the same leg wounded at Quebec. The redcoat who did it was close by and a soldier asked Arnold if he wanted him shot. Arnold said something like," No, he's a good fellow, just doing what he's supposed to." Then Arnold was carried in a blanket litter out of the action.

At that point the British had retreated to their breastworks and the battle, as managed by Arnold, was over. We had shattered an army of veterans and taken ten of their heavier artillery. Fortunately for the wounded left on the field, the sun had set and the air began to clear and cool off. Mostly, the moans of the wounded prevailed, the shrieks of sudden shock had abated, and small parties of men from both sides tended the wounded and accounted for the dead and dying. At the same time, suffice it to say, scavengers from both sides were active fleecing the dead bodies for clothes and valuables. This disgusting scenario was frowned upon by the authorities but difficult to control. As callous as it may seem, we had to ignore the cries of pain as we recovered the treatable wounded to preserve our own sanity.

Our company had mustered to see how many had survived the battle. Chief Honeoye and Trevor were there but Crispin hadn't shown up yet. We knew he had a weakness for being tardy so we accounted his absence to that. We thought he would be along any minute, apologizing with a sob story. After all, he may be one of those who, in the heat of the moment, decided to follow Arnold farther afield.

The tentative tally for casualties came to only one hundred fifty for the entirety of Gates' army. Most of our troops thought that the British toll of their losses were far higher, though final figures were not released to the papers for weeks and we suspected that, in any case, they would be understated. Over the next few days, there was a deadlock between the two armies.

Burgoyne moved his troops northward in a slight retreat and Gates took advantage of this and regained the same ground. Not a night went by but that our patrols captured or shot their pickets and reconnoitered to determine the enemy's position; mornings were too foggy to tell until the sun was high enough to burn off the fog. Colonel Fellows had crossed the Hudson and blocked the British should they attempt to cross back. Finally, Colonels Morgan, Dearborn, and Learned had circled through the woods and back to the Hudson on our side, entirely surrounding Burgoyne who now had no place to go.

The three of us waited another five minutes after muster before we started to worry—maybe Crispin was still lying on the battlefield losing his life blood.

"Where did you last see him, and when?" I asked them.

"The last I saw him was when he was running down the ravine of Mill Creek. It was about an hour ago," said Trevor.

"That's about when and where I saw him—maybe a little earlier. He was lively and not wounded then," added the Chief.

"We should each grab a lantern and look for him. Let's draw a rough map and divide it in thirds so we can scour the ground quickly. We may have no time to lose. Whoever finds him should yell out and wave his lantern for the others. Agreed? I'll take the northern segment, Trevor, you take the southeast, and Chief, take the southwestern section. Let's go!" I urged.

It was twilight but the bodies of our troops all looked the same except for those in officer uniforms. We knew that Crispin was still in the uniform of macaroni—he had hated to relinquish his status of sartorial splendor, despite the conspicuous danger of a sharpshooter, and this made the job of locating him easier.

A Hessian officer startled me by approaching and, in broken English, asked, "Are you looking for a smallish man with a van Dyke beard and a stylish uniform? He's over there just on the other side of the little waterfall. He's wounded but he'll be alright if you give him some water." I started toward Crispin when the soldier added, "I'm still alive only because your General Arnold saved me from being shot. Good luck to ye and your friend." and disappeared in the dusk. What a strange statement I thought as I rushed to the waterfall and Crispin's recumbent body. Only later did I learn the significance of what he said.

Fortunately, I had my canteen with me. I knelt down, gave Crispin a sip, and he moaned when he came to and recognized me. "I wanted to live until Saint Crispin's day, Jamie. It's coming soon, isn't it? It's in October, the same day as my birthday. October twenty-fifth?"

"Yes, that's exactly right, Crispin. Where have you been wounded? We will get you to a doctor as soon as I flag Chief Honeoye and Trevor."

He pulled his pants down and pointed to his thigh. "It's right in there someplace but I can't tell exactly because the whole leg hurts. Let me have some more water, will yuh? Please."

The only way I could signal Trevor and the Chief now was by lantern, so I yelled and waved the light back and forth. They both acknowledged my call and were at our side within two minutes. "How is he?" they both asked at the same time.

"He's got a bullet wound in the thigh. I don't know exactly where it is or how much it's bleeding, so help me turn him. Do you have a shirt or something we can bandage him with?"

As we carefully lifted Crispin into a sitting position, he didn't cry out, but he winced and we all winced with him. The entrance hole was bullet-sized but the bullet exited making a larger wound, and his flesh had been oozing blood but not pulsating. That was a good sign. The bullet had neither broken a bone, cut an artery, or a vein. Chief Honeoye took off his shirt and bound the wound with an extra wad of cloth over the worst part.

"What does it look like? Do you think I may lose my leg? Will I be able to walk again? What will Annie say?" Our friend was remarkably alert and aware of his future options. I was straightforward with him. "You don't have a broken leg. It could be much worse, Crispin. The main thing now is to stop the blood. God knows how much you've lost already. How long ago did this happen?"

"It must have been about a half an hour ago—maybe one of the last shots fired. I was walking back to meet muster when I heard the shot and felt the pain in my leg, like what it would feel like if someone hammered a nail into it, I reached around to find where I was wounded and felt the cavity and the blood. Then I passed out."

I turned to Honeoye. "Chief, you're the strongest and largest. Can you get him over your shoulder and get him back to the medic's tent? He should be in the hands of a doctor as soon as possible."

Trevor and I gently assisted the Chief in loading Crispin, who was again unconscious, and would not have to suffer the bumps and jostling of being wheeled. Litters of wounded had already been brought from the field to this center of carnage, bathed in the gloom of lantern light. I hoped that Crispin was still unconscious so that he wouldn't see the pile of amputated legs and arms or hear the moans of the wounded. The more seriously wounded were silent, as if further moaning was of no use.

Three doctors had patients on makeshift tables. It seemed that the main treatment was the quick removal of limbs except for one doctor, who had a series of bottles with powders, tonics, and balms to ease the pain and stop the bleeding. We laid Crispin down near that table but stayed with our friend to prevent someone from trampling him, and to offer any assistance.

The doctor glanced in our direction. "He must be a good friend. Don't worry, we'll fix him up so he's hale and hardy again. I'll be with him in a minute," he said.

When he finished with a soldier with a broken arm from a brawl, he signaled the nurse to place Crispin on the table. Rather than start blathering as to what might be the problem, as I had so many times before about myself or others, I stayed quiet until the doctor had time to examine his fresh patient.

He removed the Chief's bandage and had Crispin flex his leg. He then squinted more carefully at the wound on both sides of his thigh, cleaned the wounds, administered some balm on them, and lightly sprinkled some powder top and bottom, and put on a fresh bandage. Finally, he gave Crispin some willow bark, to ease the pain. All this was done in the space of five minutes, and served notice to Crispin and us that he was probably going to survive and, most likely, keep his leg.

"Keep him off the leg and change his bandage every day with freshly washed cloths. Above all, get him away from here, wash your hands before handling his leg, and keep him well fed and rested. Where's he from? He'll be using crutches after a few weeks and be home in a month." Then he sighed, "Next?" I never did get the doctor's name.

We removed Crispin to our den for the night but didn't know where to take him for rest the next day. Trevor suggested that Bemis, the tavern owner, would know suitable folks nearby and we all went to sleep satisfied that our friend would be safe.

Bemis was a gentleman who had prospered by serving the neighborhood and travelers' good hospitality and decent quarters, and was an unofficial mayor of the area. He seemed to know everyone and their history and their likely propensity to harbor a wounded veteran. He said the Schuylers would do it, only Burgoyne had burned their fine country home as a "strategic necessity," the general had shamelessly announced later. For a man reputed to have once been sympathetic to the American cause, he was a study in hypocrisy.

After the definitive second battle of Saratoga, there was a further impasse. We sensed that Burgoyne needed time to consider his options. One of them was the possibility that General Henry Clinton was still on his way to relieve Burgoyne by nearing Albany and forcing Gates to detach some of his troops to defend his rear. As days passed this became more remote, and Burgoyne presented Gates' aid de camp with Burgoyne's list of considerations. The aid was Colonel James Wilkinson, the very one who at Morristown tried to force me to build a coach for him. I had very little faith in such a sycophant, social climber, and bully. Evidently, Gates did.

But the general whipped out the terms of "unconditional" surrender so suddenly that Burgoyne began to think that there must be some truth about Clinton's advance north, and that Gates wanted to get a treaty signed before Clinton arrived to spoil the game and start the battle afresh. The one thing that Burgoyne wanted to avoid was a capitulation of his forces which had begun this campaign with such zest and confidence. It would ruin the prospect of a brilliant career.

He agreed to little that Gates had advanced but instead offered what he called a "convention," which stated that Burgoyne and his army would lay down their arms, and their colors, return to Britain, and refrain from serving in the war for independence in North America. Surprisingly, Gates quickly agreed, which again caused Burgoyne to hesitate even though he had promised his officers that he would sign the treaty comprising the compromise.

Further confusion was added when a Tory said that Esopus had been burned and that Clinton might even be in Albany. He put the question to his officers who thought it unlikely. After what seemed like endless discussions between representatives of the opposing parties, and another delay because of a second Tory's hearsay, his officers insisted that it would be dishonorable to renege; this finally persuaded the general to go along.

57

So Burgoyne signed the treaty or "convention" as he insisted it be called. The Battle of Saratoga was over; except for the surrender ceremony to be held the following day, October seventeenth. Wilkinson was sent to York to inform Congress.

CHAPTER SEVEN

OCTOBER SEVENTEENTH WAS a beautiful day in every sense of the word. A veteran British army had finally been fairly defeated, their Indians chastised, their Tories disestablished, and the disruption of everyday affairs healed over. The sky was blue and the sun shone on a landscape bathed in the full colors of fall. Enemy soldiers threw down their arms in a field out of view of our troops (General Gates' concession to lessen their humiliation) and then were directed to form up and ford Fishkill Creek and march south.

At this point, they were forever after known as the Convention Army and they marched down a path between our two columns of buckskin and homespun-dressed troops, the whole scene reminiscent of running a gauntlet. Despite the mortification of their surrender, the redcoats noticed that their American cousins were taller and sturdier in stature, and we remained quiet in near-perfect decorum under orders from General Gates. They passed a marquee where the senior officers of both sides were sharing a widely diverse dinner from field and forest, washed down with cider and rum though there was no lack of wine which could have been purloined from the British baggage train.

Gates and Burgoyne both briefly appeared, Burgoyne in his best regimentals and Gates in a worn blue frock, to accept and return, the sword of victory, and to honorably dignify the ceremony with polite denials of the others flawed generalship.

The difference in character of the two generals was stunning. Only a few days before, Burgoyne had burned the Schuyler's summer mansion and farm, where the Fishkill enters the Hudson, saying shamelessly that it was a "military necessity." Yet after the surrender the Schuylers graciously extended their hospitality to Burgoyne by inviting him and the Riedesels to stay at their Albany home, a courtesy which Burgoyne exploited for ten days.

Such magnanimity didn't exist in the ranks as the defeated troops and Tories marched past the mob of rebel camp followers who jeered and swore at them, a behavior returned by the dejected captives. The Hessians in their colorful but torn and dirty uniforms followed with their pet animals such as rabbits, raccoons, and even a dancing bear.

Captured Indians were next in train and Gates' officers had to order a special detachment to protect them from local farmers who threatened to bathe them in tar and feathers.

Our musicians played a jaunty tune written by a British officer in the last war called "Yankee Doodle." Somehow the ditty captured the spirit of our winning side.

The formal treaty had been expected for the last ten days after the Battle of Bemis Heights, but our main and immediate concern was Crispin's condition. A few days later, he was vastly improved and could even put a little weight on his injured leg, which cheered all four of us. We were still cautious since we had all seen examples of improved convalescents whose health turned sour for reasons beyond our ken. It was enough to make one superstitious.

I hiked the wooded heights above the tavern to look for straight and sturdy saplings with forks in them to make a set of crutches for Crispin. If his leg kept getting better, he would soon be able to use them. Mister Bemis had changed his mind and suggested that Crispin use a garret room since he could not as yet get around. Crispin's arms were strong and he could practice using the crutches on the landing and the large room at the top the stairs.

I cut two lengths of striped maple and peeled off the bark so the wood would dry. Then I had to have Chief Honeoye prop up Crispin to a standing position so I knew where his hands would require hand holds. By the end of the day we had a set of sturdy crutches which, with a few more days in the sun and the wind, would stiffen, be lighter and wieldier, and less likely to bend under his weight, which wasn't much.

I tied some rawhide on the feet of them for safer traction and wrapped some more around the forks, which were his main support. I tried them out by walking around the tavern despite the presence of other guests. They were a little short for me, but I was satisfied that they would be serviceable for Crispin.

One of the gentlemen guests in chairs on the lawn was interested in the way I had fashioned the crutches and showed me his cane. It was made of blackthorn with an ivory head. His own head seemed to be ivory, too, since he was bald with a drumhead-tight skin that shined in the sun. As if to make up for a lack of hair, he had a massive beard which made him appear to be a patriarch.

By God, it was Wenceslas Mochter! He showed no recognition of me for I had a beard—it was too inconvenient to shave every day while I was in combat—and I was in an officer's uniform.

I wondered if Mochter was living up to the agreement he made with Annie McLauren who's sleuthing and testimony had put him in Simsbury Mines. After he was there a month, he pleaded to give more detailed information if he was released under bond, and he pledged to root out other counterfeiters and horse thieves. He was a son of a bitch, but now he was our son of a bitch.

The last I heard was that he had produced evidence that put twenty-five others in jail. He was free to run a business (we didn't pay him) but he had resources of his own even after his mill in Hereford went bankrupt, and was sold to pay the creditors.

I had talked with him up close only that one time, when he found me up in the roots of the old sycamore which had been blown over by the snow storm. I was trying to distract him from seeing the gold ingot that had lain on the river bottom for years and been covered in the tree roots, but recently upended ten feet in the air, and which I had been striving to reach.

I thought he was going to preserve the greenwood for the community so that this ancient park could be fished and hunted and picnicked in for another thousand years since he had just acquired it and said he considered donating it to the town.

But he knew all along that he was going to sell it to the army for a recruit's training station by agreement with one of his friends in the ministry. He had by that time already acquired the town common by offering large loans to owners of the properties whom he knew would not be able to meet the payments. He even extended additional credit to tardy borrowers if their property was exceptionally attractive to his scheme.

And then he foreclosed on them when their burden became too demanding. Oh, what a blackguard he was! It was well that he moved away to the American Colonies.

I admired his cane and made flattering but innocent conversation, hoping that I would say nothing to tie myself to Herefordshire or my frightful contact with him in the Schuylkill River at Philadelphia. If ever I met an evil being, Mochter was it. I wondered what money-making bedevilment he was up to now. And, of course, he knew where the money was—the British army and investors in western land.

He said that I walked so well with the crutches he was wondering why I needed them. Had I been wounded in the battle? I said I made them for a friend, and begged off by saying the friend was waiting for their delivery.

Crispin had been watching from the garret window. "Was that Wenceslas Mochter, by chance? I recognized the cane. Did he recognize you, Jamie? His twisted mind could make all kinds of trouble for us. What's his game, I wonder?"

We both watched him for awhile and realized that he had been waiting for two young rebel soldiers, the two who had brawled in the bar of the Bemis Tavern.

On October twenty-fifth Crispin was strong enough to use the crutches and I presented them as a birthday present. He managed with 'em very well and, for the next month, he went everywhere: up and down stairs, into the bar, into the kitchen, and to the riverside, and everywhere he made friends.

A nineteen-year old, brunette cook took a liking to him and, before he could say he was happily married, she made him a special cake, changed his bandages, and offered other amenities in such a coy way, I don't feel at liberty to reveal them. He knew he shouldn't accept her daring friendship but he had had no social life except the three of us for the last three months, and we let it pass as a casual and fleeting affair.

Bemis knew about her dalliance, too, but he was in the peculiar position of wanting to chastise her for incursions on her kitchen work, but not so she would refuse him some of her generous coquetry. I brought up the subject with Crispin a few days after his birthday.

"Crispin, Jeanette is an attractive girl and a good cook and we all like her. But we also like Annie McLauren and think it would be a good idea to invite her to come from New York for a visit. You've been married for what, a year? But because of the war you've been able to see Annie only a little more than half that time. We're willing to help out with the sloop fare. How about it? Write her an express letter and by the time she arrives, you'll probably be walking without the crutches."

He looked up from his book on the military arts, ready to challenge this intrusion. "I appreciate your concern for my marriage but I think this is my personal affair. When I want Annie to come to Saratoga, I'll write her myself, thank you!" he said with a snarl. This may have been an inopportune time to intervene.

"Yes. That's what we're asking you to do—to invite her up here before the weather prevents it. Also, Annie may like to know what Wenceslas Mochter is doing up here so she can monitor him."

"Look. I'm not serious about Jeanette. She's just a passing flame, and that's all I am to her. It's nothing to worry about. She's helped me with walking with the crutches, made popovers for me and fresh apple pies, and even tucked me in bed. I think she really wants to be a nurse. If Annie knew about her, she would appreciate her helping me out."

"If it's just a passing affair, I think it's not fair to Jeanette, either. Does she know that you're a married man?" I challenged.

"I don't know. I don't think she would want to know. Women don't like to know about other women, you know." He said this as if he believed it.

There was no point in getting into an argument with him. So I dropped the subject and let him consider what he had told me and what he should do about it. Crispin was not a complete cad and we were sure he would come around and do the right thing. But Crispin was kidding himself. She "wants to be a nurse!" Indeed!

In another few days, the Convention army was going to march to semi-permanent quarters, pending Congress' deliberations over the terms of the convention. General Burgoyne had been invited by General Schuyler to his home in Albany for a few days and may have overstayed his welcome, because his visit lasted more than a week.

To my mind, this showed the difference in character between the two men: Burgoyne took full advantage of the Schuyler's hospitality and stayed overlong at their Albany home, while the Schuylers, whose summer mansion had been needlessly burned to the ground by Burgoyne (who said it was a military necessity) and were gracious and considerate of the proud, but defeated enemy. I cited this difference in every discussion I had at mess.

One of the men chosen to escort the redcoats to Boston, or wherever Congress decided, was John Hawkins. As soon as I saw John and his handsome demeanor, I hatched a fetching idea—why not introduce John to Jeanette in a casual manner so that no manipulation would be evident. Crispin had used this same ruse to successfully wean Trevor away from Annie McLauren several years ago by introducing Trevor to the voluptuous Daphne. It served Crispin's purpose and he and Annie were married not much later. Such is sweet irony.

We found it difficult to see Crispin because every minute Jeanette wasn't working in the kitchen, she was in his room or outside with him, lolling by the river or giving him some intimate attention. Bemis was disturbed by this, he didn't like his kitchen help mingling with the customers, and he asked us to persuade Crispin to remember his marital vows, otherwise he would have to let Jeanette go.

The fact is, Jeanette was considered to be a nymphomaniac, and this wasn't the first time she enraptured a guest. Perhaps we shouldn't have intruded into his affairs, but in the best interest of our friend and Annie, we thought it was necessary. We wrote and told her of Crispin's wound and the battle, but of the real gist of the matter, we said nothing. We simply invited her to come north to visit her husband and us. We also mentioned that we had seen Wenceslas Mochter to pique her interest.

I wrote the letter in the crowded den with Trevor and Chief Honeoye looking over my shoulder. It was as if we were writing a missive for the ages with each phrase challenged so that the whole resembled the proverbial camel that is, like a horse designed by a committee. I thanked them for their help, but rewrote the letter the next day when they were at breakfast, and signed for the three of us.

Jeanette was no dummy. She knew we were trying to halt Crispin's illicit romance with her and we suspect she doubled her efforts to snare his attention. Even in our presence she managed to seemingly extricate herself from Crispin's grasp only to move into a more compromising position where her blouse glanced his person.

"Pet," she said, "You shouldn't wrangle out of reach when I want to caress you. Show your honeybunch that you love her." And then Crispin would respond like a trained show dog. I suppose we have all been in situations like that with a loved one, but not in front of others.

Speaking of dummies, I realized Annie would mention the trip to Olivia so I promptly wrote a letter to her to invite her to join Annie and come to Saratoga. It had been five months since I'd seen her and it would be fun and safe for both of them, now that the army fighting was over. And I was able and wanted to help as she was with child.

I located John amidst the still-large congregation of our troops, many of whom were returning to their homes to finish their fall chores. Since writing his letter to me, he had come through the battles of Brandywine and Germantown, a far cry compared to our smaller skirmishes in New Jersey, he said. He had a much better opinion of our army than he had of the British from which he had deserted almost a year ago. Discipline was firm, but not harsh, and order was maintained in a more democratic manner. Now all that was required was that they got paid, he said, but Congress was still parsimonious and laggard with funds.

After reintroducing ourselves to each other, I suggested we go to the Bemis Tavern for a drink and relaxed conversation. As I had planned and hoped, Jeanette was serving as a waitress in the barroom in the early afternoon and she had dressed in a manner designed to capture the attention of any red-blooded youth. John noticed her right away and I flagged her to come serve us.

She was probably dressed to please Crispin for an hour before the dinner guests demanded her culinary artistry, but here she was waiting on table. John made a handsome picture himself in a special uniform that he was given in his capacity as a guard and warden of the Convention Army. (We couldn't have our guards look shoddy compared to their prisoners.)

"John, this lady is Jeanette, a special friend of mine and Jeanette, this is John Hawkins, another special friend from New Jersey whom I haven't seen in six months," I said, and then I shut up to see how they would react.

John didn't expect to meet such a charming nymph so soon after arriving but he came through smoothly without a hitch, and as a gentleman. "I am most pleased to meet your acquaintance, Jeanette," he said. "I hope to be here for awhile before guiding the Convention Army to their ultimate destination and look forward to seeing more of you."

Jeanette replied in kind, "My last name is Fontaine. It has been my pleasure to meet any friend of Jamie's and I would be pleased to serve you whatever you want, John." They sounded like code words to me. All I had to do now was to let nature take its course.

But John recovered his composure and ordered a glass of Madeira. You could tell that this was not all he wanted. Jeanette intuitively knew that, too. I also wanted a glass of Madeira and Jeanette left to fill our order and to allow John time to comment on her appearance.

"She looks like one of the society damsels in New York or Morristown. Is she native to Saratoga? Where did she come from? She seems well schooled in the social graces. Is she well educated?" John couldn't wait to escort her to some social event and expected me to complete her dossier to him then and there.

"Hold on, she's well spoken-of, and spoken for. Crispin has been her constant companion since she nursed him after he was wounded, about two weeks now."

"But Crispin's married, isn't he?" The answer whetted John's ambition even more.

CHAPTER EIGHT

JOHN COULD HARDLY wait for her to return. He wanted to court her right away. I found that he was a Lothario equal to the task of edging into Crispin's romantic territory. "Je vous aime beaucoup." he began. "Are you French or French Canadian? You impress me with your grasp of European graces."

"You're right! I am French. My father was a French merchant in Montreal and we lived well until the war and the British made us surrender. I was quite young at the time but my father told me that they were supposed to treat us fairly after the treaty. Sad to say, English merchants moved in and arranged to take all business away from the native folk. I could see why you Americans were so upset about always having to give your mother country a substantial cut of every transaction. They did the same to us. It wasn't until recently that I left home and came here to work for Mister Bemis. Where are you from, John?"

"I'm from near New Brunswick, New Jersey, just outside of New York City. I'm also new to this part of New York. I'll bet you did a lot of dancing in Montreal. Is there any place to go dancing around here?"

Just then Crispin came haltingly down the stairs. He was doing well in his fourth day in crutches but I held my breath until he safely reached the main floor and sat down to rest. I went over to him and brought him back to our table and John. Jeanette had since gone to another table to take an order.

I introduced the two to each other and we had the usual blather about what battles each had participated in. Then Jeanette came over to our table again to welcome Crispin. At that, both John and Crispin knew that a major battle for Jeanette's attention was in the offing.

CHAPTER NINE

JOHN'S TWO BRAWLERS, Robert Trainor and Bart Dickson, murderers of his father and brother, were glad to have been transferred to Bemis Heights. They had plundered many farms in the Brunswick area and knew that the law of averages would catch up with them. The local New Jersey farmers were grouping and matching descriptions of their antagonists and were soon to realize that their tormentors were from their own militia. The marauders welcomed the new venue before they realized that the pickings in upstate New York were slim because of the rebel's scorched earth policy; there was barely enough food or forage for the locals.

When they got a glimpse of the British baggage train, they reasoned that high-level officers would bring personal luxuries along with them. General Burgoyne was supposed to have as many as twenty-three baggage wagons of his own full of comforts such as wines, a commodious and colorful marquee, camping equipment, and a mistress to accompany him and enjoy the cross-country romp. Surely a treasure chest of British army cash would be a part of his retinue, they thought. Extra guards would be a give-away to discerning fellows like themselves as to where the treasure wagon could be found.

Trainor and Dickson had competition in the form of Colonel Cheyne who had been morphed into an intelligence agent and moved with the Continental Army to sniff out military secrets of the enemy from deserters. And such signs as small groups of grenadiers, not only large and brawny men, but uniformed to look even larger by the black-bear fur headgear, peculiar to their ranking, were tip-offs of caches of wealth or valuable items under their care or nearby.

Cheyne had found that his prerogatives could be self enriching. He also discovered that blackmailing Trainor and Dickson gave him an experienced workforce to do his dirty work. If they got caught and pointed a finger at him, who would believe that he had had anything to do with it? After all, Cheyne was an officer and was believed to be above such perfidy. Or, at least, Cheyne thought so.

As the battle of Bemis Heights raged, Cheyne and his two cohorts scanned the lineup of wagons on the River Road and supply boats in the river. Near the middle of the line there were more guards congregated by a particular wagon which they hoped to investigate more closely that night, but all the wagons looked the same and it would be difficult to separate that wagon from the others if, for some reason, the guards stationed themselves elsewhere.

The crooks commanded a small field piece and could take a shot at the wagon to mark it for later examination in the dark but scratched the idea for fear they would damage the sought booty and also forewarn the enemy of their intention.

During the action on the bluff, a deserter was brought to them for interrogation but they thought he must have been one of the dumbest redcoats because he didn't even understand the questions; he kept saying, "What?" Then they realized that he was deaf, possibly from the continual cannon blasts. They then wrote out the question, and gave him a quill and the paper to give his answers.

"Yes," he wrote. "The designated wagon was where the battalion treasure was kept but it was reported to be almost gone due to the extravagance of the general. Better to rob the following wagon which served as a depository for the officers accounts. It was most likely to not be tapped as there was no place on the campaign to spend money unless you were a general."

Cheyne then changed his plan— they would focus on the alternate wagon noted by the deserter and the theft would be even more satisfying and notorious for personally attacking the British officer corps. But they must pull the job off tonight. It was obvious that the British were coming out the loser in the campaign and it might be all over the next day.

After a few more questions posed to the deserter, they asked, "How can one spot the wagon which serves as a bank?" The deserter hesitated for his answer would make Cheyne feel like a fool, but he carefully wrote out, "The wagon says 'Officer's Bank' on the headboard." Trainor and Dickson laughed, but Cheyne gave the deserter a lick with his truncheon and sent him back under guard to the prisoner's stockade.

When it was dark they changed into redcoat uniforms and made their way along the edge of the River Road to the selected wagon. Each had two pistols, but kept them in the holsters to avoid appearing as a threat. This job was to be accomplished by bullying, not gunfire—they wouldn't have a chance to pull it off otherwise. As they mingled with other troops, they sized up the number of guards and where they should make their demand.

This was Cheyne's first encounter with danger in the war and he had no idea how well he could handle his fear. He had always imagined that he would be brave but with no actual confrontation to reassure him until now. He had disdain for cowards but he began to tremble. "Please God, let me handle this," he prayed, but God must have been busy answering the prayers of others. Cheyne didn't even say anything to the enemy guards. He simply stammered, turned, and ran to the river and dove in. Trainor and Dickson were startled but had the sense to just fade into the dark.

After a few days of testing to see if British authorities had been aware of the irregular activity at the baggage wagons, Cheyne decided to try again. The British guards didn't report an attempted robbery since no one of the crew said anything to suggest one, and Cheyne had aborted his feeble attempt.

With the surrender, ownership of the baggage train passed to the Continental Army so he reasoned that he had a fresh field. The scheme remained the same except the Americans had moved the long line of wagons and boats farther south behind the rebel battle lines.

Cheyne was not about to lose his courage this time, and this attempt had to be the final one. It was all or nothing. He didn't think that American officers had certified the wagons and which one had the British cash, but so little time had elapsed from the prior attempt that it was a fair bet that the same wagons as before were in the same order, and the one to approach and plunder was in the same relative spot.

To play it safe he decided to interrogate his stockade of detained British deserters. First there was Corporal John Snook, the most recent to have been caught and likely to be up-to-date in regimental affairs.

"Corporal Snook? I have reason to believe you are familiar with the baggage train that was on General Burgoyne's left front. Is that so?"

Snook hesitated, but realized that silence was hopeless. "No sir. I was in an artillery crew under Brigadier Hamilton and in the center front. General Riedesel had overall control and responsibility for the baggage train and it was on our left front."

"Snook, you should know that as a colonel of the winning army, you should answer me promptly and accurately any questions I propose. I'll give you a little time to consider your answer." Cheyne didn't know that middle class Englishmen had been well schooled in the proper grammatical construction of a sentence, but as stated, Cheyne's question was both ambiguous and confusing.

Cheyne went to another office to study a list of detainees while Snook sweated and considered to what degree of obfuscation he was willing to let loose on this bully. But Cheyne was anxious to get his needed information—he didn't have much time. He stormed into the chamber for another try. "Did you have an account at the Officer's Bank?"

"Sir, I have neither the money nor the privilege of having an account at the Officer's Bank. As the name states, that service is for officers only."

"Well, you don't have to get so riled about it. You may go, Snook." Cheyne went again to the other office to consult his list of prisoners. He thought his next selection should be more knowledgeable, he was a sergeant major who had been captured at the battle of Freeman's Farm.

"Sergeant Riley? I imagine you're happy to be out of the fray now that your general's going to surrender. But in the stockade, the war goes on and we have some questions to put to you. Do you have a bank account with your army?"

Riley had been in the military for fifteen years and recognized that this was an out-of-bounds question to propose to army personnel and a man of his standing. "What kind of an account did you have in mind, sir?"

Cheyne was astounded. 'Did all these captives behave this way? No wonder they lost.' He made an effort to cool his annoyance. "I mean, does the army extend privileges such as bank accounts to sergeant majors? And if so, where do, and how do, they make it available to you?"

"I send most of my pay to my Moms, sir. The army provides the forms on which I sign in the interest of happy conditions at home, sir, if that's what you mean."

"That's very interesting. I believe that our soldiers would welcome such a service. But isn't it rather chancy—having all that money at risk during battle conditions?

"Not at all, sir. All they have are the forms. The money's at the army's bank in London or other country depots. When Moms takes the printed form there, they give her cash from the till box. It's as simple as that, and prevents loss to gambling, liquor, borrowers, pick pockets, and otherwise losing it."

"You must get some cash. Don't they pay you on some timely basis, every week, or every month? They must carry some cash. "

"Oh yes sir, but you would have to talk to the general about that. He's a gambler, and he would think you were about to fleece him if you did."

Cheyne needed quick answers so he ignored the sergeant's insolence. "So how does Burgoyne pay for forage and food from farmers or country people?"

"He has to pay them like anyone else. And it you asked him all these questions, he would think, as I do, that you want to plunder the bank wagon. It happens to be near empty, sir, it being the end of the campaign."

Cheyne finally gave up his scrutiny of prisoners. They might blab to the jailors and blow the whistle on his plans to the highest level. He would find some other way to exploit the situation. And besides, the sergeant major said the money was gone.

CHAPTER TEN

THE MORE CRISPIN improved, the more he wandered in and outside the tavern, and unbeknown to Bemis, he entered the tavern workshop, attracted to the smell of fresh paint there. He had done line drawings and maps for Colonel Brown, but he hadn't painted a picture or portrait since his first days at Fort Stanwix, and it would help him immensely by simply painting a scene of the river. Anything to get his mind off what he considered his dilemma: how to conciliate Annie and Jeanette.

He spread some linseed oil on a dried hand towel to size and harden it, and clamped two small boards at the ends to hang and stretch the cloth evenly by the weight of a sash weight alone. On the shelf by the wall was an array of oil paints, more for woodwork or inside walls rather than portraits, but they would serve his purpose. If he painted a portrait of Jeanette, he might not be able to duplicate her shining auburn hair, but was curious to see how close he could come with plain paint. With some of the colors he thought he could approximate the color of her face and shoulders. He would worry about the color of her dress when she consented to sit for him.

That afternoon by the river, he asked, "Have you ever had your portrait painted?"

"My father hired an artist to paint my mother and I thought he was going to do me, too, but no, he didn't. Why do you ask? Do you know an artist here in the wilds?"

"I'm an artist, Jeanette. That's the way I made my living before I joined the Army. I portrayed members of some of the finest families in New York and obtained handsome commissions from them. Now,

I'd like to have you sit for me. Your beauty should be set to canvas for all time. For me it would be a labor of love."

This different side of Crispin was even more pleasing to her, and she would remember the scene for years as when she first realized that she truly loved him. As for Crispin, he considered portraying this beautiful and engaging maiden more than therapy (a euphemism he used for languishing). But their brief time was up and she went to wait on tables even though it was a slow day. Crispin thought it wise to consider how he was going to best capture her character as well as her charms, and went back to the paint shop for the rest of the afternoon.

There was a clean narrow brush handy. 'Why not try a mixture to see how true and fine I can do her hair' he mused. 'I may avoid fumbling paints in front of her when she agrees to sit.' First, he looked for turpentine to clean the brush; after that, he opened a small bottle and dabbled enough to satisfy his curiosity. Then he opened the cartons of yellow, red, and cream colors for the face and shoulders experiment, and then the brown to mix with a dab of red and a touch of yellow for her hair.

After several tries he was satisfied. He cleaned the brush, washed his hands to rid them of solvent, and went upstairs to coax her outside to digest the full benefit of the sun on her features. But Hawkins was there, waiting for her to go for a walk.

He chatted briefly about what a fine day it was to hide his disappointment, and cursed his rival under his breath.

The next day was bright and sunny, but cold. At least, he could have Jeanette to himself as Hawkins was preparing to escort the Convention Army to Cambridge. The bright room on the sunny side of the inn would do, and he asked her to put on her favorite dress and he would paint her.

She would "captivate" men for all time, he told her. She deliberated only a short while to select and exhibit a low-cut gown that exposed a shoulder—"always wear something to lead them on"—she remembered her Mother say.

As she arranged herself on a lounge, Crispin brought up the painting supplies on a tray in the dumbwaiter. When he saw her so swathed and capriciously relaxed on the platform, he gushed, "How perfect a pose! You not only are beautiful, you know just how to display yourself to best advantage." There was no need for him to make any adjustments in her demeanor but he lightly pinched her cheeks to add a tinge of color, and then set to work.

He first sketched her to include a little just above her waist and began to fill in the prominent features with a base paint on which to apply the correct and final colors. Occasionally the sun would be obscured by a cloud, but he waited for its full strength before resuming, getting just the right shade of color and texture.

Jeanette became impatient with these delays and kept getting up to see what he had painted so far. At least, she didn't make suggestions, and before noon, when she had to leave to wait on tables, he had accomplished the basic portrait; he would apply the finishing touches, such as shading her cheek-bones and other facial features after lunch.

As he ate, Crispin visualized her and the painting and realized that the color of the dress could affect the whole aspect of her vitality. Instead of a deep green which she was wearing, he wanted to substitute scarlet, it was sexier and Jeanette was a very sexual woman. He also wanted to emphasize her breasts. Next to her fine face, they were of paramount importance. Surely, every man would think so and probably every woman would, too, if only in a fit of envy. He would touch them up a bit and present them more distended and erect.

After the last lunch patron of the restaurant had left, she returned to the room promptly since she was anxious to see how Crispin would dab paint here and there to finish her character on canvas. When he brush-stroked her neck to be "oh, so graceful" she was delighted with its accurate appearance, but when he painted the top edge of her gown she was disappointed that it was not more revealing. She complained that he made her expression too severe although her very complaint showed how true to the original he had portrayed it. Even so, he accommodated her, and her pleased expression replaced the severity on the canvas as well as on her face.

When her head and shoulders were complete, he asked her if she would like to comment and she said that she had never seen herself look so well in the looking glass. Crispin agreed, but did not admit this compliment and satisfaction until later.

He was afraid she might take offense when he made the color of her gown a vivid scarlet, but he had almost completed the entire work when she applauded the color change by saying she wished only that the gown she wore was as charming.

Crispin backed away from his masterpiece for a more circumspect look and Jeanette joined him in praising the attention to detail, the capturing of exact colors, and her alluring expression. As the painting was seductive, she became more so and Crispin guided her back to the lounge.

"You should not be wasting your beauty on these yokels at the edge of the wilderness. New York or Philadelphia would welcome the attentions of a lady like you. You'd even be invited into the circles of the literati," he said, and then he embraced her. She clutched him as if doing so would make his prediction happen. After several kisses and caresses he went over to the door, locked it, and returned to further their dalliance.

As it turned out, Bemis wanted to use that room but couldn't because the door was locked. He guessed who and why, and, as "punishment" passed the word to some of his other employees. And Hawkins found out, too. When John was shown the painting, he considered the intimation as pure downstairs gossip, and congratulated Crispin and Jeanette on a fine portrayal.

November fifth was Guy Fawkes Day and, as in Hereford, a dance was held for the officers and their wives or sweethearts. I wished that Olivia was there to celebrate our second anniversary of meeting at the dance in Ross, and I was pleased to see John with Jeanette— they made an attractive pair. Crispin was not there, he had asked Jeanette to go, but John had asked first, and Crispin pouted and despaired in the barroom. He chose instead his favorite way of grieving by squeezing all he could from a bottle of rum. I tried to slow him down but he was inconsolable.

I was not as disturbed by this as I was thinking about how he would behave when Olivia and Annie arrive. He had to get a grip on himself and control his emotions, both in love and in anger, or his marriage could be vulnerable. Trevor and the Chief were with us, and tried to restrain his aggressive behavior but to no avail.

Then Mochter came in followed by Cheyne. Crispin, though seemingly unprovoked at the moment, was all set to challenge both of them to a duel.

"What a pair of bastards just came in the door!" he called to everyone. "One has fleeced a lot of people out of their homes and lifetime savings, and the other throws his weight around in the army and destroys reputations on a whim. You don't know me, Mochter, but I'm the guy who rebuilt your outhouse so it wouldn't support you when doing your morning business. Dirty and humiliating, wasn't it? Just like what you did to your townspeople!"

Trevor, the Chief, and I tried to muffle him from shouting any more abuse but the die had been cast, and the bastards spat their venom.

Mochter was first: "Yes, I remember you. You raked the manure from your father's barn and delivered milk to the Claveraques. No more than what everyone expected of you! Of course you couldn't understand business transactions, could you? The last I knew, you had joined the British army to get the King's shilling. And now you deserted and joined the rebels." Contempt was Mochter's primary style.

Cheyne cut in: "Just because the battle's over, you can't talk to an officer that way. I'll have you put on report and sent to the stockade. I should have thrashed you several years ago, and now I've forgotten your name. What is it?"

"I suggest that you take care, Colonel. Word has gotten around about your unusual interest in the British baggage train and how much cash it might carry. Soon, your days of intimidation and rumor mongering will come to an end. And what are you doing with such as Wenceslas Mochter? You either believed what he told you or failed to check on his background. If either of you wish to duel, I accept in front of all in the room."

Then Mochter and Cheyne turned and walked out with what little dignity they could muster. The crowd was gleeful and banged their drinking mugs on the table, shouting, "Baggage for cash, Baggage for cash!"

Crispin stood up as best he could, feeling triumphant, but we discouraged his further outrage. His opponents didn't have such mean reputations for nothing.

CHAPTER ELEVEN

SINCE CRISPIN WAS not willing to consider that his philandering would seriously offend Annie, I decided to have a long talk with Jeanette. I told her about Annie McLauren, that they had been married for over a year, and that Annie would most likely be coming to Saratoga in the next week or so. Jeanette had only a bed in a room for tavern employees so I had to hold this discussion in a vacant army tent and hope for privacy. Dressed for the autumn chill, Jeanette still exuded beauty and charm.

"Crispin went to great lengths to pursue Annie because he was enchanted by her looks and intelligence from the start. She was a young widow and all alone and Trevor Shaw, then a store owner, saw to her every need. As a result, she gravitated to Trevor, making Crispin's suit that much more difficult. But he persisted, even going to Philadelphia when she went there to wind up her husband's estate. Then the war started, New York was occupied by the British, and their lives went in separate directions. Crispin then—"

Jeanette gently held up her hand to interrupt, "I'm sorry to cut you short, Jamie, but I'm familiar with all of that; Crispin told me just the other day. Up to then, I thought he was single; he certainly acted like he was. So I have the same problem you have—how to break off the relationship without hurting him or anyone else."

"Well, that's a relief. I was afraid you might resent and resist my suggestion. If only the affair could be terminated as easily as it started—as you know, he's very sensitive."

"I don't think I've ever met anyone more sensitive. It won't be easy, but I've had the problem before."

I didn't have any trouble believing that.

"So, you can handle this with no help from me? He's a good friend and so is Annie, I don't want either to be hurt, so I'll do whatever is necessary."

"No. I would rather do this alone for my own reasons, and it would leave you untarnished in Crispin's mind. There's only one thing that bothers me. I would like to keep the portrait. It's the finest thing anyone has ever done for me."

"What portrait? Of you? I didn't know about that. I don't see any reason why you shouldn't have it. Except Crispin might want to keep it as a remembrance of you."

"He could hardly do that without offending Annie. Besides, he acted as if it was a gift. No, I'll keep it and make him feel that it's a remnant of our romance that I will treasure as a keepsake—and it will be."

With all this having been said, I left with the thought that I had been unduly impressed by the description and moral judgment of others: that is that Jeanette was a trollop who was nothing more than a camp follower to be taken advantage of. I now doubted that they knew what they were talking about, and hated that they so blithely thought to ruin her reputation.

But, I gladly came away feeling that Jeanette was one of those women who was not only charming, but intelligent and knew where she was going in this world. She was not made to waste her talents on Saratoga bumpkins or fraudulent colonels. I hoped we would meet again.

A brief note from Olivia arrived the morning of November tenth saying that she and Annie expected to arrive by Hudson River sloop by November twelfth. It must have come by way of Haverstraw. If it had come through New York and the British postal service, it would have taken another week.

From conversation with Crispin, I learned that Jeanette had already started to disabuse him of their continuing romance. Now, if he could only stop whining and pouting when he saw her with John Hawkins.

The romance halted just in time because Annie and Olivia arrived that Wednesday, the twelfth. As she stepped off the sloop, Olivia was radiant as usual, but had an enlarged tummy, presumably our son or daughter. Annie looked a little peaked, as if she and Crispin had had an argument that had to have been by mail.

Immediately, we took them by wagon to the Bemis Tavern for accommodations for the four of us and made plans for having dinner there in a private room. I held my breath, hoping that Jeanette would not be waiting on our table, but the dinner was a special pot roast, a feast with all the fixin's that required her culinary performance in the kitchen and all were spared any confrontation or embarrassment.

I had mentioned Crispin's bullet wound in my letter to Annie and she lavished the necessary sympathy on him and noticed how well he was walking, and without crutches, in only about five weeks. Having not seen each other for close to five months, my conversation with Olivia and Annie covered a lot of ground about Fort Stanwix, Ticonderoga, and Saratoga, as well as events at Chatham and Morristown.

"Uncle Arthur has been accused of collaboration with the enemy because he sold some cider and apples to a squad of redcoats, but he threw accusations back at his detractor and was exonerated," Olivia revealed. "He was very agitated, and so was Arabella—it was that same farmer who wanted to dig up their rhododendron." Annie and Olivia both complained that prices for everything were getting higher as our currency continued to lose purchasing power, and Crispin said he wanted to paint Annie's portrait, a favorable sign that his wayward passions had been cooled, or, at least deflected. And so our conversation was stilted by Crispin's conscience.

With dinner over and the kitchen closed, we passed through the barroom where Hawkins was entertaining Jeanette at a cozy table for two; or was it the other way around? I glanced at Crispin who steadfastly kept his eyes on Annie. I had to conclude that Jeanette had performed a sympathetic and discrete dissolution of the affair.

But, bad apples have a way of turning up to spoil the present and Cheyne and Wenceslas Mochter began to exact whatever price they could from Crispin, and later from me.

In New Jersey, we could expect that winter would not start seriously until December first, but in Saratoga the temperature plunged to zero and snow began to fly two weeks before that. Congress had considered the terms of Gates' convention with Burgoyne and refused the prisoner's return to Britain reasoning that even though they were pledged to not fight any longer, the ministry would have them replaced, and free up an equal number of others who would fight in America. The convention army was prohibited from returning to England.

Instead, they were marched to nearby towns in New England where they were spread among the populace to avoid burdening any one community for food or housing. John Hawkins was scheduled to march and oversee the prisoners so he was to be absent for the next several weeks, perhaps as long as to Christmas. Too bad, he and Jeanette were seen together frequently until he left.

Crispin convinced Annie to sit for him, though she knew it would be hard to sit still for what she thought would be lengthy periods. But Crispin had been ordered to resume painting for the army so he climbed the bluff above the tavern to do battleground scenes even though the season no longer looked like fall when the fighting took place. Foul weather excused him of this duty for days at a time and enabled him to devote time portraying Annie.

As well as thinking how he would render Annie on canvas, he thought of Jeanette and the hours he painted her. Almost a month had passed since those few, brief days—they were a charming episode in his life—but he realized they were also shameful and not to be repeated. Annie is as beautiful as Jeanette, just a little older.

He mixed his paints and situated Annie on the lounge as he did with Jeanette, and went about applying the base paint and outlining her profile. How similar, yet different they were, He must free himself of thoughts of Jeanette or he would be painting her, not Annie. 'I'll give the portrait more thought', he mused.

At lunch, the conversation began about the weather. Olivia spoke up, "I wasn't sure we could make it for lunch, the snow is over a foot deep, and it's still coming down. I don't want it to stop, it's beautiful and we never get this much in England."

Annie agreed, "It's beautiful and cozy now, but just wait until March when one can't stand it any longer. Now, it doesn't bother me as it's a good day for Crispin to do my portrait since there's nothing else to do on a day like this. Did you know he was going to do it?" she queried.

Crispin held his breath, and so did I. But neither girl had any reason to know about his painting Jeanette. It was up to me to answer with a firm "no" and to change the subject.

"We could go sleigh riding. Some kids are riding down the hill from Bemis Heights. Maybe we could borrow or rent their sleighs for the afternoon," I suggested.

"Oh, no. We want to finish the painting since I'm halfway done with it. We'll go sleigh riding tomorrow. See if you can rent the sleighs for the morning, Jamie, the snow ought to be over by then." The girls both liked the idea and so it was agreed.

We were just about done with lunch, and Crispin was anxious to resume painting, when Cheyne and Mochter entered the room; it was as if a dark cloud suffused the area, They greeted us politely, with little reference to the shouting in the bar the other evening, and sat down in the opposite corner.

But Cheyne and Mochter began immediately whispering among themselves as if arranging a conspiracy. What else would these two have to talk about?

I did have some news to break the silence at our table. "I received a brief note from John Hawkins. The Convention Army arrived in Boston a few days ago, on November eighth. He says that the prisoners were booed and pelted with garbage and housed in the barracks the British built when they were under siege two years ago. They're waiting to be parceled out to towns near Boston. That's all he said. I can't imagine that he enjoys this duty, only that General John Glover, the one who ferried Washington across the Delaware, is in charge and will take no nonsense from the populace or the prisoners."

"I understand that Congress is hedging whether to permit the army to get back to England. The British didn't turn over all their cartridge boxes, or some incidental thing like that, and Congress says it was a violation of the Convention. Besides, Congress doesn't trust the redcoats and suspects that they will simply unload the surrendered army to duties in England and, in equal numbers, send fresh troops back here to enlarge Howe's army." so said Crispin.

I added, "Congress has had a busy week, then. I understand Gates' aid, Major Wilkinson, finally completed his trip to York to report Burgoyne's surrender. It took him overlong because he lolled in Reading while courting his sweetheart. He owned up to the reason for his tardiness, they say.

"The politicians were miffed at what they considered an affront, but I'll bet that they reward him with a special sword or promotion, or both. The man knows how to ingratiate himself with those at the top. What's going on in Philadelphia now that the British occupy it?"

Annie gave her opinion, "It's a victory for the British, and after all it's the third largest city in the British Empire after London and Bristol. But it has no military value except morale building for them, or if he thinks capturing the city, where Congress sat, important. Remember, Washington still has his army—that's more important than extending your base.

"With Burgoyne's surrender, the redcoats lost an entire army of about eight thousand men, including the six thousand prisoners. The rest were killed, died of disease, or deserted. The loss will be hard for England to replace and to placate the people, who must be weary of such expensive, but poor results. The war has been going on for almost two years and all the Brits have to show for it is Philadelphia."

"You forgot New York, Annie." Olivia whispered.

"Yes. They'll probably keep New York for the duration, too. I think Clinton is their best general."

"Where is Washington going to hold out for the winter?" Olivia asked.

"Whitemarsh is headquarters now but rumor says a small place twenty miles northwest of the city and near the Schuylkill, called Valley Forge, is where he'll be for the winter. Didn't you go fishing for shad there once, Crispin?"

CHAPTER TWELVE

AFTER LUNCH, CRISPIN and Annie went to the bright Long Room to finish the portrait. Annie scanned the profile of her relaxed position on the canvas so she could duplicate it again, and Crispin mixed his paints to test their viscosity and hue.

"So, we resume the pleasure before us," he declared. "We should have this finished the way we want in a few hours, and then you can get some fresh air before it's too dark outside. In the meantime, try to hold your breath—excuse me, I really mean for you to hold your position."

As with Jeanette's painting, he had started with a base paint and began to add facial color. Then he mixed mostly brown, some red, and a dab of yellow for her hair which was almost identical to Jeanette's except the sun was shining when he did Jeanette's and it improved the depth of color. Annie's face was a little darker; almost a tinge of blue, which gave her a more serious expression rather than gay, and he added no more than a dab of gray and blue to show a more lifelike complexion.

Her throat was the same tint as were her upper arms and shoulders, but he chose to garb the rest of her arms in long, white gloves as if she was attending a debutante's ball. As he did this, he wished it was possible to scent the painting with her favorite perfume, but he fancied drawing a rose corsage instead and hoped viewers would assume and smell that fragrance.

Crispin remembered that Jeanette was at first disappointed that her gown was positioned a half-inch too high on canvas and he had lowered the top edge just a little. He would now emphasize Annie's femininity and he painted her gown a deep scarlet and recast it as velvet. He still had some details to do, but became tired and stopped.

The next day the snow had stopped and the air was clear, cold, and brisk. They had a breakfast of pancakes with maple syrup, a delightful way to start a day of sleighing down a high bluff. Some youngsters were glad to part with their sleighs for an hour in exchange for a dollar even though it was paper currency. We slogged up the road that, only six weeks ago, had been the track that numerous Americans had hiked to valor and eternity. The snow on the road had since been packed down by the kid's bobsleds the afternoon before and so the walk up, and the ride down, was probably not as difficult as I thought it would be. Then the weather turned and snow came down heavily—and we decided it would be folly to go sleighing now.

The defused light would be just right to paint in the room and finish capturing Annie on canvas, and she was more than willing to see the finished portrait. Crispin asked Bemis to have the wood stove lit and he brought up the same paints he used before from the workshop. The room was toasty warm for Annie and maintained the paint thin and easy to mix and apply. He was delighted that Annie arranged herself on the lounge in the same manner and disposition as yesterday, and when he had convinced her that she should limit her conversation, he set to work.

He had sketched out her head and shoulders down to her waist and had completed her jaw and cheeks. Now he was especially careful to obtain exactly the set of her hair as she had meticulously curled it to her natural hairline. Too much forehead and she would look too scholarly; too little and she would appear mean or dumb.

A half hour of this and Annie wanted to get up and see what he had done. After all, this would fix her twenty-three year old image for her family for all time. Children, grandchildren, cousins, and in-laws of her and her deceased husband's family would eventually all view it.

She had already disturbed her pose, so he let her gaze for a moment, and told her she was not to move again until he gave his permission. Fortunately, she assumed the same position she had before so he wouldn't have to make adjustments.

They were scheduled to have lunch with Olivia and me at noon so he had plenty of time to get the basic colors and shadings done but he was not going to rush and sacrifice the time, energy, and valuable touches of the moment that can make, or ruin, an inspired work.

He could work on the eyes and eyebrows since they were as important as the nose and mouth in expressing the subject's general attitude. He was anxious to capture her intelligent but capricious expression through the sparkle in her eyes and the slight upturn of her stubby nose. When he finished these particulars, he let her get up and take a look—he valued her opinion and wanted no disappointed criticism when the painting was completed.

There was a knock at the door. "Mr. Johnson, what do you want me to do with this sketch?" It was Mr. Bemis wanting to catch a peek to satisfy his curiosity, although he really wanted that Crispin discard the portrait.

Crispin was visibly shocked and thought, 'Didn't Jeanette take the picture and put it in a safe place? What can I do or say to avoid a terrible scene? Thank goodness the door is locked.'

"Just leave it where you found it, Mr. Bemis. I'll handle it in the morning," he blurted.

"Have you been doing other portraits, Crispin? Have him bring it in here so I can see the progress in your technique."

"I hate to interrupt our progress anymore this morning, Annie. There's a necessary flow when painting which artists crave, it's when we do our best work. We'll look at it in the morning, all right?" Crispin said this with finality. But, he thought, 'what can I do to further stall the inevitable scene? It could ruin her entire visit and make her suspicious when she goes back to Chatham.' He was fearful that his nerves would collapse and cause unsteady paint strokes just where they had to be most seamless and smooth.

"Sit back so I can resume painting and accomplish what I want by noon. We're having lunch with Olivia and Jamie, you know."

He waited to see if she would still insist on seeing the sketch, and there was silence. Then he chatted about trivia to further take her mind off of what could have been an embarrassing reason for argument. He decided that his nerves were too upset to continue; he would plead a headache and suggest that they seek fresh air and hike up the hill.

Crispin had been thinking that he would surprise his superiors and paint the snowy aftermath of the scene at Freeman's Farm that he was sure they wanted. Knowing that Annie would not want to trek all the way there in the snow, he borrowed Trevor's spyglass and, as they reached the cusp of the Heights, trained it on the dilapidated and shot-up farm buildings and the British redoubt, and stored the scene in his memory. He could paint the image at a later time.

Two men were there in the distance, digging as if they wanted to clear the snow for what purpose he couldn't imagine.

Then he remembered; that's the spot where the British buried their officers—of course British military protocol decreed that they couldn't be buried with the enlisted men. The two men were not interested in the snow or tidying up a cemetery; they were digging up the bodies of the officers to plunder the dead! Who would want to do that? He held the glass firmly to a tree to steady it and saw that it was Mr. Mochter and Cheyne. "Of course. Who else?"

Crispin and Annie rushed the body snatchers as if they were officially authorized and the scoundrels dropped their shovels and ran down a ravine. At that distance, they couldn't see that our friends were no more challenging than a man and a woman having winter fun. When told this somber story, we decided that the two scoundrels must be desperate for funds for them to stoop so low as grave scavenging.

The exertion chasing them and sleighing down the hill one more time was enough fresh air and excitement for the day and Crispin and Annie came back to the tavern to have late lunch with us. We doubted that Mochter and Cheyne would show their faces in the dining room.

Annie's complexion had changed: the fresh air and exercise had reddened her cheeks and, rather than wear her out, they had invigorated her. After lunch, Crispin added a little more red to all skin surfaces and added a little more twinkle in her eyes. She couldn't wait to see the difference and joined Crispin as he took the next-to-final gaze of the work in progress.

Annie was delighted. "It's amazing what a little exercise will do. We did nothing but sit in the sloop the whole week when coming here, and now look—I look young again."

Crispin agreed. But he wanted to finish the portrait and call Olivia's and my attention to it. We both were impressed by Crispin's artistic sophistication since sketching the crew of the Raritan when we crossed the Atlantic. He was quite professional to our eyes and it was plain that he considered Annie a treasure.

Crispin was also a showman. Despite our impression that he had finished, he advanced several steps and made a few brush strokes to an already fascinating portrait of Annie, and signed his signature with a flourish in the lower corner.

This was cause for celebration and we went to the dining room for drinks and a snack. We were just finished ordering when Cheyne and Mochter entered the room again; it was as if a dark cloud suffused the area. It put a damper on not only our conversation but on the entire assemblage; it couldn't have been more startling if King George and his court had marched into the place.

But they were so experienced in criminal activities that they acted innocent as choir boys and ignored everyone in the room.

Then conversation picked up and I mentioned something that had bothered me. "I still don't understand the British taking over Philadelphia. It doesn't disrupt the economy of the locals, nor does it really threaten Washington's army. You'd think that Howe would want to smash the Atlantic ports to destroy the shipyards and privateers, who are raising hell with English shipping; they're especially ruinous to his supplies so that his troops have to eat rations of hard tack and salt pork, if they can even get that. Or he should attack Morristown and its depot of our supplies."

"You forget, Jamie. Maybe Howe just wants a change of social scene. Remember, the campaign year is just about over and his army and ours will be dormant until spring. Time to meet the local Tory debutantes and exact patronage from their fathers. And probably the foraging around New York is no longer sufficient to feed the troops and keep their horses fed. Without horses, they're immobile.

"Besides, it's Germain and the King who are running the show from London. With leaders like them, it's as if they're on our side." Crispin could surprise me with his perspicacity at times.

Just then, Trevor and Chief Honeoye came into the bar and then to our table. We had them join us and the conversation took a different turn: "We just heard that Washington took another pasting at Germantown, a suburb of Philadelphia. The Continentals started the attack early in the morning, but the plan was too complicated, and the brigades were from too many points, so it failed. Fog also confused the situation so that we actually shot some of our own men," Trevor almost cried.

Honeoye added."You forgot the Chew Mansion fiasco, Trevor. The British occupied a large Tory Mansion in the middle of the main town road and our troops wanted to annihilate it. They were outgunned at the mansion and it took too much time, so they missed coordinating with another brigade down the road, and the planned attack fell apart. It disappointed everybody.

"It was a serious bungle where discipline was not carried out and timing was botched. We need to train both our men and officers. In my opinion, that's our main necessity this winter."

So far as Crispin and I were concerned, it was mid-November and Germantown happened more than a month earlier; it had taken that long for this information to reach us.

CHAPTER THIRTEEN

THE NEXT DAY, Olivia and Annie wanted to go shopping and there were only a few shops including the blacksmith's so I thought they would be back soon. I lingered over my coffee and began to wonder—what makes men like Mochter and Cheyne behave as they do?

I didn't know much about Cheyne's background, but Mochter came from Ross on Wye, in Herefordshire, as I did. The roster on him was well known and detestable. He came from a notable family in London but his parents died young from a smallpox epidemic and he was brought to the West Country by his uncle when only eleven. The uncle, Peregrine Mochter, was of the old school that believed children should be seen, but punished for expressing themselves.

Peregrine had no children of his own, having been unsuccessful in wooing a wife, and realized that Wenceslas was the last of the Mochter line. Perpetuation of the family name was going to be due to his ward's charm, dedication to work, professional perfection, and hoped-for success, so he sent him to the local academy, Winton Arms. Here, Mochter applied himself at his uncle's urging and was usually the one to first raise his hand to answer questions posed by the matron.

As this annoyed the other students, it pleased Mochter, and he studied even harder to please the teachers and increase the social gap and prestige between the other students and himself. Even at a young age, he was called Mochter rather than "Wes," or a more endearing name. His sole friends were the kind that wanted to pull the wings off dragon flies, to throw boiling water at cats, or raise the most mischief on Guy Fawkes Day.

The main business in the region was the Peregrine Mochter Granary and Mill located on a tributary of the Wye River. Every harvest season farmers lined up their wagons to have their grain ground or stored, depending on the market. It made the Mochter fortune, but even that was not enough to arouse the local spinsters to smile and make conversation with the curmudgeon when they encountered him in the stores. He was a pinch-penny and, except for a handsome contribution to the church for his prominent pew, he was renowned for retaining his first guinea.

This routine went on for years until one evening; Peregrine became dissatisfied with his evening gruel and berated his cook so much that a mouthful at the wrong moment choked him to death. Wenceslas was twenty-two when he inherited his uncle's estate, including the business and his residence, which was a stone building, built like a church without ethics.

He was smart enough to retain the miller, the bookkeeper, and most of the employees and, over time, learned much about the operation and the reason for charges earned and expenses paid. Aside from meanness occasionally, such as denying service to Sally Bushnell's father when she refused to be courted by Mochter by reason of fidelity to my soldier brother, he was ethical and honest with his customers. He became prominent on his own and rose to become secretary of the local grange which, in turn, somehow put him in touch with members of the Ministry, or their clerks. So far, there seemed nothing to direct him on a path of deceit, malpractice, or spying for the government during the Revolution. True, there were both sides of the issues, but he made a profession that, in circumstance other than war, would have led him to the scaffold. That is when I became privy with this pillar of the community.

First, he invited patriarchs of the oldest, but poorer families who lived on the common, to a party, the intent being to loan them more than they could pay back on the security of their property. There had been a regional epizootic that killed off an important share of the Merino sheep population and he'd foreseen an opportunity in the wool market.

If a borrower was even a day late in his loan payment, his property was foreclosed and confiscated. To appear lenient, he loaned more to tardy parties who had the most desirable properties, only to secure title to those grounds when the inevitable day arrived.

The commons, which had been owned in common for close to a thousand years, became a sheep meadow for the sole use of Wenceslas Mochter, Esquire.

Moreover, he did the same thing with respect to the Greenwood, a beautiful park of ancient trees and other greenery which under Royal Grant, or some such, had been a hunting and fishing garden for our town going back to the days of King Alfred. Numerous generations had enjoyed hunting and fishing, and frisking the teen-age girls, and expected their children would do the same until Mochter cast his eyes on the grant.

Under some legal trickery called the law of enclosure, he claimed the property and turned around and sold it to the Ministry, to be cut down and made into a recruiting base for the army. Who could refute the prerogatives of the King?

I had always fished there, as did Crispin, and I hooked my largest trout in the stream as well as stumbling on a rock on the stream bottom. The rock glittered as the sun briefly shined on it and I suspected it was more than just a rock, it was an ingot! I found this a certainty later in the autumn when a windstorm blew over the ancient sycamore, the tree roots had snagged fishing lures and entwined the ingot over the years, and curiously, to my benefit they had risen ten feet in the air because of the blow down.

I'm sure that Mochter didn't see the ingot, but he claimed that I had stolen something from him because he came by when I was up in the tree reaching for the ingot which was wrapped almost completely by the roots. But he didn't know the true nature of my arboreal gymnastics and I tried to divert his thought and attention by feigning that I was grasping for the tied fly that lured the trout. And that was the beginning of my prolonged feud with him.

Crispin was despondent because of his menial life and servility to his father, so he joined the army to get to America. The King's shilling also lured him. But two weeks later, when he learned the army was taking over the Greenwood, and he and an army crew were ordered to destroy it, he bolted the army. He told me that he hadn't planned to do this, but the Greenwood was essentially Crispin's world and the thought that he was forced to ruin it made him take off.

In the eyes of the nation's army, this was a near-capital crime. I was his only savior and it became incumbent on me to take him with

95

us on our honeymoon to my uncle's farm in New Jersey. I wouldn't recommend this for a romantic honeymoon, but I had to save my friend from certain maiming or possibly his death. Further thought meant we had to literally tuck him in a barrel and get him on our ship.

As it happened, Mochter sailed to the New World on the same tide, but on a Navy ship, and we fought tooth and nail on the few occasions we met since.

Not knowing what exactly I may have taken, he changed his story and said I had stolen Olivia from him. To Mochter, everything had a price and could be owned, bought, or sold.

Most of Mochter's motivation was greed, but it seems much of the world caters to that mode of life. He has plenty of life's pleasures and the funds to meet any desire. Why should he traipse all the way to America for yet even more? And spending large sums to keep his maliciousness going to further extremes, his business went bankrupt when other mills charged less and gave more. He had been living the life of a grandee, but his expenses exceeded his income. When finally caught, he was already out of counterfeiting and into monopolizing the horse market for General Howe.

Annie's testimony convicted him, and a month in the unconscionable Simsbury Mines so drove him into melancholy that he pleaded for mercy and promised to reveal all he knew about subversives. Rather than waste him and his connections, Annie suggested to the authorities that he become an agent with inducements of loyalty to the United States.

Now, even that terrible experience in the mines seems to be forgotten and he and Cheyne have found each other. They are "birds of a feather" flocking together. We have to suppress both of them, but not yet—not until the girls go back home to safety and out of harm's way.

CHAPTER FOURTEEN

THE HUDSON HAD frozen at Fort Edward and it was likely to soon freeze at Saratoga, and if a cold snap settled in, it could freeze all the way to Troy overnight and navigation would cease for the season. More snow could also sock the girls in here for the winter, so it was best they soon go back to Chatham. We weren't sure that the British were done with their mischief—talk was that St. Leger was dickering with Ethan Allen about Vermont becoming a province of Canada. Wasn't Allen still in an English prison?

The girls had seen that our social life was dismal and didn't want to be trapped, so they engaged to return three weeks before Christmas. A week later, our unit was ordered out to Valley Forge, a small, bankrupt ironworks twenty miles northwest of Philadelphia. We had been merged with Washington's army, a sign we considered relative stability between the opposing armies in southeastern Pennsylvania.

Annie was right: Crispin had fished the Schuylkill upstream for shad, but at Matson's Ford, not Valley Forge, five miles upstream. The Valley referred to contained Valley Creek, a stream pure enough for an encampment with ample trees for fuel, building cabins, and shelter from the wind, if you were one of the lucky who were assigned to locate on the southern side of Mount Misery. We found it curious that soldiers often called paradoxes by their opposite names though the season at Valley Forge wasn't as cold a winter as commonly thought. I wondered if this was the stream that John Bartram said was his favorite. Crispin will probably find out if there's trout in it.

A few stone houses stood for the use of senior officers but it took a month to build enough log cabins to house twelve men each. What were missing were adequate clothing, shoes, and food. All these items were close by, but only in exchange for hard money, not the paper we had, but the silver and gold the British traded in abundance from Philadelphia and Germantown. At least, the Schuylkill didn't freeze as had the Hudson above Newburgh.

Over a period of six months we lost twenty-five hundred out of ten thousand men due to our weak currency, poor quartermaster work under General Mifflin, merchants lacking patriotic zeal, and disease. Had it not been for a shad run up the Schuylkill in the spring, we would have lost more.

One of the more beneficial arrivals was that of Friedrich Wilhelm Augustus von Steuben, a Prussian officer with specific attainments of immediate value to the American army. He was now forty-seven, had been schooled by Jesuits when young and was a staff officer during the Seven Years War. Because of his training and service in the German general staff, he could be of particular service useful to us as Benjamin Franklin saw when they met in Paris after a series of introductions. Through the Count de Saint Germain, then to the French agent and playwright, Beaumarchais, who advanced funds to Franklin who wrote Washington who referred him to Congress as "a Lieutenant General in the King of Prussia's services." That's how he came to America. I hasten to warn that the Count de Saint Germain shouldn't be confused with Lord Germain who wangled his way into leading Britain into war to the death with us.

By the time von Steuben left Marseilles on 26 September and reached Portsmouth more than two months later, the "Baron" was celebrated and dined in Boston for several weeks before reaching York and then Valley Forge, February 23rd, to serve without pay. He was immediately asked to fashion a military training program which he did with the help of Hamilton and Greene, since he knew no English and little French. He submitted it to Washington in March who approved it and asked that it be put into action then and there.

He started with a one-hundred man platoon shivering in the cold as they listened to his German and French coming from an over-dressed, gold braided officer, perhaps the only one of his kind that existed. (Crispin's came close) But soon they came to understand and carried out their orders by proudly marching and counter marching on the parade ground of the rustic post. They also were taught the manual of arms, the language of command under fire, how to aim their muskets, and to properly parry with the bayonet.

When the first group had learned the details and maneuvers, he had them fan out as drill masters themselves, to teach others the rudiments of the parade ground, the discipline, and, above all, that they were coordinated, able to understand and take orders on the spot as a cohesive fighting unit.

In turn, the second unit taught a third, and so on, and by early June, the whole base could proudly march and wheel in line and column. Of the utmost importance, as an officer gave an order, it was carried out, and on the double!! When General Clinton, who had taken over from Howe, was called back to New York, we saw how well this influenced our army's fighting ability at the Battle of Monmouth.

Baron Steuben was not the first emigrant to receive recommendation to this country. Two or more years previous, Doctor Franklin had interviewed Thomas Paine and written favorably to a Philadelphia newspaper for him. It was well he did, for Paine was an example of miscast careers, all of which had failed and caused him much sorrow.

But Paine had accurately read the measure of this country's problems with England and put it better than most of the Founders when he wrote Common Sense, and a desperate year later, The Crisis. The first pamphlet explained why we should become a country of our own, and the second gave us the resolve to do it in the face of despair.

The Marquis de Lafayette was an orphan. His father was a Colonel of Grenadiers and was killed at the battle of Minden when the Marquis was not yet two. Then his mother died before he reached thirteen. When he was sixteen, he married Marie Adrienne Francois de Noailles, of one of the most powerful families of France going back four or more centuries. In the fashion of his class and the times, he joined the Royal Army when he attained thirteen, three years before he married.

On the eve of the American Revolution, he attended a speech about the issues of the opposing parties and the attendant revenge and glory for a materially sympathetic France by joining the Americans. To do this, the young Captain had to get permission of

King Louis the Sixteenth who had recently assumed the throne. The king referred him to the influential Compte de Broglie to dissuade the young man. The Compte tried, but unsuccessfully, and introduced the Marquis to Johann Kalb, who was similarly minded.

They came over with flattering agreements from Silas Deane, sort of a gatekeeper, with a group of adventurers eager to gain glory for the rights of man, to embarrass the British, and seek revenge for the inequitable Treaty of Paris of '63. The adventurers were also eager to embellish the list of their military achievements, past, present, and future.

They disembarked on the coast of South Carolina in early June, and were directed to Philadelphia where they arrived in six weeks. They had some trouble convincing Congress that they could be useful until they said they would pay their own way and expected no command until merited. It was now August 1, 1777. They were just in time to participate at Brandywine where Lafayette fought honorably and was wounded in the thigh, a respectable beginning.

On the embarrassing side of the scale are a few who dishonored themselves, usually by partaking too much of the bottle. General Matthias Fermoy readily comes to mind. He was French, but came from the Caribbean to join the rebels and soon found himself at Ticonderoga. When Burgoyne challenged the fort with a barrage from Mount Defiance, General Sinclair decided to save his army rather than try to save the fort, a futile task, and the word went out to abandon the place in the middle of the night. Darkness was essential to not tip off the British and to get a head start.

Fermoy was drunk and, in his haste to pack and leave, he knocked over a lamp. His tent caught fire and illuminated the surrounding camp in the act of leaving, so that by dawn's light, most of the few trails were jammed with rebels being chased by redcoats, Hessians, and Tories, thanks to Fermoy. Gondolas crammed with personal baggage and supplies were overtaken on Wood Creek by the British. Surprisingly, it took six months to cashier him out of the Continental army.

A different fate waited for French chef de brigade Tronson de Coudray. He had risen in the officer corps after sixteen years in the French army when our Revolution began. He was smart, hard working, and had connections to Royalty through his brother and by teaching the Comte D'Artois the arts of war. He saw to the selection of artillery and engineering officers who would be assigned to America as military advisors. He impressed Gribeauval, Beaumarchaise of Hortelez et Cie, and Silas Deane with his knowledge and cooperation and arrived in America in May of 1777.

A problem with many adventurers was their arrogance which didn't go over well with Congress or other officers, especially when the French expected high military rank. It was difficult to deny them and endanger the already touchy relations with France. Congress solved the problem by inventing non-command titles in which the work was incidental or non-existent.

In Coudray's case the solution was provided by the movements of the stars and Coudray himself. While about to cross the Schuykill Ferry on horseback, he refused to dismount a skittery horse before crossing and the horse plunged into the river. Coudray could not dislodge his feet from the stirrups in time and drowned.

There were a few more like Fermoy and Coudray but most of them were cordial, wanted to cooperate and were competent, like Lafayette.

Another Frenchman, this one from Bavaria and peasant beginnings, was Johann Kalb who left home at sixteen and joined the French infantry. He was a good student and gravitated to the Diplomatic Corps and was approached by Choiseul (who oversaw intelligence vis a vis England) and was sent to America to sample American opinion of the English in 1768. When he returned with shrewd and detailed reports that were the opposite of Choiseul's opinion, he was demoted, and he resigned, having personal security from marrying a rich wife.

With the crowning of Louis the Sixteenth, which brought back the influence of Compte de Broglie, he rejoined the army and served under Broglie. By November of '76 he was promoted to Brigadier General and decided to make his career in America, signed a contract with Silas Deane, and sailed with Lafayette and the others, in April of '77.

When he arrived in this country there was some Congressional confusion about his contract, but it was squared away, and he became Major General attached to Washington's army, was at Brandywine, and German-town, and arrived at Valley Forge as the winter began.

I can't leave this roster unless I include "Thadeuss Kosciuszko, a Polish son of poor gentry who graduated from the Royal School at

Warsaw in '71. As a captain, he was trained further at the school of military engineering and artillery at Mezieres, France. He returned to Poland but found little opportunity for advancement, and despite a love affair there, which also turned sour, he returned to France.

He had become attracted to the American dream and borrowed the fare to get to Philadelphia where he got a position with the corps of engineers working on the Delaware River forts in August of '76. From there, he was assigned to Ticonderoga two months later, and performed well in designing defenses there and later at the Saratoga battlefield.

It's been said by several officers that his designs at Saratoga helped defend our redoubts and entrenchments against British attempts to breach them. I also heard that he would probably be assigned to improve the defenses at West Point.

At any rate, it seemed that every man involved at Fort Stanwix, Ticonderoga, or Saratoga was at Valley Forge. The weather was chill, but the friendships were warm.

CHAPTER FIFTEEN

BY THE END of January, cabins had been finished for the entire camp at Valley Forge, a total of about ten thousand men. With twelve men in each cabin and a fire going, it was comfortable provided you had all your clothes on your back and shoes on your feet. But from when General Greene became Quartermaster General, most of us became suitably clothed. To be honest, it was also a mild winter.

Just as in Morristown, Mrs. Washington came to stay with the general, this time in the Pott's stone house by the river. She was anything but a frivolous woman, but we had more dances and occasions to better know other officers and their wives. Then Steuben came and continued to leave his imprint on every platoon in the camp until mid-June when the camp was ordered to vacate to pursue the British. Several members of Congress appeared with Washington and Greene about food and clothing shortages, and then sought out their prominent constituents before going back to York, the current congressional seat. Gouverneur Morris, was one of these gentlemen, known for his support against the Crown but a moderate of some Congressional extremes.

I cite these aforementioned because the entire camp fell out to honor them on the parade ground and in much better order after Baron Steuben took over the management of the drilling and the training of the men. There was one more man of distinction: General Charles Lee had been exchanged by the British but that was not until May, only a few weeks before the camp was abandoned to follow and harass General Clinton and his army's exodus from Philadelphia across Jersey to New York. Lee was also honored, but with some reluctance due to his jealous attempt to oust Washington and his dubious relations with the British. But more about that later.

Trevor, Chief Honeoye, Crispin, and I managed to stay together when we made a slight fuss with Captain Straus of our new regiment. But he didn't know we were friends. Building a log cabin was a new experience for us. With the help of some woodsmen from the western part of the state, we were able to complete it in two weeks, just before the weather turned foul. It so happened that the Swedes, who had a settlement in Chester a hundred years ago, invented the log cabin. Sweden had a lot of forests as the Delaware Valley did, and they brought the log homestead idea with them. We were assigned plots, but Straus favored us with a southern slope protected from the north wind by a grove of pines. It was when others tried to cut our pine trees that we had trouble.

It was plain that our antagonists didn't know how to wield axes. They had most likely been clerks in the city---their language was too genteel, their hands had no calluses, and they lacked a large arc when swinging an axe. Besides that, they had plenty of trees. They just wanted to cut them all down instead of thinning them. They finally saw the merit in our argument, and built their cabin, but I won't go into that complication.

They invited us over when they finished, only finding out that they didn't know how to build a fire, either. When the Chief saw the blaze they had going, he said, "At that rate, you would have the entire North American continent up in flames and nary a stick of wood to heat your tea!" He explained how Benjamin Franklin had designed a fireplace and chimney to save a farmer almost half his labor by not having to cut up so much firewood, simply by his new design. "Get a copy of Poor Richard's Almanac and you'll find out. Doctor Franklin didn't patent his design or charge for it."

The Chief then knocked their fire apart and rebuilt it using only half the wood. "In addition to using too much wood, you would have made it too hot in here and have to spend the night outdoors to be cool enough to sleep," he scolded.

Of the twelve men in our cabin, four were clerks or otherwise didn't know the proper usage of axes or other tools. We taught them, but only when the door was closed. To avoid embarrassment, we don't talk about it in the presence of strangers.

At about the same time, the end of January, Olivia wrote to say she had moved from Chatham to Tredyffrin, Pennsylvania, halfway between Saint David's and Paoli. Doctor Iverson did, too. He was now somewhere in the vast labyrinth of Valley Forge and his wife and Olivia shared an abandoned farm just off the Lancaster Pike. Not a bad idea to keep in touch about your baby with your doctor through his wife.

When I went to see her and the new farm home, Olivia and baby were all right but she complained of looking like she swallowed a watermelon. Iverson said she had about five weeks to go but not to worry. She said the same.

There was some hickory growing nearby on the post and we selected a few limbs of the proper size to bend them into rails for sleds. We found more than enough hickory to make extras for cabins that had tubs large enough to boil the whole lot so we could bend them to shape. This made friends of the neighboring cabin mates initially when we celebrated the boiling and later when we sleighed down the hill, which was a challenge to those from farther south.

Despite her precarious condition, Olivia went down the hill, the less steep part, on a sled and said it was the most fun she had had since boating at Saratoga.

Making sleds was a good project from the beginning. It brought about a mixing of men from New England with those from the Carolinas who rarely see snow and the fun things you can do with it. Captain Straus was impressed and congratulated me for thinking up a way to make our forces more cohesive. He said he was putting me in for a promotion. It really didn't make any difference, no one was getting paid anyway, and the purchasing power of our pay was less and less. So far as the sledding went, the weather soon turned for the better and we had only a few rides down the hill.

On March 30, as predicted, Olivia gave birth to George Hedley Claveraque II, a seven pound eight ounce maker of shrill cries far into the night. His name sounds like that of a king and his disposition was, too. But, can one do better, under the circumstances, when one has a doctor's wife in the house?

Occasionally, I went into Wayne, newly named after our heroic General whose brigade suffered, but survived the so-called Paoli Massacre and was from around these parts. While our army was barely subsisting, this town on the Lancaster Pike was enjoying the blessings of a bounteous summer crop and the British were purchasing food and forage from them with gold and silver.

Washington was furious at this duplicity and insisted that farmers and businessmen all along the Pike accept army pay, and provision the army that protects them. This effort by the nation's leader was only partly successful until he realized the man to correct financial matters was right here in Philadelphia: Robert Morris, a successful trader, financier, and member of Congress. He had helped pay the soldiers when they were about to stick to their contracts and go home, even in the perilous times before Trenton. Morris provided Washington civil authority as well as financial help when other members of Congress had fled to Baltimore. What cured the currency problem more than anything else was hearing that the French had finally agreed to support the United States both militarily and financially, but notice of this didn't occur until May of 1777.

By mid May of '78, most of our clothing and commissary problems had been solved and the better weather relieved the sick and lowered the disease rate. I asked Crispin if he would join me in a climb up Mount Misery, (that's what the soldiers named it) to relieve his sorrow of missing Annie McLauren, and maybe Jeanette. (I didn't suggest either but recognized his petulance and sad pout). The trees had leafed out, wild flowers bloomed, and the air was fragrant so that enduring the miseries of last winter now seemed worth it.

From the top of the ridge, we could see all around; farmers were planting their crops and the roads to Pottstown, Wayne and Bryn Mawr, and Matson's Ford, were speckled with wagons and carts. The air was noticeably cooler, too, and with spring advanced, what had been a charming valley was now a pasture of stumps, and slashings that had not as yet been burned. Valley Creek had been used to wash clothes and blankets so much that the lower part had to be off-limits for potable water.

Crispin turned to me, "The British will soon be leaving Philadelphia. It was hinted by a man I feel sure is a Loyalist. He didn't say where they're going and I didn't think to ask, but where would they go that would make sense?"

"Well, they wouldn't go to Charles Town, they've already tried that and lost; they wouldn't go to Boston for the same reason; they must be going back to New York.

"Just think, Crispin. After more than two years, the British with the most powerful army in the world, is no more advanced in winning the war than when they started. In fact, they're behind since they've squandered the friendship of so many. Most of the bad judgment is because of the men pulling the strings in London---I mean Lord Germain, Secretary of State of the Northern Department and the King. I understand that even Lord North wants to resign but the king won't let him. Well, we don't even know for sure if the British are evacuating Philly so we may have just wasted a lot of time skylarking."

Crispin had been patient listening to my rant about the British, but he quickly got in a word edgewise. "The main reason I mentioned the British leaving is that if they do, we do, and we haven't fished much in any of these streams yet. You told me that John Bartram traveled through the entire Northeast and some of the South, but he preferred a spot near here where a small stream entered the Schuylkill. Do you remember that?"

"Yes, I do, but he never told me the name of the stream. You don't have your rod with you, do you? You don't happen to know the name of the stream?"

"We ought to be able to sneak to Bartram's Gardens and find out."

"I am truly sorry, Crispin. Olivia told me that Bartam died last September, just as the British were occupying Philadelphia."

As we climbed down from the ridge of Mount Misery, Crispin wanted to know more about the Conway Cabal.

"It's a simple sounding name, but a complex tale of jealousy, intrigue, congressional favor, and back-biting by senior officers and officials who should have known better. Some knew better and got out before disgracing themselves.

"It may have started with General Charles Lee. Just before he was captured at Basking Ridge, he had signed and posted a letter to General Gates, in which Lee tried to smear Washington as being inferior in his military efforts. Of course, the tone assumed Gates felt the same way about the Commander in Chief and set the stage for what was to follow. Our army had suffered severe damage at Long Island, New York, White Plains, Fort Washington and Fort Lee, but Lee was made captive only six weeks before Trenton and Princeton and had he complied with Washington's several pleas to join

Washington's gathering across the Delaware, he could have claimed credit for the army's success at Trenton...and probably would have.

"With Lee out of the picture, Gates saw his chance to acquire more status by ousting General Schuyler, head of our Northern Department, who was then trying to manage the invasion of Canada under Generals Montgomery and Arnold. Schuyler had seen service in the French and Indian War, was a landholder of substantial tracts in Central New York and along the Hudson, and had wangled for land along the border of the Hampshire Grants, making him unpopular with homesteaders and speculators on the Vermont side. He was also rich and considered haughty, adding to his unpopularity. For these reasons, Gates lobbied New England Congressmen every time he had the chance to get Schuyler's job.

"Enter James Wilkinson. He was only nineteen and was with Arnold in the Canadian Campaign, had risen quickly to become Gates' aide de camp before Burgoyne started his campaign of invasion, and as Gates finally replaced Schuyler, he rose in rank accordingly.

"Much of the credit for winning at Saratoga is given to General Gates (Gates didn't even mention Arnold's name in some of his important and boastful dispatches to Congress) but many who have studied the battles credit Arnold for winning both, especially when it's known that Gates spent most of the battles in his tent. With the credit for this most marvelous win, it would have been easy for even a bashful man to try to remove Washington. Don't let me hear you say that I ever said that!

"His supporters were Wilkinson, of course, Samuel Adams, General Mifflin, Doctor Benjamin Rush, and a number of congressmen whom I don't know.

"How about Conway, the Cabal was named after him?"

"He was ambitious and drawn into it, but it was not created to benefit him. He was actually innocent of any collusion, except for one slanderous statement, and that's what did him in."

"We read little of Conway in the papers, yet he's a general, how so?"

"First of all, he was born in Ireland of Catholics who sent him to a series of military schools in France for his education. He rose to a major ranking just about the time the Revolution started, and was interviewed by Silas Deane. Like many, Deane gave Conway a favorable recommendation and when he reached Philadelphia, he was given a rank above his abilities which rankled other contenders from the start."

"He sounds like a blow hard---like Wilkinson." Crispin spat.

"He was. I don't know Conway, but I met Wilkinson in Morristown and the comparison fits.

"Anyway, he was in time for Brandywine, Germantown, and Whitemarsh. Then he's been chummy with some Congressmen. But Wilkinson was sent by Gates to Congress with word of the surrender at Saratoga. On his way to York, he stopped overnight at Reading and happened to hear some army gossip from General Stirling's aide. A few days later the aide sent a note to Washington enclosing a statement by Wilkinson to the aide which demonstrated "such wicked duplicity of conduct" he felt duty bound to report it. The enclosure read:

"In a letter from General Conway to General Gates he says---Heaven has been determined to save your country; or a weak general and bad councilors would have ruined it."

"Intrigue indeed!" said Crispin.

"Yes, Washington handled it coolly. He was shocked that two of his officers passed disparaging remarks about him and sent a brief note to Conway saying: "Sir, A letter that I received last night contained the following paragraph," and enclosed a word-for-word copy of the damning letter.

"You can imagine how upsetting this must have been for Conway. General or no, he must have been like a little boy being apprehended by God! He scrambled to write a note to the Commander in Chief assuring him of his respect, bravery, cunning, and other attributes. Of course, the very fact that it was written so promptly, was evidence that his supplication would fail."

"What happened then?"

"Pretty much what one would expect. Word leaked out as to the conspirators. Arnold's part in both battles at Saratoga became generally known, dimming the luster of General Gates' fame. Conway had submitted his resignation to the Board of War and was shocked when they readily accepted it. And he went back to France.

"The whole thing blew over and Washington's deft and gentlemanly handling of the main conspirators added even more to his respectability. By the way, Wilkinson did receive the honorary sword and promotion to Brigadier General from Congress!"

By now we were back at camp and some were reading of events posted on the news board. On the front page of the Philadelphia Gazette so all could see: "British to Honor Howe at Mischianza."

"Where is Mischianza, Jamie? It sounds like an Indian name!"

"I don't know, Crispin. I've never heard of the place."

Then, I realized that it must be some kind of an unusual celebration or they wouldn't use such a high-falutin name. And I was right. Howe had reached the pinnacle of army rank, after being knighted by the king, and was determined to retire as Commander in Chief of British forces in America. He was replaced in that role by General Henry Clinton. His aide, Captain John André and Captain Oliver De Lancey, a Loyalist, planned the extravaganza.

"I don't know either, Crispin, but I think Mischianza is a fancy name for a party honoring General Howe, who is due to return to England. It looks like it will be an elaborate fiesta with hundreds of guests and British officers. You can bet that security will be tight that day. I hope we have "guests" who can find out British plans now that Sir William will be gone. It says here that May 18th is the big day of the party."

The big day came down by the waterfront; a series of regattas, medieval festivities, and drinking that everyone endured for a planned twenty-four hours, before going home at four in the morning. It must have been expensive and riotous with everybody, who is anybody, there. Howe was on a ship bound for England within a few days, but the day after the big party is the one that caught our attention.

British activity in force was beginning to be apparent. Somebody said it was similar to before when the Brits were preparing to abandon Boston. Then the placing of General Knox's artillery on Dorchester Heights was the reason; we could have blasted all of Boston Harbor, including their fleet. And they were having trouble feeding the troops because of our sea blockade.

About three weeks ago, General John Lacey, who commanded the Crooked Billet post a few miles north of Philadelphia, suddenly found his post surrounded by an overwhelming British force. He originally had over four hundred militia, but because of expiring enlistments and sickness, he was down to less than sixty effectives.

Lieutenant Colonel Abercromby was in front of him with four hundred men and a detachment of light horse and to his rear was the notorious Major Simcoe with three hundred Rangers.

Fortunately, there was a wood nearby into which Lacey retreated. For an hour he held off his opponents and then reversed course, and left the wood leaving the enemy perplexed by his absence. Even so, his losses were twenty-six killed and ten badly wounded.

The day before the Mischianza, our spies reported more activity and all units were told to be on the alert; it might signal the evacuation of the city.

On the same day, a hint arose to be investigated.. I was part of the brigade assigned to the Marquis de Lafayette, now a Major General, probably to please the French, by honoring the young Frenchman. He commanded over two thousand troops and we had five guns. We left Valley Forge May nineteenth, crossed the Schuylkill at Swede's Ford, and assumed a position near Matson's Ford downstream a little.

The British always had good intelligence, probably from Tories, and they knew of our plans. They expected our exact location at a major crossroads and were ready to move in on us so that we were trapped, as in an enclosure, one side of which would be the river. We were greatly outnumbered and in danger of being wiped out. Lafayette was calm under this threat and expected the attack the following morning.

It seems that Lafayette knew of this special location before leaving and doubted the British knew it as well as they should. One of his men told him of a small road that led down to Matson's Ford that couldn't be seen by the enemy. It was a risk but had to be chanced for escape. But it worked, and we pulled off the escape with no casualties. As lucky as this was, it was due to Baron von Steuben's drill and training that paid off.

The action was not only to protect our base at Valley Forge and to prevent British foraging in preparation for their trek to New York, but to test Lafayette with a command, It could have been expensive in casualties, some charged, but it was worth it.

I might add that at the lowest point on the river road was the Brown Belt and Transmission's factory in which I had invested two years ago. I wished I had time to stop and visit the company officers, but as someone said, "war has its drawbacks."

Chapter Sixteen

Before the false dawn on June sixteenth, Crispin tapped me on the shoulder to wake up. "Get up, Jamie. We're going to New Jersey to do some reconnoitering."

"This is a hell of a time to tell me that. What time is it and why didn't you tell me a few days ago? And why do we have to rise so early? New Jersey can wait."

"Just get dressed, but don't wear your uniform. I'll tell you all about it over a quick breakfast."

"Why not wear my uniform? Are we going to play spy? Well, why not. It'll feel cooler."

Crispin didn't answer.

It's not often that Crispin is so serious and so I did as he said, and at the tavern in King of Prussia, he filled me in with the details.

"The brass knows that Clinton is definitely going to cross Jersey to New York and the most recent information is that it will be very soon. Clinton has loaded a ship with heavy equipment, invalids and the sick, and as many vociferous and prominent Tories as it'll hold. He's short of ships, which are the only ones he has, so he's going overland to New York with the army. We're supposed to map the path we think he'll take, me to do the mapping, and you to protect me from disgruntled farmers and maybe redcoats. I have asked Captain Straus to order Chief Honeoye and Trevor to go with us, but I haven't had any answer yet. Any questions?"

"That sounds like a lot of mapping. How do you know what to map in such a short time?"

"It's been explained to me that Clinton may cross the Delaware at Cooper's Ferry and then proceed north through Bordentown,

Hightstown, and South Amboy. Or he could go to Moorestown, Mount Holly, Monmouth and points on the coast between Sandy Hook and Amboy—then to New York. That narrows it down so that our work could be done in two or three days. But it's best if we do it in one.

"We'll only have to select the area leading several miles east of the river. Once we know where he's going after he crosses the river, we can guess the rest of his path. Finish your coffee and we'll be on our way."

"How many in his army?"

"About ten thousand troops, sixteen guns, and fifteen hundred supply carts. It'll be a long hike for them, and a ten-mile long caravan, but we should report to Washington before any clash."

"We should be pretty well matched. Are we supposed to take their entire army on? It's going to be damned hot in New Jersey."

"They didn't say anything about that. They'll probably play it by ear. Let's get to our horses and get out of here!"

Thus began a series of the hottest days of my career.

We trotted alongside the Schuylkill with the idea of taking the Cooper's Ferry. That took us past Bunny Bunting's house, where Olivia and I stayed almost exactly two years ago. It looked pretty much the same except for the ill-kept look of an occupied city. We felt privileged to know that that would end soon.

When we reached the river, there was Chief Honeoye and Trevor Shaw, but dressed in uniforms of the British Army. What to do? We were leaving the city and didn't want to be shot by our own.

Chief Honeoye answered the question in everyone's mind. "Let's chuck the uniforms. We can go wherever we want easier and the uniforms are too hot on a day like this. The owner of City Tavern is a friend and customer of mine and we can leave them with him. First we better buy some everyday clothes."

They bought indifferent shirts and pants and changed in a back room of the tavern to avoid questions of every suspicious mind as to whether they were rebels in plainclothes or Loyalists. As they came out to the bar, the Chief had a satchel full of something heavy.

"Those uniforms must be very heavy, you're lugging in the bag. What else do you have? A jug of rum?"

"Something better, Jamie. I've got a fresh load of Doctor Honeoye's Seneca Oil Elixir. It's come in handy during the most perilous times and I suspect that's what we're going to be getting into.

Properly suited we cantered to Bordentown.

On the way we appreciated the cool breeze off the Delaware, but as we left the river, the heat became sweltering and made distant views shimmer. The British were out in small patrols, no doubt to learn where to guide the exodus along the selected roads.

After a few miles, when Crispin thought the terrain had some feature that could help or hinder an army, he stopped to set up his easel. It was getting dark but the picture didn't have to be artistic, a line drawing was enough, and he was fast. After only minutes, we were moving again.

We soon camped in a wooded grove by a stream and again, woke early to reach our destination at noon of the second day.

At Crosswicks we stopped for a late lunch and sat in the shade by the creek of the same name. A British patrol stopped and asked us our business, our first interrogation of the mission. The lieutenant surprised me when he said, "Don't I know you? I've seen you someplace before."

Then I looked more closely at his face. Of all people, it was Strawbur Topping! I blurted out," Of all people, it's Strawbur Topping!"

He had put on a little weight, probably the result of success in the army, and he seemed less exuberant than I had known him. At any rate, I was surprised and glad to see someone from the West Country.

My friends stood up, expecting an introduction. Strawbur took off his helmet while he searched his mind for my name. "You're Jamie Claveraque of Ross on Wye! I wondered what happened to you. How come you're not in the army? You favored the rebels so."

I looked at my three friends and winked, "I was in the army, Strawbur, but I was wounded and my enlistment ran out." I introduced my friends and explained our common background in southwest England. There was no point in using false names; the situation was strange enough.

"Let's sit over in the shade," Strawbur suggested, and we moved away from the rest of the patrol. To them, he said "Take a break, Mates. It's too hot to not be at ease." To me, he said."What a strange circumstance to see you. Now our prior discussions about government have some substance. But we need not talk about that. Situations change, you know."

"Well, I'm glad to see you in this manner; I'd hate to see you in my sights, although, if I knew it was you, I'm sure I wouldn't squeeze the trigger." I answered. We both chuckled at this nervous repartee..

Strawbur squinted and he became serious as he moved closer. "We're on patrol, looking for odd situations or devious people. My mates are going to wonder about you and your friends. I don't want to arrest you, so give me a good reason why you're about today. Anything reasonable will do," he whispered.

Though he spoke softly, the three of us heard him clearly and Chief Honeoye spoke— a little louder than usual. "I'm going to have a horn full of Doctor Honeoye's Seneca Oil Elixir. Would you care for some, Lieutenant?"

"I've seen that stuff on back bars and I never knew what it was. Is it whiskey?"

"It's sort of a cross between a recreational drink and a medical elixir. First of all, it tastes good. Second, if you feel badly it clears you out and makes you feel better. And if you have any number of maladies such as jaundice, peristalsis, or corns on your feet, it cures them and relieves the pain. Try it." and he offered to pour some.

"That's kind of you, Doctor. I am feeling out of sorts today. This ought to satisfy my curiosity," and he dumped the contents of his canteen and held it up for the elixir.

This gambit gave me time to think of a reason to satisfy Strawbur. When I had a reason, I spoke a little louder so his troops could overhear it.

"Do you remember that I have an uncle in the northern part of Jersey, in Vaux Hall? He's ill and I was going to see him when my friends said they would accompany me. Crispin, the one with a beard, likes to draw country scenes, the Doctor said he'd like to idle through the countryside instead of his usual race from one customer to another, and Trevor is not familiar with this part of the colony. So here we are, and we foolishly chose the hottest day of the year to do it."

Strawbur said, "That's good enough, Jamie." and upended his canteen to his mouth. In the next second, he coughed and scolded, "For Christ's sake! That stuff will kill you before it cures you! Where'd you get it?"

"It comes from a special spring in upper New York, in the middle of where the Iroquois live. I treat it with special herbs that give it its power. That's why I'm called doctor. But finish it. By sunset you'll see how beneficial it is." He winked at me as he declared this.

It must not have bothered Strawbur that much, for he did finish it and stood up and waved us goodbye, saying to me in an aside, "There's another patrol coming this way from the north soon. Better take care and watch what you say. See yah."

Before we left, Crispin made a note saying "fresh, sweet water here, and drawbridge," but made no sketch. Then it clouded over to very dark and we had a raging deluge with lightning and thunder. It was so dark that, even though it stopped raining abruptly, we lost our orientation on the unfamiliar and dark road and went north rather than northeast, and met with the patrol that Stawbur cautioned us of.

This was upsetting and we tried to hide any anxiety, but we were detained again. This was a larger squad and led by Captain John Brigandi, a personage also from my English beginnings. I recognized him first, but said nothing, afraid I might not be so lucky as in the last encounter. But Trevor said hello to him. Brigandi had been a frequent customer in his store, and they were friends. Brigandi had even seconded for him in the duel with Charles Chipping and recognized Trevor right away.

It was like a school reunion. "Trevor, how nice to see you in this God-forsaken countryside on this bitch of a day. I wish we had bathing garb to both go swimming. And Jamie, too! Well, why not, you're both good friends. Tell me what you've been doing."

The Chief spoke up, "Don't freeze me out of the conversation. I didn't know you all knew each other!"

Trevor introduced the Chief to Brigandi, a formality we had overlooked.

Brigandi told his company to be "at ease" and they were quick to relax and dwell on the weather. "Did you just see Stawbur? He preceded us by a mile or so. Surely, this is like old-home week." Brigandi said.

"Yes, we saw him, too. He seemed less argumentative less sure of himself. The last I saw you, John, was in New York. Have there been any more duels there? Chipping committed suicide, you know. He was at Fort Stanwix and single-handedly tried to urge the British army to attack us just before a Seneca brave threw a tomahawk at

117

him. Poor chap, he let alcohol and gaming get the best of him. He was driven to extremes."

"No more duels. Clinton got sore about the bickering among his officers and threatened demotion to the next set of duelists. Then he made that attack on Forts Clinton and Montgomery and Vaughn burned Esopus and Clermont as a diversion to Burgoyne. Now, Howe's gone back to England to retire and to defend his actions before Parliament, and Clinton is going back to New York. I guess you know all about that.

"Look, I don't want to detain you fellows. You probably have business to attend to and I have to be on our way with my company. It's been great to see all of you. When this damn war is over, I would love to see you all at a reunion of the Revolution. Until then"— then he saluted as if to credit our status for the benefit of his men, reformed them, and was gone.

We resumed our trek to the northeast and took the road to Allentown. It was getting hotter and humid by the moment and the ground turned sandier, so that it absorbed the heat and reflected the sun's rays back at you from the ground; a double whammy, so to speak. At least there were several streams that were all cool and clear and welcome in this heat.

Crispin stopped us again; this time to investigate a small wood. "What is significant here? The wood doesn't have military value, does it?" I asked.

"It has shade, which the four of us need badly if we're going to finish this mission. If this heat continues, both armies might stop here for the same reason," Crispin said. Indeed he was right because fifty yards into it was a small contingent of British regulars resting in the shade, on the side with a slight breeze.

They acted surprised as we didn't hesitate to crowd in beside them. Alas! A civilian doing this to a squad of regulars wasn't done, don't you know. The lieutenant of this group was not pleasant or known to us as before, and obviously was annoyed at such an intrusion. As soon as he opened his mouth, I recognized him; he was the British equivalent of Colonel Cheyne, a critical bully looking for victims. In every army it seemed necessary to have one of these.

"What makes you men think you can pull off the road here? Can't you see that this is army domain? Get your own piece of woods. Be gone with you!" he spat.

118

As much as we hated to cave in under this petty rage, we moved off, glad to get out of his sight. Someone like that, even in your own army, could make life difficult. At least, we had a few minutes of relief out of the sun. But we weren't here to take issue with the British army.

Crispin did little sketching after this. The British were obviously reconnoitering themselves to find the most direct and supportive path to New York, via Raritan Bay. Crispin said he could make the images of important sites stick fast in his memory; all he needed was a notation of what the main feature was and the image would appear for sketching when we returned to Philadelphia. He didn't want to be caught with a folio of sketches as Nathan Hale did a few years ago.

But he was pleased with the rendings of countryside he had already done, and kept them. I remember when we were traveling to Philadelphia several years ago and he made a brisk business sketching and selling people paintings of their homes. Perhaps he remembered, too, and was trying to accrue a little extra cash for when we return.

The next town east, Imlaystown, was a hamlet of only five houses and a crossroads store where Trevor wanted to purchase some sausage for an afternoon snack for all of us. But we stayed overlong at the well-stocked store and another British detachment must have had the same idea, and we felt challenged as they crowded in on us. Certainly, the Brits had something in mind with all these detachments afield. Our intelligence unit must have been right.

The hamlet and the store had no particular significance until a wagon with wine kegs pulled up and unloaded the whole cargo into the store. I could tell the four of us thought as one: the store was a depot for storing the wine supply of the British officers, soon to come by in large numbers.

The delivery was ill-timed considering the heat and its effect on the wine, but the wholesaler was not about to lose the business by delaying delivery because of the weather. With the four of us there, it was an embarrassment; I thought the detachment would probably detain us so we couldn't report it as a likely sign that Clinton's army would be coming though here. Unfortunately, I was right.

A captain, who was taller than the others and was very dignified in his uniform, stepped over to us and, looking at me, said, "Who's in charge here?" As soon as I said, "I was", I realized it was a trick. In only a few words he had found that we were a unit in the military and that I was responsible for it. Crispin was actually in charge, and he tried to speak up, but I held up my hand and silenced him, hoping that his portfolio wouldn't be examined.

The next thing I knew, the captain ordered a sergeant to take five men and escort us back to Allentown where we were to be incarcerated in the town's combined jail and post office. The captain barked, "If only one of them tries to escape, shackle them all. Keep 'em there until you hear from me or are otherwise notified."

I wondered what "otherwise notified" meant as the captain and the rest of the detachment filed out of the store. Trevor reached into his pocket, and our new hosts went for their pistols. When Trevor showed some coins, he said, "It's for the sausage." and put the money on the counter. The sergeant and his detail laughed, as did Trevor, and we had no trouble on the hike back to Allentown.

So far, the British we met were pleasant and not aggressive, except for the lieutenant who kicked us out of the woods, but in the army that sort is expected. The jailor was different. Not only was the jailor a woman, but her husband, a Tory, had been in the British army and was killed at White Plains. Anyone under suspicion of being a rebel was immediately branded by her as a murderer and subject to punishment for her sacrifice. She assumed that we were rebels and took it for granted that we were there to wrack havoc on British plans to make it to New York.

The jail was about as large as my parent's dining room table when no leaves were placed in it, and there was only one place to sleep. For a place like Allentown, the jail was sufficient to accommodate two drunks, and that's probably the only service it provided the town. But there were four of us, it was hot, and our jailor was bound to make us even more uncomfortable.

My friends thought I was wrong when she brought in some water. "You men must be hot, here's some water for you." she said, and she put down a pitcher and a tin cup. When she left, Crispin said, "That's surprising for someone who feels so hateful for anyone on our side. She's thinking of our welfare after all."

We all drank so much to make up for our sweating, that we emptied the pitcher and called for more. She came to the door and asked for the pitcher and went outside. We heard her out in the yard, working the pump. These exertions removed any doubt as to her compassion, even if we were rebels. But we said nothing to make her think we were partial to the rebels so maybe she'd think we had committed some innocent mischief for the army to put us here.

She came to our cell with the pitcher of water, keyed-open the cell door and smiled as she threw the water on the slab of stone floor which had been absorbing the sun's heat all day. In an instant, the steam filled the small space, engulfing our clothes and ourselves so we could hardly see to the end of our outstretched arms. We didn't realize that the hot air could hold any more moisture or that one could harbor so much hatred as her cackle confirmed. But we knew we had to figure a way out of this hellhole and beat it back to General Washington.

CHAPTER SEVENTEEN

WE STUDIED THE walls, the ceiling, the stone slabs, and the cell door, but could find no immediately conceivable way to escape this oven. We were afraid that the heat would drive our guards to some cooler place like a lake, a hillside, or just the deep shade of a maple tree. "Otherwise notified" gave them the latitude they needed to just abandon us, especially if the battle went through this way. Fortunately for us, they went no more than a hundred yards to the shade of a clump of trees.

"If we can't see our way to get out, maybe we can think of a way someone could get in. "I said, and we concentrated on that prospect. After a few minutes of unrewarding thought, a customer of the post office came in to that part of the building to open his box. We heard him turn the key, slide out his letters, and slam the box shut. The wall shuddered because it was flimsy. Three of us thought there was some significance to this, but Crispin didn't.

"So what if it shuddered and was flimsy. That doesn't mean we can dismantle it and break out of here. It's just a cheaply made wall. Look! Where would you say that guy's box is on this side? Here? About breast high? I'll bet I can stick my knife through to it." And he stabbed and his knife went right through. The wall was only a quarter inch thick, so that if he wiggled it, he could lever and split the wood apart.

The compartment was empty so it probably was the same box that the man opened. It also meant he wouldn't come back soon and we had the necessary time to enlarge the hole. Crispin quickly became a thinking hero and began willy-nilly grasping adjacent sections of wall and breaking them to enlarge the hole towards the floor.

Each of us took a turn in doing this and before long; we could shove head and a shoulder through if we bent over. Trevor broke one of the upright joists to widen access and made a wrenching sound of yielding wood. We all went "Shush" and made more noise trying to quiet him than Trevor had made.

I suddenly had an awful realization: "What happens if someone comes in to get his mail and he can't help but see this hole? What do we do? What time is it? Maybe the post office closes early. We certainly don't want the lady jailor to come in." We sat like a group of dummies, baffled by not anticipating this horrific possibility.

The Chief slapped the cot. "I know. We'll tear strips of cloth to tie up packets of letters meant for the same address so it looks intentional. There's probably only about a dozen boxes with mail in 'em , and we'll put the packets aside to give to the customers who come for them. We can tell 'em we've been hired to rebuild and strengthen the wall."

Crispin said, "What happens when the lady comes with our dinner? She'll know what we're doing."

I wasn't bothered by this."Always a worry wart, Crispin. After her performance in bringing us water, I doubt if we'll have that problem. She doesn't care if we don't have dinner." We cleaned up the mess and tied mail into packets to look businesslike and waited quietly for darkness and escape.

Trevor broke out the sausage and divided it in four parts, and we devoured it in ten minutes. A late afternoon breeze caressed the cell window and our sour-sweated bodies so that we could finally endure our own stink. With nothing to do, we just sat there, idle as the packets. The sun slanted shadows in a sharper angle and had a tinge of amber in the light. I pulled out my watch and it was six o'clock. It was almost the longest day of the year. My God! It certainly seemed like the longest day of the year in this place.

We now assumed that the post office was closed and no one else would come. We could continue enlarging the hole. This occurred to all of us at the same time and we systematically resumed wrenching the thin wall and mail boxes. With pieces of the uprights we could leverage larger portions. Even the metal doors of the mail boxes came in handy: we used the edges to score the wood evenly so that it broke in a straight line, and we laughed at our silliness for such an unnecessary diligence.

By eight, it was dark and we were done enlarging the hole. Allentown was as completely dark as it was before whites came to New Jersey shores when the Lenape Indians held sway. We had to feel our way through the hole and into the post office part of the building. The entrance door was directly across from the wall we had ruptured. All we had to do now was to open it and follow the road back by starlight.

But the door was locked and from the outside! Of course. They had to lock it to keep stupid intruders, like us, locked inside.

Trevor asked what the trouble was. We told him and he came to the fore with one of the metal mailbox doors. "I did this to myself in my store once and spent all night trying to get out before the customers came. At least, I had candle light then. But first, let's see if the hinges are on this side." We felt along the pivoting edge, and sure enough, the door swung inward and they were on our side of the door. Trevor put the edge of the boxdoor metal against the protruding ring at the top of the hinge pin and tapped each of them out. Then he levered the door off the threshold and swung it firmly so that it pivoted on the lock mechanism and broke it off. We were free, but not home.

Our horses had been confiscated by the regulars and we had to walk back to Crosswicks. We could have stolen some in Allentown but didn't want to risk the regulars jailing us again. It was hot enough that horses were kept in the pasture rather than in the barn, and in Crosswicks, we were able to coax some to us in the dark.

Fortunately, there was a peach orchard near the paddock so we had our fill before skedaddling off to Bordentown where we rented a rowboat and watched the sunrise as we crossed the Delaware. In Pennsylvania we began to feel comfortable again. We also had a normal breakfast at a tavern near Pennsbury Manor, William Penn's family mansion. Here we rented horses and rode back to Valley Forge via Willow Grove, near where the Crooked Billet skirmish took place over a month ago.

Crispin brought us with him when he reported to General Washington. The general was surrounded by chaos and high-level officers with questions and suggestions, and messengers waiting to deliver dispatches. Nearby was one of his aides de camp, ready to write down every word of Crispin's report and the general's response.

Crispin told of our several encounters with British patrols: "We thought we were in the right place because of the intensity of British units in the region of small towns such as Allentown. While in a store near there, we knew we were on to something when a wagon full of wine kegs made a delivery much larger than could be expected. It signified that a large group of people, (should I venture to say army officers?) were going to be there in the next few days or week.

"We were calm about this information, but the British weren't. They got excited and promptly arrested us, and sent a guard with us back to Allentown where they had a jail."

Crispin was taking out his sketches as he continued. "I sketched these on the fly so they lack detail, but not the significant details like bridges and swamps—Washington cut him off. "That's just what we wanted to know! You've done a good job, Captain. We want you to go back and beyond Allentown towards Sandy Hook. Anything that you think could be used to detect their proposed track, or harass and delay the enemy, even wine deliveries, will be useful. But you have the idea."

He hesitated a bit and added, "One thing more: If you are somehow caught and they grill you, or find yourself in a situation where you can divulge inaccurate information, act reluctant to do so, but give in after a while so they think it natural. After all, the British think Americans are disloyal poltroons. Tell them we have twenty-thousand effectives, twenty heavy guns, and two hundred and fifty dragoons with extra horses. Scare 'em. They have half that. Worry Clinton and Cornwallis.

"Then report back to me. Any Colonel will know how I can be reached, either in person or by messenger. That'll be all." he said, and stood up. Our report was over.

Crispin saluted. Then we all did, the general returned the salute and we left headquarters.

Outside, Crispin pulled a map of New Jersey out of his portmanteau, pointed to a relatively blank space, and pronounced, "Englishtown and Monmouth are where we go next." and he pulled out a compass to test its accuracy.

We dared not go through Philadelphia again, there was too much activity. We got fresh horses, circled the city, and went to Newtown where we picked up supplies for a few days and aimed towards McKonkey's Ferry, near where Washington had crossed the river a year and a half ago. Half way to Lawrenceville, we made cold camp. There was little activity but we thought it best to be as obscure as possible. We were about half way between Trenton and Princeton on an unmarked stream but the water was clear and refreshing and the heat had subsided some.

We didn't trust the map or the road signs which were largely to direct travelers from larger towns to other larger towns, so we went south east and intercepted an east-west stream and rode upstream to Edinburg, a small town on a road leading to Hightstown. The stream happened to be the Asunpink, the stream that feeds into the Delaware at Trenton.

We expected to encounter British or Loyalist patrols because of what happened three days ago, but none appeared either near or far. This seemed to be a good sign that the British were concentrating on Allentown as part of their path to the coast. But Washington wanted us to go beyond so we were ready to go another five or ten miles past Hightstown on a better road that went due east.

A farmer had a fruit and vegetable stand and it was already one o'clock of the second day of our second mission. All of us were hungry and we dismounted and made sandwiches out of their fresh bread and strawberry jam, and ate fresh-picked tomatoes. How cool and tasty they were! I thought Crispin was smarter than saying, "Don't eat the tomatoes. Don't you know that love apples are poisonous?"

At least he recovered his respect slightly when he said that sandwiches are the best thing the Earl of Sandwich ever did for the Colonies. The three of us shamed him for not knowing better about tomatoes. But we still couldn't get him to eat one.

CHAPTER EIGHTEEN

WE MOVED OFF on the way to Englishtown on the best quality road we had yet seen in New Jersey. It was wider, had few stone walls for surprise attacks, and had frequent streams running through mostly open meadow-lands. But the road disintegrated into sand which was difficult and tiring to walk in, especially if you had a heavy pack to lug. It was true that the whole area was sandy, so a traveler wouldn't have much choice. Crispin doubted that Clinton, as an astute General, would choose such a road. We all thought so, and Crispin wrote a note to that effect. He decided not to waste time on sketches since Washington didn't even look at them.

He also decided that we should not all be on the road, but spread out, like flankers, to note conditions on either side fifty to a hundred yards out. Crispin stayed on the road, but I was on the right side, Trevor was on the left, and Chief Honeoye weaved back and forth, especially if he was called to give an opinion on conditions. I should mention that none of us were armed—it would only raise suspicion and, if attacked, we would be overwhelmed and most likely shot or hanged.

It happened that this part of New Jersey was thick with Loyalists, why, I don't know. Possibly the better off had official jobs with the former government under William Franklin at Perth Amboy. But that's a long way to go to work; ten to fifteen miles, so I doubt it. We saw a few people who seemed to know that something was about to happen. The closer we got to Englishtown, the more we saw them in groups, watching us with caution or suspicion.

There was a tavern in Hightstown but Doctor Honeoye wasn't familiar with it and said it was best to avoid places where solid groups of Loyalists might collect. If they were drunk, all it took was one disgruntled guy to start a mob, and an outsider could easily end up hanged. Trevor said he could easily vouch for that.

As we went farther east, the suspicion and dislike of strangers became more palpable and I remember the episode in Clinton, New Jersey, almost two years ago.

Crispin had been out painting early one morning, and a Quaker, on his morning walk, struck up a conversation with him. Later that day, Crispin was bitten by a rattlesnake and we were directed to a doctor, who happened to be the Quaker gentleman of the morning. So we all met him and, in the after-noon, he invited me to have a drink at his home by the creek. I found out all kinds of information from the doctor, who had been a stranger but twenty-four hours before. He was quite cordial.

I would have to think of some pretext to start a conversation and maybe the townsman I approach may not be as sociable as the Quaker doctor, but I have to start some place. As we rode, I thought of a scheme of acting as the agent for a company looking for an additional factory location, since most towns were hungry for an improvement in their economy. Of course, we needed a river for driving machinery and Englishtown became a candidate.

I suggested my plan to the others and they agreed to play a part as my associates in the scheme. We settled on being a cordage company, what with the land suitable for growing hemp and marine facilities only twenty miles distant.

We made it a point to be seen investigating the river, the roads, and other businesses so that someone of importance would ask us why we were so curious. It was best to have them try to sell us rather than us trying to sell them. After that, we would have to play the part by ear and expected to be welcomed rather than rudely disparaged.

For appearances sake we stayed in the English King Inn, a gentleman's hangout, and awaited the first act of our scenario to begin in the bar.

After we had a round of Madeira, men were not glaring at us anymore and one, who was dressed in a vest and waist coat (curiously warm clothing for such a hot day) came over to the table. He wore a monocle like a school master, and had heavy jowls which trembled as he spoke. He introduced himself as a lawyer and former mayor and we followed suit by using our true names.(It's too easy to mess up with made-up names.)

"My associates and I noticed that your delegation seemed interested in aspects of our town, and we welcome this attention. Perhaps I can be of service." He gave his name and his offer was more of a demand than a question, a good sign of genuine interest.

I had been delegated to be the spokesman; "Yes, sir, we represent the Chatham Cordage Company from Chatham in North Jersey and are concerned about opening a new branch of our company, provided we are welcome, and the town selected has to have the necessary features for our success. You must be the very man to render this information. Or, is there someone else we should count on?"

"Gentlemen, it is remarkable that our town council was just talking about expanding our economy. The war is not over yet, but we should make plans for when it is so we can be "on the ground and running," as they say. I will be honored to have you as our guests' tomorrow morning here at breakfast. Just appear and ask for Squire Arcularious. Say, eight o'clock?"

When he departed, we all thought we had started well. But we had to get information fast. Washington couldn't wait long.

Trevor immediately said, "I hope they don't check anyone in Chatham for veracity." Crispin shot back, "If they do, they won't get an answer until we're long gone. Don't worry about it. I'm more concerned that we'll make a misstep, and we could end up empty of information and hanged at the same time."

"This is not a good way to talk. We've started well and we'll get better playing these parts as we go along. Let's rehearse what information Washington wants. Crispin?" scolded Chief Honeoye.

Crispin was concise:"First he wants to know what route General Clinton will take. That means we should look at attractive avenues of travel like bridges, swamps to avoid, sources of water for horses, (he has over three thousand of them), good roads, (the sand road we just left is lousy; their fifteen hundred baggage wagons would slow them so they would be sitting ducks), and level ground.

"Judging so far, this part of the state has nothing but flat land. The whole area has prosperous farms, but the harvest for most foods is not quite yet, although the cattle are sleek and plentiful. Their army will subsist on forage as they go and I see no signs of scorched earth because of the Loyalist population. I think that's about it.

"If there's anything along those lines or whatever you might think is worth passing on, now's the time to mention it. Comments anyone?" No further comments were forthcoming and we retired for the day. The next day would be pivotal to our mission and our success counted on our being careful and retentive.

The next morning, Arcularious was there, dressed in a wool suit, with four other gentlemen, presumably from the town council. After introductions and a benediction, we began breakfast and all concentrated on eating a heavy meal. As the last of the scrambled eggs was consumed, Arcularious repeated what we had told him yesterday for the benefit of the others, and they responded with interest.

I continued to be our spokesman and casually mentioned, "We have not combed the state but we have examined Salem, Bordentown, and Toms River." This was a fabrication, but I said it to tease the town leaders to consider and to disseminate it throughout to the citizens. "You may think that some of those places have factors which would eliminate them right off, and I concur, but we had to satisfy ourselves that we did not leave any stones unturned. As businessmen, you must agree, I'm sure." I paused here to allow for signs of agreement and was not disappointed; they were in an agreeable mood. Then I continued with specifics.

"We need a strong current of water for our machinery, a hard-working ethic in the labor force and plenty of them, (that means good schools and a healthy past birth or immigration rate), proximity to our marine market, and fertile ground for growing quantities of hemp, even cotton.

"I forgot our visit to Cape May where they said cotton could be possible because their location on the cape between the Atlantic and Delaware Bay is warm and has as many growing days as Atlanta. Imagine that!" I thought I was doing so well that we would have to actually form a cordage company to make this fancy a reality.

Crispin must have thought I had said enough, for he stood up and was brief with a closing statement: "Gentlemen, I hope you can show us with a field trip this morning, or afternoon, the virtues of your town as they apply to our necessities. But first we will be glad to answer questions." He looked at each of the council members expectantly, but only one had a question.

"I hope you don't expect a money contribution to induce your establishing a branch factory here. Do you?"

Crispin did not wish to discourage the interest these men had in our quest. "No sir. Our treasury is bursting with dollars. We fully expect to enrich your town and its various businesses." I whispered to him, 'Just the right answer, Crispin.'

There were no further questions and Arcularious suggested his group huddle for a moment. In no time, they agreed to personally escort us through their environs at one o'clock after lunch.

We met outside the hotel and were first escorted to the river, and Arcularious began."As you can see, there is a steady current and this has been a dry summer so far. There are other places more suitable for a mill, of course, but we will show those to you in due time. The road crossing the river goes north to Amboy and a branch goes east to numerous towns on the shore and to Red Bank at the head of the Navesink River, only ten miles distant."

Crispin said he wanted to see the ground upstream so we went to the eastern side of town a few miles. He acted disappointed. "This looks swampy, not a good place for a mill." Arcularious paled but countered, "I showed this ground to you as the source of three streams which join and make up the river you saw on the other side of town. It's sort of a sump to collect water from the watershed that makes it reliable throughout the year—no downtime, you know," he almost purred, he was so satisfied with himself.

We all noticed the bridges that crossed the three streams and would have to be destroyed. "Excellent point, sir! How many students in the graduating class and the next two junior classes?" Crispin insisted. Arcularious asked one of his associates who whispered in his ear, "Twenty-three graduated. There should be seventeen next year and twenty-five two years from now."

Again, Crispin said "excellent," encouraging our suitors. They glowed with satisfaction. He threw another question, "How many farmers grow hemp?" Arcularious answered this one directly, "Two. Goerk has twenty acres, and Bird has forty. There's plenty more land for the same crop." he hastened to say.

Crispen was handling this expedition magnificently, I thought, as he said. "I would like to see the downstream portion of the river for mill sites," and we rode five miles or so west to see what bridges might be there. There were no bridges as the stream was shallow. One horse or a thousand pulling wagons could cross anywhere here. This was important information for Washington to know.

We acted like we had made our minds up and rode back to the hotel to pay our bill and check out. Just as we were dismounting, one of the council members bent over and whispered into Arcularious' ear. I was close enough to hear the lawyer say, "Are you sure?" and the other assured him, "Definitely, I've seen him in his store!"

Arcularious bellowed, "Seize that man, "pointing to Trevor, and they immediately surrounded our horses with theirs.

"What's this all about?" I spoke calmly although I felt as though stabbed at this point in our mission. "What do you think he's done? —sold you a ham at a high price?"

"No. This is Trevor Shaw, former owner of a store in New York. He was challenged to a duel by a British officer and knocked him out. He didn't follow the acceptable convention of using a pistol or saber, he fought with his fists! He was also put in prison for fighting us at Bound Brook but escaped and wasn't seen again until now. I think there's a bounty on his head." The challenger seemed to know the details.

A crowd gathered, the council collectively jumped from their horses and grabbed, not just Trevor, but all four of us, and led us to a jail. We were cited for treason to the Crown. In this Loyalist area, that meant hanging, and the citizens were all for it. How to get our information to Washington immediately perplexed my mind.

CHAPTER NINETEEN

OF ALL PEOPLE, I didn't expect Arcularious to come in to the jail to see us. He acknowledged that it must seem peculiar, and he shut off his usual spigot of bombast and quietly explained. "I'm a lawyer and I recognized Trevor Shaw, since I've been in his store, too. Ever since your John Adams took on the task of representing the British soldiers in what you call the Boston Massacre, I've admired such legalistic courage. None of the other Boston lawyers, except Josiah Quincy, had the guts to oppose the mob and the so-called Sons of Liberty, and take on what Adams's cousin, Samuel Adams, was branding as cut-and-dried murder.

"I want to do something courageous, so I'm offering my services to all of you because you're all in trouble. Adams got the judge to delay the trial 'til fall so tempers could calm down, but I've got to act fast or there may be a lynching party with you as the honored guests. Are you with me? Do you all want me to represent you?"

We agreed yes, but still in disbelief that we were in this fix, and he said, "Fine," and that clinched the deal. We hoped that he was as fine a man as his little speech.

He got out a pad and began writing down questions and our answers. We still played the Chatham Cordage Company game (why admit this scam, lose our chance to get information to Washington, and make things worse?) Besides, Arcularious was probably a Loyalist and might back out of the case if we withheld important information. Since we had given our correct names, we didn't have to fudge there, but we did have to be careful to not reveal our military or political connections.

One of the jailors stood nearby and heard everything said. He was possibly posted there to do just that for the benefit of the prosecutor, so Arcularious asked for a private room. The council member who had recognized Trevor came in, looking like a cat that had caught a mouse; he even had hair tufts in his ears, like a lynx. He refused us privacy by saying "This is not a public building to offer privacy, stay where you are." This contemptuous attitude made us aware that our case was going to be even more catastrophic.

Of course, the sheriff's office was both public and provided privacy, but we didn't pursue the matter. Arcularious, whose first name we found was Al, said it was best to have more of this discussion later, which I think meant that he would get an order for privacy from the judge. Our acting the part of executives looking for a branch location was so good; Al didn't even question us about it or the faux company.

In this hostile town, we wondered how he was going to get us exonerated. But, he had the determination of a rhinoceros and, as the day ended, we felt less uncomfortable, even though we had planned to be halfway to Philadelphia, or seeing the commander in chief, by now.

After a meager breakfast served at jail, Al appeared and said he had arranged for a court appearance this morning. He had worked on our case all evening and thought he could get us freed by noon. We were startled by such quick action. Most attorneys acted as if they were members of Dilly, Dally, Doolittle and Stall.

We pressed him to see what he had in mind to get us out of this mess so quickly, but he said he'd rather we find out during the session; he didn't want any chance of leaks to the prosecutor's office. Crispin, ever hopeful, got out the map to find the best way back to Washington's whereabouts, since time was important. Al went to his office and said he would see us in court at ten, and not to worry. Time held heavy on our minds while we sweated that hour.

Promptly at ten, we were led into the court; the building was of the finest architecture and had the best furnishings in town. The room filled with people, most of who were clamoring to see us suffer, and the bailiff directed all to rise as the judge came in and assumed his seat behind a massive desk which impressed all with the supreme majesty of the justice system.

The prosecutor was first to speak: "These four men (he read our names) are charged on several counts; Trevor Shaw escaped from captivity, and was on the battlefield at Bound Brook fighting on the rebel side; they have invaded our town in an attempt to disrupt government and aid the rebel enemy. A bounty is on Shaw's head," he declared in a morbid monotone.

Then, the court turned to our lawyer when it was his turn to make an opening statement. Al stood and radiated dignity: "May it pleases your honor to recognize that Trevor Shaw is the only one to be charged; the others had nothing to do with his escape or being at Bound Brook. As to the prison escape and fighting for the enemy, these are military matters and outside this court's jurisdiction. The charge of disruption and aiding the enemy is a matter of hearsay and intent, not capable of determination. Finally, there is no bounty on Mister Shaw. I am sure the British army has more important matters to attend."

"With the court's concurrence, I recommend that all charges be dismissed and the prisoner be released immediately." He said this as if he were the judge.

There was an angry outcry from the full house of hangers-on; the prosecutor slammed his brief on the table and swore, and the judged rapped his gavel several times to quiet the room. He cleared his throat (for this was politically unpleasant for him) and announced that "It is the court's decision that counsel for the defense is accurate in that this is the wrong court, and the other charges are over exuberant and of no merit. The prisoners are dismissed!"

The court room was again beset with boos, anger, and outrage, and required the judge to hammer his gavel and dictate quiet.

"What a great piece of work!" I told Al as I shook his hand. "You should be in New York or Philadelphia where they would appreciate you more. How much do we owe you, sir?"

"I don't want to charge you for this was easy— a simple piece of work. The prosecutor made the mistake of being too influenced by his constituency and not enough by the terms of the law. It was my pleasure to serve you, to retain honor, and make a name for decency. As to Philadelphia and New York, I'd rather live an easier life and I have, or had, many friends here."

The lynx-like councilman, who spotted Trevor, approached Al. "How could you go against town opinion, especially with General Clinton coming this way?"

"How could you be so petty, to attack a group to whom you want to sell your river property? It was obvious that to prosecute them for what you thought the crowd wanted to do, was unjust. We don't have a jail big enough to house all those who have thoughts of murder, theft, rape, and shop lifting, as if merely thinking about it were a crime. Sorry, but I couldn't, in all justice, do anything but defend them."

I interrupted "One more thing. How do we get our horses back?"

"I'll go with you to the sheriff's office. They'll know you're free to go."

As Al had forecast, it was eleven o'clock and we were free! We spurred our horses and left for where, we weren't sure.

Despite the risk of encountering British patrols and deep sand, we went due west until we met one of our army units. That was at Manalapan where we met a Captain Johanson and sent our report via his dispatchers. Washington had crossed the river at Coryell's Ferry, gone to Hopewell, and then to Princeton, probably with a large battalion. We cut over to Cranbury near the Millstone River since it seemed to be close to where Clinton would pass. There we would most likely find our regiment.

I still had affection for the Chatham Cordage Company; it had served us well.

CHAPTER TWENTY

THIS WAS JUNE twenty-sixth and General Clinton had settled on the path we thought he would, based on the density of British patrols and ease of passage. Our engineers had been out destroying bridges, mucking up wells, and otherwise hindering Clinton's path. Washington had the regulars under observation and was tentatively ordering harassment rather than a full-force attack. Defeating Clinton on top of Burgoyne's surrender would likely end the war. But if Washington was defeated it would also end the war, but in Britain's favor. Hence the caution.

All the battalions that had wintered at Valley Forge, and more were there, but it was a better trained and disciplined army, thanks to the efforts of von Steuben. All, from the top officers down to privates, were encouraged and eager to test their new-found strength.

I was not privy to one of the significant episodes of the event since the problem dealt with high-level officer's courtesy and protocol. In the beginning Washington wanted to send a brigade to harass the enemy and assigned its command to General Charles Lee, who was still second in command. At Valley Forge in May, we had just gained back Lee as a result of an officer exchange with the British, and I hoped we had gotten the better end of the bargaining; many of our high officers had a high opinion of Lee and felt more confidant under his direction at the battle's beginning.

I was dubious. (I kept it to myself) He had been a prisoner of the British for a year and a half, and since he had formerly been in the British army, may have made some concessions to them that were not favorable to us. I didn't know this for certain, but he'd already been in cahoots with Gates and both were bad-mouthing Washington before Lee's capture.

Lee knew it was appropriate to take the command when Washington offered it at Monmouth, but when he found it was to be only a brigade, Lee deigned the offer as being beneath his official station and Washington delegated it to Lafayette. Then Lee changed his mind again when the C in C became more aggressive, and enlarged the force to four thousand. Lee finally accepted the command, making an awkward situation at the last moment. Fortunately, Lafayette didn't raise a stink, but graciously accepted the decision. Then Washington increased the command to five thousand and the battle began.

The layout of the ground where the battle was destined to be fought was just east of Englishtown, near where we had looked for mill sites, and almost barren of farming, being largely swampland bordered by low ridges surmounted by hedgerows. Three streams oozed from swamps at the base of ravines that were no more than fifty feet deep. There were a few short hills which were later used for batteries for our guns and had a significant effect on the outcome of the battle. The terrain was similar to what we saw the day before, but the main factor was the heat and humidity which drained the strength of both sides and, at sunset brought an end to the fighting.

Our regiment was part of General Maxwell's command and we saw only our sector of the fighting, which continually changed from attack to withdrawal, from one side to the other. But I'll try to piece together our action with my own observations and what few I heard from others.

On Sunday, June twenty-eighth, General Henry Clinton planned an early start when he sent German General Knyphausen north with the baggage train to Middletown. This was good strategy as it removed valuables from harm.

A few hours later, Lee began our advance against the redcoat's left rear flank in a hesitant manner which was recognized by General Cornwallis, one of the better British officers, who took advantage of Lee's slow approach and charged over the open ground from just east of the Middle Ravine. Lee's orders must have been confusing for there was a jumble of uncoordinated movement by such officers as Generals Wayne and Dickinson, Colonels Richard Butler, and Henry Jackson, plus Woodford's and Varnum's Brigades. Then, General

Maxwell and his New Jersey Brigade, which had come up from Mount Holly, to which we four friends rejoined. All in all, Lee's command amounted to over five thousand men and twelve cannons.

Fearing that he had lost the initiative and would be overwhelmed, Lee called for Lafayette to draw three regiments from Wayne with some artillery and assault the redcoat's left flank. Lafayette did so, but was dissatisfied with his first position and as he dropped back to more favorable spot, other commanders thought he was retreating. Accordingly, they dropped back as well, which appeared to be the beginning of a rout, either because it was ordered or of individual initiative (later, an arguable point).Actually, Lafayette was jockeying to block a British thrust to his right.

By now, it was noon and with the fighting and the late-June New Jersey heat, tempers were rising as well as the temperature. General Washington got wind of the confusion and arrived to hear from one commander that Lee's command was attacking, and another said he was retreating. As the commander in chief topped the ridge overlooking the swamp in the West Ravine, he saw a large group of our men retreating from the British farther east. Washington was usually cool and calm under fire, but this lack of leadership and confusion he abhorred, and approached Lee to deliver one of his most damning condemnations, one that will go down in history as resulting in an improvement in the Continental Army's management.

Lee was already in a state of confusion and Washington's withering comments belittled him as if he were a corporal, not an easy accomplishment to such a proud officer as General Lee, the second in command. Lee offered a few excuses for the order he gave to retreat and added that he had not agreed with Washington's plan of attack at an officer's council held several days before the battle.

Washington said that if Lee didn't agree to the plan, he shouldn't have accepted the command. But regardless, he should have obeyed orders. He then relieved Lee of command and sent him to the rear lines. Later, at a court-martial, these points were argued by contradictory witnesses and what with later events and bad judgment on Lee's part, the general's military career was over.

I don't know why the twelve-mile long baggage train wasn't attacked. With all those wagons it would have bottled up Clinton's exodus from Philadelphia and the schedule of loading troops from Sandy Hook to New York might have been screwed up. But it wasn't—not to any serious extent, anyway. As it happened, General Knyphausen had led the baggage train north and it was not involved in the fighting.

Washington seemed to have confusion too often and retreats he had to remedy on the battlefield. It was true at Long Island, Kipp's Bay, and at the Brandywine. After the encounter with Lee, he organized to counter the attack that Clinton had initiated to push Washington back west, and the fighting was mainly on the ground overlooking the West Ravine. There was a hedgerow of holly (prevalent in this part of the state) and cedars (also plentiful) which made a good protective shield to fire volleys of musket fire at the British advancing from the east along the Monmouth-Englishtown Road.

Though the hedgerow shield was originally Colonel Livingston's idea, Washington recognized its delaying value to give time for an organization of artillery placements. It was the middle of the hot, stultifying heat of the afternoon and many of our casualties were from heat stroke rather than bullets or grapeshot, but our men could see how the battle might end in our favor by Livingston's tactic. So the regiments of Livingston, Varnum, Stewart, and Ramsay were aligned behind the hollys to fend off the British by small arms until the artillery shelling could finally be arranged for behind the swamp of the West Ravine.

Colonel Oswald brought up four cannon and General Henry Knox (of Ticonderoga transporting of guns fame) supported Oswald with four more. General Greene mounted a battery of four guns on Comb's Hill which overlooked the Monmouth-Englishtown Road along which enemy troops could be enfiladed as they marched toward us. All twelve guns and their artillerymen were safely protected by Woodford's infantry brigade. Next to officers, men that served the guns were the most sought-after targets for infantry and riflemen on both sides.

Because of the pressure from grenadiers and dragoons, those four forward regiments of Livingston's, Stewart's, Ramsay, and Varnum were pushed back, so his final attack against the British was stymied. However, there was still enough daylight left in the day for the enemy to mount an attack against us. An officer from this locality pointed out to Washington how the swamp between the East and Middle Ravine could slow the enemy and a ridge west of the swamp would shelter a brigade which overlooked the soft ground, a perfect deterrent. Behind the ridge was a tract of trees to hold a reserve force for follow-up, if necessary. I should also mention that, at this time of the day, the British had the sun in their eyes.

In anticipation of the impending attack our forces organized a large U-shaped defense consisting of General Wayne and his five regiments in the center, with General Alexander (Stirling) on the ridge to the left and Greene similarly on the right. Lafayette was in the rear and between both of them.

We were on the right flank and in the rear. The British attack was expected soon. Crispin suddenly tugged my arm, which was annoying since I was sighting my rifle on an officer's white cross straps, and waiting for him to get closer before firing.

"Look! There's a civilian on the edge of the field. He must be nuts and has no weapons, what's he out here for?"

I couldn't believe it either—a middle aged man in a business suit walking onto a scene about to explode, and trying to get somebody's attention.

Trevor answered the question, "Don't you guys recognize him? That's our attorney, Al Arcularious! It's got to be something important, he's no dummy."

The man stopped and talked briefly to one of our men and then followed the man's arm which pointed straight at us. There was some musket fire but our stranger was not in the least disturbed and came to us as casually as if we were at a table in the City Tavern.

I called to him. "Al, get down! The British are about to let loose Holy Hell on us any second and they won't hold off because some fool is in and out of their sights. Crawl if you have to." He seemed to finally recognize his danger and bent into a low run to the shelter of some yew bushes we were using for cover. Unbelievably, his only words were, "I've been looking for you guys all morning. I'm glad you're alright and I feel better already."

"What is so urgent that you had to get to us just now? Has the judge changed his mind?" I meant this sarcastically.

Just then, the British began shelling our position as well as those on the left flank. Al had started to answer but all I heard was, "...It's probably safer out he—" The cannonade obscured the rest of his sentence, but the meaning was clear. One of our soldiers was badly hit in the hip and fell to the ground unconscious. He was out of the fracas, so I grabbed his rifle and gave it to Al, saying, "You must know how to use this, get his cartridge box, too!" Al hefted the rifle as if he were about to shoot a deer and I had no more qualms about his being on the field with us.

I still had my sights on the officer and he was close enough for me to fire a shot. In the early days of the war, General Stephens had said to "shoot 'em in the legs, then it takes two more to carry them off the field and three are out of the fight with only one shot." It worked. Al saw this and fired at another officer waving his sword to encourage his men. The officer fell, but his men rushed closer with their bayonets at the ready. Fortunately, not all our men had fired their guns and there were enough still loaded to change the minds of the gallant survivors of the enemy charge.

The initial cannonading, both ours and theirs, slacked off and Al still wanted to say why he'd come on the field so desperately. "The town's people are mostly Loyalists and couldn't tolerate me getting you fellows off the hook. They gathered outside my house, brandishing pitchforks and yelling to hang me from the tavern sign. The councilman, the one who recognized Trevor, was angry because he lost a reward as well as hearing a contrary verdict, and led the mob of fifty or so to gain back his stature, avenge him, and take me down, all at the same time.

"I doubted I could change their minds in time to save my life. So here I am, bereft of property, reputation, a practice, and nothing but the clothes on my back. Bombs and all, I feel safer here than there."

This was but another case of the reality that, in war, there are many casualties besides those on the battlefield. The lull in the fighting was over; both sides had taken a breather to rustle the grit to mount the final action, and there was only an hour's sunlight left in the day to decide the winner.

General Alexander's division was the first to be assaulted by the elite veteran troops of the "Black Watch" and their field guns. They were pummeled for an hour but the left held with the help of Steuben and Washington. Lieutenant Colonel Carrington answered for our side in an artillery duel, but the efforts of all showed the value of Steuben's training and discipline of the troops over the winter.

General Greene's front was then attacked by similar elite troops, the "Cold stream Guards" and others under the command of General Cornwallis, and again, our brother soldiers held their ground and gave back as much as they suffered. Cannon shot from Comb's Hill also played a part in Greene's defense. I would like to add that our fire, whenever the enemy came within range, contributed to our success in holding our own against the full fury of the British army. Trevor stood up to take a shot. Chief Honeoye pulled him down. "Hey, Trevor! There's fifty muskets aimed at you when you do that!"

The center under General Wayne came under attack three separate times but Wayne had his men hold their fire until the redcoats were about to execute their famous bayonet charge when he gave the order to fire, which among many, mortally wounded their valiant General Monckton, and captured the colors of his unit.

Infantry on both sides were exhausted by the heat, humidity, and maneuvering in the deep sand as they fought during most of the day. Even before the sun was setting, it seemed that a mutual agreement pervaded the ranks of both sides, and the fighting stopped except for the artillery which dueled sporadically for another hour.

I've heard it said by civilians after a battle, that camp followers are a raunchy, wretched type, especially the women who were considered whores. Some may have been, but most were soldier's wives or sweethearts, or otherwise helpful. During this battle, they were like angels, and brought pitchers of water from wells and springs.

The heat had been as menacing as grapeshot and musket balls, and many hardy and able soldiers died of heat stroke. I'm sure many more would have if it weren't for these damsels of distress. I know that I was close to prostration since I passed out briefly in the early afternoon. Whores or not, these ladies were heroes and should be treated as such; to show our thanks we shared our rations with the ones who aided us.

The sunset was as blazing hot as the sun was at noon; more bloody red than orange from a sun that seemed as large as a rising harvest moon. Al was proud of himself, "I didn't think I could ever shoot a man, and I hope I never have to again. But when I felt the entire British army was trying to get me, after my experience in town, I found it easy to pull the trigger. Oh good. I could use a cup of that rum," he pleaded when he saw the canteen. He was still dressed in a business suit and sweated not at all.

He looked at each of us and said in a serious tone, "I guess I should explain myself. I grew up in Englishtown and have always been agreeable to the idea of independence. When Paine's pamphlet on Common Sense came out, I was more sure than ever despite my clients and others claiming loyalty to the crown. I seemed to be a party of one in a sea of Loyalists, but I kept my thoughts to myself—my practice demanded that I did, and I served all, regardless of their political affiliation.

"When you gentlemen came to town, I thought you were probably rebels, but I wanted to defend you against a strong-minded populace. It's what we lawyers are pledged to do; to represent all who ask for our services. Because Clinton has been in Philadelphia for ten months, this part of Jersey has been comfortable with the British, being conservative anyway, and they're upset that he's been ordered back to New York: the rebels could now gain the upper hand and they could make the townspeople suffer in many ways, primarily in their income. I can't blame them—most political opinion is formed by economics, not loyalty, despite what many in the country claim. "So I took your case to live up to my profession's ethics and to gratify my wish to gain some degree of fame, however briefly. When you posed as owners of a rope walk, I became certain that you were reconnoitering in connection with Clinton's abandonment of the Quaker City. How? Because businesses don't go looking for new ground to do business in the middle of a destructive war. But you presented your story in a persuasive manner to me and the others on the welcoming committee."

"Frankly, I feel better about myself now, even in the middle of death and destruction. After the trial, you suggested that I go to the big cities for my practice and I think you may be right. My thought that they were not as honest and sincere as small-town people is a myth, and more ambitious professionals will better regard me so I'll have reason to thrive in their warmth and intellect. Again, I thank you for your timely opportunity to redirect my life. Now, how do I get out of here?"

We watched him go to the rear in the dusk. I had given him a letter of protection that I think would be honored now that the battle had abated. Al Arcularious was a rare and notable man who I hoped to see again in the future. I have no idea where he went; whether it was Philadelphia, New York, or Kingston, I knew not, but there was some city that would be favored by the likes of men like him who steered their own way and benefitted all by their good works and self honesty."

Most of us had no trouble falling asleep in the night's heat and mosquitoes. When we woke, we knew our prayers had been answered to know that General Clinton and his troops had left their camp and the field early. They caught up with Knyphausen and the baggage train in Middletown the next day, and departed the Jersey shore at Sandy Hook for New York two days later.

Some say this was the last major battle of the Revolution in the northern part of the country, but that's because they paid little mind to the factionalism and resentment fomenting on the northern frontier.

CHAPTER TWENTY-ONE

I WAS APPALLED that I was getting so used to war that the casualties no longer upset me. At Monmouith we had seventy-two dead, of whom thirty-seven died of sunstroke. Twice those numbers were wounded and over three hundred missing. But many of the missing returned later, having passed out or wandered away due to the heat. The British casualties, we found out weeks later, were comparable to ours, but over sixty died of sunstroke, probably due to the heavy uniforms that officialdom insisted they wear. Many Hessians deserted and showed up in Philadelphia within the week. They were probably going to Germantown to someone they knew. Good for them to escape the British army.

Only a few days later, the border war in New York and northern Pennsylvania erupted in an attack Iroquois and Tories led on the Wyoming Valley settlements. Devastation of people and property was thorough and showed that the three-day mayhem was carefully planned. Because of atrocities throughout the frontier of New York and Pennsylvania, it was fearfully expected by everyone and many abandoned their homes.

The attack was two-pronged: beginning in early June, Tory Colonel John Butler marched from Niagara through much of the Iroquois area with his Rangers, picking up warriors from the Senecas, Cayugas, Onondagas, the Mohawks, and Tories. They stopped at Tioga, where the Chemung River meets the Susquehanna, so they could build canoes for the rest of the trip to the Wyoming Valley towns, only sixty miles farther.

The Loyalists must have spied out that the four valley forts were poorly garrisoned because the townsmen had recognized their danger

149

and organized two regiments of the best young men, only to have them taken over for the Continental Army elsewhere. (The battle of Monmouth was shaping up as General Clinton was moving his troops to New York.) A militia was then formed and again, the company was drained away. It's estimated that only about five hundred men, most of them old or too young, were on hand to oppose twelve hundred Tories and Indians.

Gucinge, one of the Seneca chiefs, set off southwestward with his band to assault settlements along the West Branch of the Susquehanna, and the rest went down the North Branch under the leadership of John Butler. The two met twenty miles above the main settlements before they sprung the attack on the valley. Some Loyalists, who had kept mum regarding their loyalty, rose to help the marauders by giving up their stockade home, Wintermoot Fort, making the rebels most uneasy.

The Indians used a tactic that seemed to never fail: they sent out a small group to lure rebels out of their fort but gradually fell back to where their comrades were hiding in the tall grass and in great numbers, an ambush strategy that usually overwhelmed the innocent. They must think we're dumb to continually fall for this. At least, I do.

At the end of three days, over a thousand homes were demolished, three hundred and sixty men were killed, and over a thousand head of cattle were marched off. Because of Butler's control over the Indians, women and children were not molested, but many died of starvation or exhaustion as they fled to Stroudsburg or Shamokin.

But to understand this horrific situation, a little background may explain why this powerful coalition of British soldiers and savages could be.

The encounter of Europeans and Indians occurred even before Columbus claimed he discovered America when ambitious fishermen from Western Europe explored the fishing grounds off the coast of New England. They would cross the Atlantic in season, fish for several months, and then dry their catch on the shore before returning home to cash in their crop.

The native people were curious of the whites and their large ships propelled by the wind, as were the whites interested in the furs obtained in abundance by the Indians, but no longer available in such numbers in Europe. Trading between the two parties ensued: metal knives, hatchets, cooking utensils, traps, and muskets, lead and powder revolutionized the Indian culture, and myriad furs, bought cheaply, enhanced the wealth of the traders from overseas.

Word of this bonanza circulated as fast as gossip on a grapevine, and monarchs begrudgingly financed expeditions to further explore North America, particularly since Spain had been profiting ever since Columbus, not only in furs, but in gold and silver, beyond the Spaniards wildest dreams. During these explorations, England, ever competing, organized land companies to settle territories and exploit a whole new market for goods to the Indians, and those who traded continually explored farther with the Indian's guidance. The French, through the efforts of the Sieur de Champlain and others, explored what later became Canada, Quebec, and the north-western states while England still concentrated on the eastern seaboard.

The Dutch entered the contest and explored what later became New York State, including New Amsterdam on the island named after the Mannahata Indians, and Fort Orange, after the House of Orange from which their monarch had sprung.

Because of the waterways like the St. Lawrence River, the Great Lakes, and western tributaries to the Mississippi River, the French explored as far as a thousand miles west of Lake Michigan by 1740. This was largely for the fur trade and the conversion of the Indians, so the population of Canada was sparse with most settlements concentrated along the St, Lawrence.

But the English were busy developing seaport trade in New England and Virginia and remained blocked by the Appalachian Mountains until just before the Revolution. People from Europe, such as the Huguenots and the Palatine Germans, fled their countries during times of political oppression and populated those regions more than France populated Canada.

In 1664, the newly restored English King, Charles the second, decided that the Dutch settlement of New Netherland (New York and New Jersey) was an intrusion on an otherwise continuous English seaboard so he sent four naval ships to make good his claim. The populace was multi-cultural, not solid Dutch, and they weren't happy under Peter Stuyvesant's Dutch rule, so they agreed to become English without firing a shot.

The province was renamed New York, New Amsterdam became New York City and Fort Orange became Albany, named by the king for his brother, the duke of Albany and York, who was given the new territory and later became the infamous King James the second.

During this period of exploration and settlement, the Indian tribes had suffered loss of land, European diseases for which they had no immunity, decimation through war, and a radical change in their culture that made them almost totally dependent on the white man for essentials. They could no longer hunt or make war with bows and arrows, their clothes were mostly European made, cooking and trapping equipment was supplied by the whites, and even tomahawks were made in an English factory.

Indeed, if they had had the wherewithal, they should have declared independence themselves.

But most of all, they craved alcohol and all varieties of it. It weakened their morals, their minds, their strength, and often left them drunk and robbed in their trading with generally greedy white traders.

The Iroquois occupied most of New York for over two hundred and fifty years, and what it didn't populate, it ruled and extracted tribute from adjacent tribes such as the Lenni-Lenape in Pennsylvania and New Jersey, and the Susquehannocks in Pennsylvania. They were a confederacy that had existed for most of that time, consisting of the Seneca, Cayuga, Onondaga, Oneida, and the Mohawk, their domain going from near Niagara Falls east to just short of the Hudson River. The Tuscarora came up from the south and joined the Confederacy later, under the sponsorship of the Oneidas.

They were shrewd statesmen and knew how to play France and England against each other to their own advantage. During many centuries before in Europe, England and France were constantly at war, and conflicts which started in Europe often gravitated to America, and involved the Iroquois and their subject tribes. Consequently, they acquired arms which enabled them to dominate tribes as far west as the Illini Indians and the Catawba to the south, from both a military standpoint and their middleman status in the fur trade.

Largely due to the understanding and savvy of Sir William Johnson in the Mohawk Valley, they were persuaded to be on the English side. But when England won the last of the four French and Indian Wars, the French lost Canada and the Iroquois lost power because they could no longer get the leverage of negotiating with one country against the other. They then colluded with the English simply because they no longer had a choice. But Johnson's death just before Revolution began didn't help them either.

Just before the Revolution broke out and the migrants from the seaboard began to cross the Appalachian Mountains in large numbers, all the Indian tribes felt rebuked because they had been promised by a treaty made at Fort Stanwix in 1763, that England would prevent white settlement west of the mountains—a promise based on a vague boundary and which was impossible to enforce and carry out. This fomented Pontiac's Conspiracy, a coalition of many Upper Lakes tribes that, for many practical reasons such as the trade, was brief, but bloody.

With peace, the migration began anew and the Indians wanted redress and a more precise boundary line as well as enforcement. To assure themselves that their domain would remain unsettled, the Iroquois sold the British government a large tract they'd claimed south of the Ohio River for ten thousand pounds at the Fort Stanwix Treaty of 1768.

So this long-winded, but only partial background, explains why the Iroquois were on the English and Tory side. They were formidable but not unformidable.

Many in the army thought that because of the good performance we put up harassing Clinton's army, we would get some time off. Clinton was not likely to make any further move what with his army exhausted by the more than week-long trek during the hottest summer in some time. His officers would be looking for a restful interlude, too. They would very likely care to spend some time in the summer reacquainting themselves with the Tory girls of New York society.

I must confess I would be remiss if I didn't want to see Olivia and my four-month old son we named George after my father. Crispin would no doubt like to see Annie also and reassure her that he's a good husband—and maybe he'll soon be a father, too.

Trevor hasn't mentioned Daphne since last fall when we all attended the service for her estranged husband. Is she back in New York—is he interested in her anymore? He hasn't said a word and keeps his personal life to himself. But he's getting on, and needs a companion. Perhaps Olivia could introduce him to a girl friend; she's been in Tredyffrin long enough to meet widows and other single possibilities.

Chief Honeoye is another close-mouthed friend whom I value highly and want to help. I should write Olivia a note, if I can get some time off, and ask what she would think if I bring Trevor and the Chief home with me. I'd like to show them my son, too. I promptly went to our captain to see what our prospects were for a week off and to Trevor and the Chief to see when they wanted time to relax and where.

Captain Straus was the kind of officer one had to wheedle with to get what you want. I asked for two weeks of leave, sure that if I asked for only one, he would cut the request in half. I was right; he cut it to a week which was all I wanted, anyway.

When Trevor and the Chief went to Straus, he granted them a week without any quibbling and I dropped a note to Olivia as to when we should be arriving, and asked where in Tredyffren her new abode was. "It's about two and a half miles past St. David's Church in Radnor," she wrote; "Stay on the Lancaster Road until you get to a small cafe, The Chesapeake House," turn left and back-track down the slope along a ten-foot wide stream, and you'll be here."

In two and a half hours we arrived from Cooper's Ferry, but there were two houses, not just one. I recognized the right place by Olivia's dress hanging on the line. She ran out to greet us, lovingly kissed me, and hugged both Trevor and the Chief.

"You finally got uniforms! You look so official and warrior-like—and you're all in one piece. Come; let me show you our yard on the creek. Would you like some cider? It's been another hot day." She snatched the dress off the line and went inside.

We marveled at the refreshing scene after our long ride weaving behind laborious oxen pulling Conestoga wagons going west. The brook was a hundred feet from the house and fronting on a meadow, our meadow. The brook was crystal clear, cold, and had two-foot deep pools as it burbled its way down and under a small stone bridge. A wagon lane ran out to a field where there was a majestic white oak. I wanted to take off my boots right then and wade in the inviting pool, but I could do that later, so I resisted.

Across the stream was a small swamp. I could see at a glance cardinal flower, jack-in-the-pulpit, yellow aster, Joe Pie weed, Oswego tea, turtle head and other pretties; no wonder Olivia had chosen this place to stay.

She came out of the house lugging a chair, and the three of us hastened to assist by each bringing out more chairs and a small table. Then she went back in and brought out our baby, our son of four months.

I must confess that all babies look the same to me; large bald heads, tight-fisted hands, pink and smooth skin, bowed legs looking like they rode a small pony, and drooling as they try to talk. But he was ours to be proud of and to continue the line of Claveraques well into the next century. Trevor and the Chief were courteous congratulating us. Olivia then swept aside a wind-blown lock of her sleek, black hair and smiled gratefully before she went to get the cider.

With her came one of the ladies who shared the house with her. She was thirty-ish, blonde, had an attractive face and figure, and acted as if she had just come from an Earl's drawing room in London. Olivia seemed pleased to introduce Natalie Latterlea, originally from Chelsea on the edge of London.

She snidely let it be known that she didn't favor Americans: her husband was a captain with Burgoyne and was now part of the Convention Army. "I don't know where he is. The last I heard from him, he said he was in a town outside Boston. It may have been Cambridge; he didn't know that or when he'd get home. Your Congress has stopped the army's transport to England, and what they'll do next is anyone's guess. Nothing seems to help, not even the King's signature."

I thought, 'What'd you expect?' and I went to get another chair.

Then Annie Johnson, formerly McLauren, arrived and heard just the last of Natalie's complaint. "A good thing he's not dead, my dear. Burgoyne's men fought as well as they could, with much bravery I'm told, and still they couldn't win. Be glad he's alive and able to come home when Congress thinks the British ministry will behave honorably." I hoped that their usual banter was not as brutally barbed as this.

Trevor tried to sooth the scene with the usual amenities. "Was your husband garrisoned in New York, Mrs. Latterlea? I think I remember a Captain Latterlea in New York. I used to own a general emporium there." This was the first time I heard Trevor refer to his store as an "emporium." He seemed to be aligning himself with her style of speaking. "I believe he was a close friend of John Brigandi and Charles Chipping."

"Why yes, he knew both of them. John was a friend, but Chipping was a drunkard, spoke disrespectfully to his wife, and generally was obnoxious." she agreed.

"That's him, to a tee. Five years ago he was an interesting conversationalist, and engaged in, not just the army, but in history, sailing, and athletics, and knew how to tell a story or a joke. He became ambitious, tried to ingratiate his way with the higher-level officers, and drank heavily as he gambled his fortune away, Naturally, Daphne found this infuriating and the marriage went down the drain, too. At the end, he tried to one-handedly urge the army to attack a fort under siege in upper New York when a Seneca Indian tomahawked him."

"How awful! Is Daphne still with the army?"Natalie asked as if in a near faint.

"I don't know what became of her, but she was resourceful and was able to get along. I liked her, but was never worried about her future. I would bet that she has another husband by now." This was an honest appraisal by Trevor.

Yet other guests appeared. Doc Iverson arrived with his wife, Maryann, and joined right in with his old friends who had escaped British captivity with him. "Trevor and Jamie! How nice to see you again, and on such different conditions. If it wasn't for these guys. I might be in that sugar house still. Tell me what you've done to upset the British this time."

Of course this caught Natalie's attention and an ugly scene could have erupted, but Trevor again had a soothing way with her. I went to get two more chairs, but there was only one and I had an excuse to roam the yard as I yielded the seat to Maryann.

After Olivia got everyone into a convivial conversation, she came over to me, proud to point across the stream. "See the wild flowers over there? It's partly the reason I chose this place. It's a wonderful spot to wander and forget about the war. I've also planted this garden so I don't have to go to market every few days. The other girls help out, too."

Trevor and Natalie had wandered over. "Did I hear you say you made this garden? You could fetch good prices for those tomatoes at the market. And I'll bet you have to fold your lettuce twice to get it in a sandwich. What's the secret?" Trevor hadn't known Olivia gardened or had been in the seed business.

Olivia was pleased to hear compliments on what she had been quietly working on all spring. "I think it's the soil. It's largely shale, but I've improved it with humus from last summer's leaves. I've also top-dressed it with mushroom soil, which is highly-manured soil used in the culture of mushrooms. A lot of mushrooms are raised around here, and since the special soil can be used only once, I got a lot of it very reasonably."

Trevor, a seasoned business man, was impressed. "Jamie told me you were in the nursery business in England. I guess you sold flowers for corsages for m'lady's important social affairs, is that right?"

"We did that, but our main business was selling plants and seeds of new or unknown plants from America to gentlemen who were busy landscaping their estates.

"What kind of plants do you mean? Like tulips or peonies?"

"No. Like mountain laurel, rhododendron, moccasin flower and Oswego tea—all from the wilds of northeastern America. We have many of these specimens right around here, but in England, they're still new, exotic, and highly sought after. John Bartram, from nearby, was one of our suppliers. His gardens border the Schuylkill only an hour from here."

"So you got your plants and seeds right here. Who runs your business now?"

"My brother and I were working in the business when my parents died and we carried it on—I relinquished my share when I came over here—I doubt very much that Jamie and I will go back to England. Bartram, in his younger years, hiked through the back country for his specimens and seeds. He went into the Appalachians and as far south as Florida as recently as ten or so years ago."

"As this country grows after the war, it'll need plants to beautify stumpy fields and line boulevards and parks. Take a look at Valley Forge, the army left it in a mess! Perhaps, with your know-how, you might start a nursery business here. Maybe Bartram could stand some competition."

"John Bartram was an older man and he died about the same time General Howe occupied Philadelphia. His sons are carrying on the business because they worked with him for years, including the

157

traveling. I doubt if I or Jamie would hike into the mountains, but I suppose we could train someone to do it."

"This business with the Indians will open up a lot of land for settlement. People are going into the Ohio Valley and now that the Proclamation Line is no more, migration west will cascade like when the Huns invaded Europe. It'll grow even more when we push the Indians west of the Mississippi.

"The Iroquois even know it. Nine years ago at the Fort Stanwix treaty, they sold a large tract south of the Ohio to the English government, to divert migration away from their domain. If they keep attacking the frontier, this country will devastate them, take their land, and sell it to fund our government."

I had no idea Trevor knew all this. He's probably going to use his money from selling the store to finance a land company of his own.

CHAPTER TWENTY-TWO

THE NEXT DAY, I suggested to Olivia that we go visit the Brown Transmission and Belt Company at Matson's Ford. I made an investment in that company two and a half years ago after I first arrived in this country, and had never seen or talked with anyone about it except briefly with the broker. I wanted to see how well they had survived the British and what the prospects were for the future.

Natalie assured Olivia that she would take care of the baby and that she should enjoy a day away from the garden and child raising. The weather had cooled and the day promised to be pleasant and informative. She might want to put some of her money into the company, too, Olivia said.

We went near enough to Valley Forge to remind me of more difficult times, and rode down along the river among the odd small hills. The factory building looked undamaged and even spruced up. We went in the front door and asked for Mr. Brown, not knowing the names of any of the management.

Mr. Jonathan Brown was about forty, was dressed as an artisan with a leather apron, and curious that one of their shareholders had actually stopped to visit the business. He invited us to his cubby-hole of an office, even though he was the president. I felt embarrassed that chairs had to be brought just for us—I think he did, too. We had to speak louder all this time since the building was aquiver with gears and belts turning their machinery and making a constant racket.

"I admire the condition of your building and grounds. The British must have left you alone. They've made a mess in the city, as you probably know. So you should be congratulated on your diplomacy. But how did your sales and finances do all this time" I tried to be sparing of his time and not waste our few minutes with irrelevant chit-chat.

"We were lucky that they knew something about business and did little to bother us. I think that they expected to win the war this year and then take over the business. But they were ordered back to New York. So no damage was done and we continued production and even increased it some. Have you seen the most recent report?"

I hadn't, so he went briefly into detail. "Sales increased five percent and our revenue increased ten percent, largely due to installation fees. Some of our expenses increased as most of what we buy, like iron for gears and the cost of office supplies, became more expensive due to the armament and paper industries. This was more than offset by the lower price of hides, with so many cattle in Valley Forge and the city being slaughtered to feed the armies.

He continued: "As settlements increase west of the fall line, we expect larger sales, especially when the war dwindles, as it seems to be doing now. Companies will expand and build sawmills and grist mills in the more hilly country. All in all, this year we increased our net income and increased our dividend by five cents a quarter. Would you like a brief tour of the plant?"

As Brown took us along an aisle, a lengthy leather belt hummed as it rotated from a large pulley to a smaller one. Everything was spinning rapidly and attached by belts or gears to either speed or to increase the power from the water wheel. I could see the importance of the bonded connection between the two ends and how taut it must be to not slip off their spools, or whatever they call them. As expected, the place smelled of leather.

Part of the space outdoors had a putrid stink as the hides were processed in large trenches by employees wearing thick leather aprons. Back in the building, gears of different sizes and angles, even small chucks for holding drill bits, were being cut out of iron, and displays of uses were predominant to show prospective customers the benefits and quality of their products.

The company seemed to make fine serviceable goods and knew how to present them from the customer's viewpoint. I felt comfortable that we had a worthwhile investment. But the noise and stink was insufferable and we indicated our thanks and intention to leave. I also think that Brown was so busy with orders that he was glad to see us go.

As we went down the front steps, Olivia sighed, "Whew! How would you like to work in that place?"

My answer was brief. "Frankly, my dear, I'd rather own shares of the stock."

After a circuitous ride down past Bartram's, we rode back to Tredyffryn. The rest of the week was spent meeting new neighbors and lounging around the house. The Chesapeake House sold Philadelphia papers and it was pleasant to sit by the brook reading about changes in the city since the British evacuated. Articles about Arnold were frequent and expected since he had been as active and vocal as a military commander.

But he got a little high-handed and made enemies with the wrong people, as he usually did. Some even accused him of profiteering and one called him greedy and treacherous to the country.

General Lee was swiftly given a court martial in Brunswick in early July. He was charged with disobedience of Washington's order to charge the enemy at Monmouth; misbehavior for making a shameful retreat from the enemy on the same day; and disrespect of the commander in chief in two letters which were wildly abusive. General Alexander officiated and Lee was judged by his peers as guilty on all three counts, but he was still with the army in Philadelphia until September.

A much later article said that Congress had finally agreed with the sentence, which restricted Lee from command for the next twelve months.

The month of August provided day-to-day stories in the paper of General Sullivan's fling at diplomacy with the French at Newport. General Henry Clinton had been sent there at the end of '76 by Howe to keep the Bostonians uneasy. (Some say Howe sent him to get him out of his hair) He had six thousand army troops and a strong fleet plus General Robert Pigot was there with another three thousand.

The sand bar off Sandy Hook prevented the timorous French Admiral d'Estaing from entering New York Harbor (he had just missed encountering Clinton ferrying his troops from Sandy Hook) and Congress decided the French fleet could instead be used to attack the British at Rhode Island. In addition, Washington sent Lafayette, Glover and Varnum so that Sullivan had ten thousand troops to make his attack on Pigot.

The French fleet, with three thousand troops, arrived on the scene at the end of July and the usual compliments and pledges of cooperation were said, but Sullivan and d'Estaing didn't hit it off. Despite this, the two planned their assault. A few days later, French Admiral Suffren handled his squadron of two frigates so fearfully, that the British panicked and destroyed six ships of their own fleet to keep them from coming into French hands.

The diplomatic trouble began over whether Sullivan or d'Estaing should attack Newport Island first. British naval reinforcements were coming and Sullivan's army was spread among the several islands and bays so that a desperate stance had evolved.

Jockeying for the advantage of the weather gage by the two fleets took place and then a furious gale erupted, breaking ships' masts of both fleets before they could begin to fire broadsides at each other. The British considered a fight, until more French ships arrived, so they made their way to New York for repairs, and d'Estaing returned to Newport. Not a shot was fired.

After the storm, Sullivan pushed his harried men against the British, fully expecting d'Estaing to lead his troops in a pincer's movement on the other side of the island, but the Frenchman refused to land his troops, who had been on board ship since the storm began. In the middle of the night, d'Estang abruptly sailed to Boston for repairs, without giving notice. Lafayette rode all the way to Boston to persuade his stubborn countryman to come back and participate in what seemed to be a certain win, but he had no luck and returned the same day.

The French refusal so roused the anger of the militia that twelve hundred deserted. The battle raged to and fro on the island for several days, but Sullivan was getting the worst of it. He managed to get his troops to the mainland, but what had appeared to be an easy triumph, turned into a rout. Mobs in Boston even hinted that they wouldn't make repairs on d'Estaing's fleet. Lafayette and Greene did their most to rectify the frayed feelings of the French and avoid weakening the important coalition that Sullivan still antagonized. The French-United States Treaty had been endangered, but cool heads smoothed over indiscretions by both sides. Sullivan's career seemed on the downside.

In mid-September we read of an Indian attack on German Flats and in October, the rebels retaliated at Unadilla. In Cobleskill, they suckered the militia out of the fort and ambushed them. Other depredations of the Indians and Tories occurred and served to increase the friction between them and us.

What had more influence on the rest of the year, and the following year, was the Tory-Indian attack on Cherry Valley on November 11th. The New York village ten miles south of the Mohawk was brutally assaulted by a large party of Mohawks, Seneca, Cayuga, Onondaga Indians, and Tories. Joseph Brant was with the marauders this time, as he was not part of the Wyoming Valley raid in July. You had to admire the determined pluck of these people to march all the way from Niagara, down the Chemung River to Tioga, and up the upper Susquehanna to hit this outpost.

Tories, such as the infamous Walter Butler, were in the attack force (he escaped from jail in Albany) and the townsmen knew that they were wide open to attack. Even though Colonel Gansevoort had been recommended, Colonel Ichabod Alden got the appointment to command the new fort, and was in charge of his Massachusetts Militia regiment.

In view of Indian troubles, a new fort had just been built. It was inspected by Lafayette who happened to be in the area inspecting military facilities of this sort. Embrasures had not even been cut to allow a field of fire for their guns, but Alden said he'd been so busy, he hadn't gotten around to it. The lapse characterized his and his troop's sloppy management and lack of Indian War know-how.

Alden reluctantly sent out two patrols to see if rumors of enemy activity were valid; one patrol was captured in their sleep and the other reported nothing, which allowed a relaxed and less alert attitude to continue. After a two-inch snowfall on a foggy dawn the Indians swept over the town, first hitting the fortified Campbell house where thirteen officers were lodged; all were killed. Alden was hit by a thrown tomahawk as he was running to the fort and many of his other officers were killed, too. The outpost had been carefully scanned and selected as the target because of their ineptitude.

Over thirty people, including officers, were killed, most of the barns and homes were burned, along with both the mills, and seventy hapless victims were captured and marched south a few miles the first night. The next day most of the captives were released, but a few were held as hostages because the wives of Sir John and John Butler, and others were confined in Albany.

The whole northeast border was alarmed as these attacks were reminiscent of the French War tactics twenty years earlier.

Even Washington was alarmed to the point that he started planning an invasion of the Iroquoian to wipe out the power of the Longhouse so that they were no longer a factor in our fight against the British. I felt sure that our unit under General Maxwell would be a part of Washington's plans. I even relished it, but it was several months before we were called.

The first assault of Washington's plan was in April of '79: five-hundred and fifty militia from Fort Stanwix made a hush-hush hike to near Fort Brewerton, camped for the night, and then raided Onondaga Castle near Onondaga Lake. Colonel Goosen van Schaik, son of a successful old Dutch Albany family, who had seen action at Crown Point and accompanied the Fort Frontenac capture under Bradstreet during the French and Indian War, commanded this raid, in which he and his men went a hundred and eighty miles, there and back, in less than six days. It was very satisfying to see Chief Hannyerry of the Oneidas join in with sixty braves and lead the affair.

During this time, they destroyed the major Onondaga village, burned fifty homes, took thirty-seven prisoners, killed thirty warriors, and brought back a hundred muskets. All this was accomplished without losing a man! This served notice on the Iroquois that their days of arbitrary destruction were at an end, or so it was thought.

The plan against the Iroquois was mostly planned by Washington and contained three separate parts, of which the raid on Onondaga was the first. The second is a two-fold plan in which General Sullivan (the command was first offered to General Gates who refused it because of age) would start at Easton with twenty-five hundred men, cut a trail to Wilkes-Barre and collect stores before working their way up the Susquehanna to Tioga, where they'll rendezvous with General Clinton.

Clinton will leave from Schenectady, go up the Mohawk with fifteen hundred men to Canajoharie, carry his boats and supplies twenty miles cross country to Lake Otsego, and travel down the Susquehanna to meet Sullivan at Tioga.

From there they'll jointly follow Washington's orders to "destroy and devastate the Iroquois nation and capture as many prisoners of every age and sex possible," to be used as hostages for good behavior.

Washington emphasized that the country was to be "destroyed, not merely overrun." This meant that all the Indian towns and Chenussio, the major Seneca town, and possibly Niagara, would be laid waste, including their orchards and fields, and stored food supplies. Washington was harsher in this planning than any issued before.

The final part of the plan is for Colonel Brodhead to leave Fort Pitt, go up the Allegheny River with six-hundred men to destroy the more western villages of the Seneca, and meet Sullivan at Chenussio. From there, they'll go to Niagara, if conditions are right, and wipe out the British, Tories, and any Indians there. Because of this last possibility, some think the plan is coordinated with George Rogers Clarke's expedition against the northwest.

It's an ambitious plan and requires a major part of Washington's army, which up to now, he couldn't spare. But it should stop the destruction on the frontier, and curtail food supplies in upper New York from going to the British army.

I put the paper down and thought what a terrible dislocation for the Indians this would be. I knew they were cruel and vicious, but that's usually a sign of despair, and not knowing what to do against overwhelming forces. We've done the same in our numerous wars. They've made treaties with reliable leaders of the province and sold land to the whites. Their under-standing of a "sale" was not identical to ours; they thought they were just letting us have the use of the property, not the exclusive use. But they lived peacefully with us, as long as we didn't try to cheat them outrageously. Our outlaws and others who fled law-enforced areas were usually their closest neighbors, which made the Indians easy prey for mischief.

It boils down to oppressive leaders in Europe who aggressively hound their citizens because of religious or other reasons. The people leave their country and come over here in large numbers, looking for freedom and land. The land is eagerly acquired by land companies, who are favored, by the King or local governors, with land grants. The land is finally sold to the new arrivals as they move west.

Individuals move west, clear the land and build a cabin for their family, and work hard to raise enough to feed them, maybe even a little more to improve their lives. But this usually encroaches on the Indian's hunting grounds. Then, the disgruntled Indians try to kill the owner, and burn the place down. They take his kids; maybe adopt them into the tribe to make up for attrition due to wars and disease, and the whole process recycles for the next generation.

Chief Honeoye's parents were victims of that scenario. It happened to him twice, when his parents were massacred by Onondagas, and again when his adopted Oneida parents were killed by white renegades.

What can we do about it? Not much more than ride with the tide: educate oneself about government and aspiring leaders, vote for the good ones, work hard and get along with the neighbors, and join the army when you have to. And have heart.

Trevor was right though. We'll push the Indians west of the Mississippi in succeeding generations, and life will be calm in the east. Making money this way is part of the game.

CHAPTER TWENTY-THREE

EASTON IS A relatively new town at the confluence of the Lehigh River with the Delaware. It's been proposed as a supply base because it could be supplied by water easily, and is out of easy reach of the British; so it was to be used for the Sullivan Campaign. It was also a portal to the trail used by Indian traders north to the wilderness. Because of some unavoidable delay in appointing officers, the first to arrive didn't get there until May seventh.

It was a natural place to begin the march, but the trail had to be widened for wagons to carry our supplies through rugged country to the Valley towns on the Susquehanna River. Brigade troops were there in early May hacking a road north through Wind Gap, which is not a town, but merely a notch in the Blue Mountains, and on to Wilkes-Barre. It was tough clearing a road and laying down logs in corduroy fashion through laurel, virgin forests, and swamps, but getting loaded Conestoga wagons, cattle, and heavy equipment north was the first order of business.

Crispin was excited by our going to Easton. "We couldn't go there several years ago because of my rattlesnake bite. Now we can fish the falls where the Lehigh enters the Delaware."

"What makes you think you'll have time for that? We'll be working all the time, more than usual even." I had to tell him.

"This is good trout country." he pronounced, as if nothing could deter him.

Wanting the last word, I said, "When the road's finished we'll have plenty of time to fish." How right I turned out to be.

General Sullivan's army consisted of four brigades totaling twenty-five hundred men; General William Maxwell (we called him Scotch

Willie for obvious reasons) and his brigade of New Jersey Continentals; General Enoch Poor and his New Hampshire and Massachusetts regiments; and General Edward Hand's Pennsylvania regulars which included Daniel Morgan's famous riflemen, constituted the main army.

General James Clinton, the New York governor's brother, had fifteen hundred New Yorkers and two small caliber guns. In addition, both divisions had the usual camp followers composed of wives and sweethearts, but mostly they were loose women, and too many, were considered an important part of the army. They did the laundry, cooked, cleaned up after meals, and performed other services.

The road to Wilkes-Barre was finally completed so that the army started north by June eighteenth, but because of difficulties on the way, such as passing through Wind Gap, and the swamp known as "the Shades of Death," and troubles with the artillery, we didn't reach our destination until June twenty third.

However hard to believe, we languished in Wilkes-Barre until the end of July. This was due to supplies that arrived but were poorly packed; unsalted meat, poor commissary management, or no supplies at all, was not an uncommon feature of our army in this war. We had the same problems at Valley Forge, so the problem wasn't because of distance.

General Sullivan, who saw this mission as a chance for promotion and fame, was frustrated as any man might be, but he handled the problems in what I thought was an efficient and calm manner. As this was my first connection with the general, and though I had heard adverse comments, I developed a liking and respect for him. I think most of us did, and we did our best to speed up deliveries, often by way of the West Branch from Sunbury.

Besides, there was an unusual adventure waiting for us and we wanted to get started on probably the most exciting event of our lifetimes. Proof of this was not only constant conversation about Indian atrocities, location of their villages, Tory leaders, and natural problems of navigating the Susquehanna, but that many of my friends were keeping journals of day-to-day events.

Crispin got in some fishing and the Susquehanna yielded not only what was left of the shad run, but trout, bass, and occasionally a salmon. It wasn't virgin water, but it was close to it, he said.

Our presence was appreciated by the local people as we had improved the economy of the valley and certainly the social life of the daughters of families who had to suffer a catastrophe, unique in one's lifetime, only a year ago. They were sorry to see us leave, but on July thirty-first, we finally did.

A hundred and twenty boats, twelve hundred pack horses, and seven hundred cattle had been loaded, or herded, and started moving up the broad river that swept this beautiful valley. Half the community of several thousand must have been on the banks waving us goodbye and good luck against an adversary that had cost them so much grief. At the confluence of Lackawanna Creek, the river turns sharply northwest, cutting off our last view of civilization. From now on we had to make do with what we had.

The Susquehanna in this part of the state runs swiftly among hills as high as eight hundred feet, and has many curves interspersed with stretches of rapids or riffles. Where the river loops are around more or less level ground, we could cut across the flat to save ourselves from unnecessary labor. Here and there are small islands, which in many cases, are farmed. Other stretches were like proceeding through canyons with high hills on both sides, some-times with majestic splendor. While the boats had to follow the river, where we made our trail was carefully considered as we went along. Regiments moved in a column, rather than a mob and flankers on each side spread out, making it a difficult trek. It was the "warrior's trail," meant for single-file passage, so narrow ledges hundreds of feet high had to be by-passed or we'd lose cattle, horses, or men on the rocks below, as happened occasionally.

One place was called Standing Stone. A large and thick slab of rock had fallen from the heights and dug itself in the river bottom so that it stood twenty feet straight up. Another of nature's miracles was farther upstream; a spring gushed out of the rocky eminence and fell free for what we guessed was two hundred feet. A breeze misted the falling water and, if you were in the right spot, small rainbows appeared to delight the eye of the lucky observer. I'll bet that was noted in many journals.

As I said, flankers were sent out one hundred yards to avoid sudden danger, and we sensed that we were being watched by many eyes, but we saw no Indians. After several days, Crispin said it was the sixth of August, the anniversary of the Oriskany Massacre, as it was now called. We saw an Indian youth, but he dashed into the woods and we saw no other until we arrived at a small Indian village, curiously called Newtychanning.

The place had recently been abandoned; we saw three red men run into the bushes. Pots were still boiling over untended fires and foot prints were all around, but nary a person was to be seen. I suppose that our numbers frightened them off. We became more alert, especially when entering the edge of the forest for answering nature's call. What a time to be so vulnerable!

According to our guides, Hannyerry, the Oneida chief, and Jehoiakim, a Stockbridge Indian chief, we were approaching Tioga, where the Chemung enters the Susquehanna, and we were looking for a shallow place to ford to the other side. It was found near another Indian town called Sheshaquin, only a few miles from our rendezvous spot. The town had been destroyed over a year ago by Colonel Hartley in retaliation for Indian raids. Some called the place Queen Esther's Town, for one of the Montour family sisters, a powerful and long-lived family in the Iroquois realm. Their brother had been on Sir William's raid of Canisteo in '64.

Overall, we had come sixty miles to Tioga, and General Sullivan sent a messenger to General Clinton ordering him to start his run down the first stretch of the Susquehanna River, which had Otsego Lake as its source. It was August tenth. That's a correct date since we checked with the general.

The two generals had been in constant communication by messengers and we knew how far Clinton had come: he'd started at Schenectady and went up the Mohawk to Canajoharie, where he portaged over two hundred batteau across twenty miles of rugged trail to Lake Otsego. He saw that in the dry summer, the lake had risen very little. In addition he had scouts reconnoiter the outlet, which they reported hadn't enough water to transport the loaded boats for about ten miles, where another stream entered with enough flow to eliminate the problem.

Clinton was clever; he built a dam across the narrow outlet and had his men clean up the brush, stumps, and other objects that might obstruct the first ten miles below the lake. Now, it had been seven weeks since he built the dam and the lake level rose over three feet, more than enough to relieve everyone's mind. Some said it was God working in our behalf; I kept quiet, but thought it was God who gave us the sense to think out and solve the problem.

When Clinton received the definitive order to start south from Sullivan, he positioned the bateau below and to the side of the dam where the rush of water would cause no damage, and then broke the dam. The flood washed away any remaining obstacles, and as the torrent receded, he launched the boats, each manned by three men. Only a few boats were badly damaged.

The rest of his force marched on both sides of the river and destroyed all the Indian and Tory towns as they went downstream to Tioga. There were a considerable number of them either on or near the river: Oneonta, Otego, Aleout, Conihunto, Oquaga (Brant's town) Ingaren, Choconut, Otsiningo, Owego, and Packtowanuck, all occurred before reaching where they were to meet us and where the Chemung River added to the Susquehanna.

Some of the towns had been burnt by Hartley the previous year, especially if they belonged to Tories, but if there was any doubt, they'd been spared. Rather than wigwams or longhouses built to Iroquois tradition, many were built like white residences one would find in any seaboard city. They even had glass windows.

I thought it curious that many of the towns began with the letter "O." Perhaps that was a key to understanding the Iroquois language, but I forgot to ask Chief Honeoye.

When we finally reached Tioga, one of the first things ordered done after the celebration was building a fort to store our supplies and lighten our load. Fort Sullivan was four blockhouses built and positioned in a diamond shaped layout, one blockhouse at each corner, with a stockade linking them. It spanned most of the narrow neck between the Chemung and the Susquehanna, and was manned by a full regiment. This took about a week before it was finished, but it was good enough to be defended, and left the major part of the army free to advance up the Chemung.

Just before the supply depot was finished, Sullivan sent Captain John Jenkins, one of our guides (he had escaped Seneca confinement with the help of Red Jacket, a Seneca shaman), to go up the Chemung a few miles to a small Seneca town to reconnoiter. Sullivan wanted to prevent the congregation of Indians to attack our position while we waited for full completion of the fort, and Jenkins and Jehoiakim were the best ones to do this.

General Sullivan had been surprised that the Indians didn't resist our invasion of their homeland, and made aware that a sizeable Indian village was not far, he sent Generals Hand, Poor, and Maxwell, which included us under Colonel Dayton, to destroy the village to prevent an ambush, a favorite tactic of the Indians. We did this at night over a trail that narrowed to a precipitous ledge as we advanced, and, to make things worse, a fog crept in so that we had to go very slowly and the five-mile march took all night.

In the morning as the fog lifted, we saw that there were only a few warriors still there, and General Hand was sent to the far side of the village to block an escape of any that were there or would pop up. On the way, we were gunned by fifty warriors who used the technique of baiting a trap with a small contingent of braves to lead us to where many were in hiding, and if they were good shots, could wipe us out. Six of our men were killed outright and nine were wounded. With that, Hand directed that we charge the savages and we shot a few before we were withdrawn.

The rest of our mission had found the town of Chemung empty, and we burned or trampled most of the verdant fields of vegetables, but left a field of corn for our use for when we returned from the campaign. As General Sullivan said, this was "first blood," and we anticipated a violent clash ahead. General Clinton's arrival seemed to be taking longer than expected and Sullivan sent out a thousand-man detachment under General Poor to locate and escort him to our camp. Clinton's division didn't have any trouble on the way down the river except for heavy downpours the last few days, which made them wish they hadn't burned the house in the last village; they didn't make any headway when they crowded together, stalled in the rain.

On the twenty-second of August, they were alerted by Clinton firing six rounds of his cannon to announce their presence only a mile distant. We replied with thirteen shot of our own. When they appeared around the last bend in the river, they looked exhausted, but glad to finally join and enjoy the companionship and the security of us, their comrades in arms.

The looked-for meeting was greeted with cheering, so much so that General Sullivan allowed a quart of whiskey to each officer and a half pint to each of the rank and file. The army band played festive music, some men danced and pickets were sent out wide during the celebrating. Lanterns in tents were lit longer than usual as certain of us caught up in our journals. As to the revelers, they were disappointed that orders came down that their whiskey ration was to be watered.

Crispin was one of the revelers. "Why don't the others get as much rum as us, they do as much to contribute to the campaign as we do? And they might be shot, too," he said. He was spoiling for a fight and I was afraid he'd had too much already so I casually eased over to his place at the campfire.

"This is the first I've heard you complain in behalf of the rank and file. What's come over you?"

"I shot a turkey with the bow this afternoon and I wanted to give it to the boys in my company, but an officer claimed it for his friends. He was high enough that he could get away with it, but I resent it."

"You're probably up for promotion and will bask in such preferment yourself some day. You can shoot another turkey but you shouldn't get in trouble with one of the higher-ups."

"Yeah, but——." I cut him off.

"Get used to it," I said, and I meant to be harsh for his own benefit.

Just then one of General Clinton's men walked by with a strung bow and a deer slung over his horse. I was glad to see that someone else thought to bring his bow and take advantage of virtual virgin hunting grounds. I grabbed Crispin's bow to wave and catch his attention. He came over, smiling and accepted a gourd of rum.

"That's a handsome buck. Did you just get him?"

"He was just off the trail so I asked Colonel Dearborn if I could take a few men with me and go after him. They're all archers and know to approach game slowly. The buck was just north of here. My first shot got him; I knew I was close enough."

"What's your name, Captain? Where are you from?" I was curious.

"I'm Joshua Lang from Claveraque, over near Vermont. What's yours?"

"I'm Jamie Claveraque from almost anywhere you can think of."

"You gotta be shittin' me! What's your real name?"

Crispin barged in. "He was from Ross on Wye, England, same as I was. Since then we've lived in Vaux Hall, New Jersey, near Newark. Then Morristown, Fort Stanwix, Bemis Heights. Monmouth, and now, wherever we are in Iroquoia. But we don't own anything in

173

those places. By the way, I'm Crispin Johnson. I'm here both to fight and to draw maps. I also hunt with a bow."

Lang shook hands with both of us and turned to me. "Your name really is Claveraque, then. I just never thought there was another with such a name. I think the guy who founded the town was Claveraque, he was a Huguenot, you know. So were my folks. But that was seventy years ago."

"Did you see anything out-of-the-ordinary while coming down the Susquehanna? I understand you had an easy time once you made the carry to Otsego Lake."

"I'm sure it must sound like it since we went most of the way by boat, but we stopped and burned about a dozen villages including their crops which were almost ripe. I wouldn't want to do it for a regular living."

"You also didn't really need a map—just floating along the river took you where you wanted to go. Any problems?"

"Just one. The river was raised by Clinton building a dam across the outlet of the lake, and we broke the dam so the water would take us quickly along. But it also flooded a lot of rattlesnakes that were forced out of their holes and in no mood to be friendly. They were more than a nuisance in the lower places along the shore trails. Nobody got bitten but there were several hundred, and that was surprising."

Crispin was practically invited to say something after that comment. "I was struck and bitten by a rattler about a year ago and it's no joke. It hurt like hell and took all the strength from me for three days. Trevor said I could have died. I better keep my eyes open for 'em."

The rule was instituted that no one could whoop like an Indian, or fire a gun, even at the enemy, or under any circumstance, because it would confuse others since signals were sent in the form of musket shots. Consequently, no one could take advantage of the myriad game animals that, unused to a blundering army, came within an easy shot of our path. Because we were to be traveling through such a hunter's paradise, Crispin and I brought along our bow and arrows. Between us, we were able to supplement the diminishing rations, to the pleasure of the generals and our friends. Rather than have nothing better than salted pork, it was glorious after a long march to sit by a fire and eat venison, too.

Crispin was with one of the detachments and it was the first serious encounter with the enemy on the expedition. He was to draw up-to-date maps since the ones we had from General Clinton disagreed with those of General Sullivan, and began to be inaccurate. Some maps had intentionally been drawn incorrectly to throw us off the track. Obviously, spies had been at work.

I told Crispin, "I don't envy you. You have to carry the usual equipment and rations, and a musket, and your surveyor tools. How are you to protect yourself if we're ambushed?"

"I try to look like a shaman so they'll leave me alone."

"That might make you more of a target," I said reluctantly, I didn't want to scare him.

"I'm sure they're continually watching us, so I stop, set up my easel, and draw the usual lines on the paper. So far it's worked. That's what I did when I was working in the lower Hudson, and I came out alright there. I drew a lot of maps, too."

That seemed to be more luck than sense. "Can I help you in any way?"

"All you can do is walk next to me with your musket as if you're guarding me from harm."

"Well, I would be guarding you from harm."

Just then, we saw a flicker of brown recede into the laurel, and we both became more aware of our intrusion into Iroquoia.

The day after Clinton joined us at Tioga, and we overcame the effects of celebration, the two divisions began the march in which we were certain to meet the enemy in large numbers. So far, our casualties were nine dead and fifteen wounded.

We also had some loss of men because of sickness and an accident. A private was cleaning his musket in his tent and he thought the piece wasn't loaded. But he was wrong: the trigger was nudged and a ball and some shot fired through several tents and slightly injured some men. But the ball went through three tents and struck Captain Kimball through the heart, killing him almost instantly. The shot pellets caused damage to others, but it was miniscule.

Another soldier died of a heart attack and another of camp fever. And a fifteen year-old who had begged his way onto the campaign, was shot by Indians as he was rounding up some stray horses.

To lighten the load, we left a lot of supplies at Fort Sullivan under the care of a hundred and fifty men plus the boatmen, more than fifty sick, and the camp followers. The way was now by the Chemung River and our scouts thought there were several large Seneca villages close by so we went unburdened and cautiously to be on the lookout for an ambush. The Chemung wove its way among steep hills and narrow valleys so that we couldn't have flankers spread sideways except for the scouts who went ahead several miles.

For that matter, the trail became so narrow that we had to ford Baldwin Creek, which ran east to west along the base of the mountain until it emptied into the Chemung. Then, where the valley broadened, we forded back, but in both fordings some of the supplies were ruined because of the depth and strength of the stream.

Chiefs Hannyerry and Jehoiakim both said that Newtown was about three miles up the river and was regarded as an important Seneca town from which raids on New York and Pennsylvania towns were made. This information made us even more wary and we were far ahead of the division headed by General Hand. Captain Thomas Boyd warned us not to be tricked into an ambush. The usual Indian gambit wasn't to be tolerated here. The idea was to draw the unwary to an area where a large number of warriors wait to pounce. We heard of this practice working almost every time.

Crispin and I were constantly scanning the woods ahead for places where the enemy might strike. So were most in our regiment. We were deep in Indian country and didn't expect to come upon abandoned villages anymore. We hoped not because we came all this way and wanted some action.

Lieutenant Boyd held up his hand and slowed the vanguard to a stop where they were about three-hundred yards from the hillside ahead. He had sharp eyes and earlier, with Clinton's division at Lake Otsego, he had spotted two spies wanted for previous crimes. He went into the woods, back tracked to catch them and brought them in for sentencing. They were hanged and Boyd was promoted to Captain and became a favorite of General Sullivan.

Here something looked funny or familiar to him. He pulled out a small telescope and scanned the hillside in front of us. Baldwin Creek was slightly ahead of us, soft swampy ground was to our left, and a steep hill was behind—it was perfect for an ambush. He gave the scope to a sergeant and told him to climb a tree to get a better view. The sergeant climbed a pine tree, swept the hillside with the scope, and saw nothing but a normal growth of trees, but looked again, more slowly a second time.

Sometimes we look at something, but have a preformed opinion of what we're about to see. But if we take a second look with a fresh and more exacting scan, we can penetrate our previous view and see what's really there. This must be what happened to the sergeant because he stayed in the tree for ten or fifteen minutes before shimmying down. He whispered his findings to Boyd who ran off to General Hand with the information. This was about noon on August 29th.

We found out later that the sergeant saw that there was a barricade up about a hundred and fifty feet above the river which wound around the six-hundred foot high mountain, to the east and northeast, for at least a mile. It had been carefully camouflaged with recently-cut saplings of like trees and laurel to obscure perhaps five hundred warriors and Tories waiting to hear Chief Brant's war call. I thought at the time that Boyd might get another promotion for this saving service.

Hand was born in Ireland, trained to be a surgeon for the British and in 1767 came to Fort Pitt to be a surgeon's mate. He quit the Royal Army in 1774 and practiced medicine, but joined a rifle battalion in the Continental Army as Lieutenant Colonel at the siege of Boston. He was just in time to be at the Battle of Long Island and at White Plains and Princeton. His unit's stalling General Cornwallis at Princeton made the battle a victory for Washington. After that, he was part of George Rogers Clark's early missions. All in all, he impressed Washington who recommended him as a Brigadier General. And we were lucky to have him with us.

He was a quick thinking general and dispatched eight three-man patrols to reconnoiter the territory. With his topographical knowledge, Crispin was in one of these. When they returned, Hand told Sullivan, who ordered a council of war of his generals. After familiarizing themselves with the land features, the agreed-upon plan was to have his troops ring the Indian fortifications first, and then at a signal blast of artillery, aggressively attack so that a pincers movement would block the enemy on their hillside. The fighting was vicious from both sides and lasted no more than two hours for the whole battle. The Indians were almost trapped but managed to

177

escape just before the ring was closed when Brant signaled the Indian call for retreat.

The leaders, John Butler, and Joseph Brant survived but a number of Seneca, Cayuga, and Onondaga chiefs were killed in the battle.

Among the Indian dead were Gucinge and Kayingwaurto of the Senecas, Rozinoghyata of the Onondagas, Captain John of the Mohawks, and Queen Esther, the middle-aged Seneca woman who tomahawked fifteen captives at Wyoming a year ago.

The American dead amounted to eleven, with thirty-two wounded; the British and Tories dead came to five, seven wounded and two captured, and a total of twelve Indians were dead. We didn't know how many wounded they had since they removed them from the grounds. In view of the significance of our victory, it was a minimal casualty count. But we were only half through with the campaign and certain that more encounters were to come.

The following day was spent destroying the Seneca village of Newton. Many of our men were farmers and they appreciated the quality of care that had tended the orchards and fields. Pumpkins, watermelons and squash were monstrous compared to the usual products at our markets and it was apparent that we had much to learn from the squaws who were responsible. We also felt badly that we had to destroy fields of corn eighteen feet high and corn ears twenty inches long, but this was the specific order by George Washington so that the Iroquois could not continue their wanton destruction of our frontier farms the rest of this year or the next. It was the opposite of a labor of love. We ate as much as we could even as we worked hard to destroy it. This helped reduce the drain on our rations.

The pincers movement that took so long to arrange, had concluded so fast that we almost were able to round them all up, but they fled quickly, so fast that John Butler's commission, personal papers, and battle plans were lost in the scramble. A quick study revealed that the next stand might be at Shequaga, or Catharine's Town, near the head of Seneca Lake, twenty-five miles north. That was our next goal.

CHAPTER TWENTY-FOUR

AFTER YEARS OF reading about the French and Indian War, Pontiac's Conspiracy, and the friction between Indians and the frontier, it suddenly dawned on me that the Sullivan Campaign was a two-object plan to destroy the Indians' capacity to wage war and, at the same time, a way for the colonists to rapidly increase their land holdings at little cost. It was planned by Washington who had a history of acquiring land ever since he started surveying for the Fairfax family in the Northern Neck section of Virginia.

Ever since the beginning of settlement on the seaboard, the colonists had bullied and bought land from the Indians and now the edge of the frontier was crossing the Appalachian Mountains. Iroquoia was a vast tract of choice unsettled land right in our backyard, and as a country, we had done little to add it to our ownership. New York had gotten as far as the Unadilla River but that was the boundary by treaty. I was so impressed by this large tract of land, lakes, and rivers, that I wanted a plot for Olivia and myself. If the Iroquois squaws could grow such specimens of fruit and vegetables, so could we.

But my mind wandered as we trekked the twenty-five miles along a tributary of the Chemung to Shequaga, or Catharine's Town, and Seneca Lake. Catharine was the sister of Queen Esther who was killed at the battle of Newton. Both of them were Montours and could trace their ancestry back a hundred years to the time of Governor Frontenac and some said they were even related to him. But they were eminent in their own right: they attended councils in Onondaga and traveled to Montreal and Philadelphia on diplomatic missions. Even now, Queen Catharine was spending the summer in

Canada. Both had been respected by Indians and whites alike, and had acted as judge and mayors in their communities. Now we were headed towards her town which was located on the flat near the head of Seneca Lake.

Another important Seneca town was Kanahwaholla on the Chemung River. And nearby was Rumonvea, a smaller town on a creek the name of which I don't remember. We destroyed both of them, again leaving some of the crops for our return.

We went due north until we came to the end of the tributary and found ourselves at the watershed separating the Chemung from Catharine's Creek which enters Seneca Lake at its head. The valley became so narrow that we had to cross and re-cross Catharine Creek, someone said seventeen times, and then, in the late afternoon, we were in a swamp. A swamp is manageable by a few men, but thousands herding many cattle, and heavily loaded packhorses, can muddle the whole into a pudding in which many struggle or get lost, but at a minimum, all are exhausted.

It was getting dark and we didn't want to retract our steps, so we continued on what the map said was our trail.

I suggested to Crispin and Trevor that we hold hands in the dark so that we didn't get lost or step in a hole and drown. It was so dark that nothing could be seen to reassure us that we were where we wanted to be; not even the stars were out. This was country familiar to Chief Honeoye, except for this swamp, and he was scouting far ahead. West of here was where he obtained his snake oil elixir from a little pond not too far away. But, as he said, it was difficult and out of our way. I suspected that he didn't want to reveal the source of his elixir, and how inexpensive it was to produce it. Too many would be tempted to take the profitable business away from him.

I also thought that since the Indians are so superstitious, perhaps the Perseids in the night sky at this time of the year was interpreted by them as a bad omen, both now and a year ago, just before they abandoned the siege at Fort Stanwix. Mid-August is the astronomical date which coincides with both of their hapless occasions. Shooting stars falling all over have to have had some effect on primitives. I'll have to ask Chief Honeoye—he'll know the answer. I looked back along the line of march and thought what a good idea it was to load the boats with wagons and our artillery, especially the two six pounders and the two weighty howitzers; they had continually slowed our march. We had to guide them on solid ground and retrieve them where mired. Now, they weren't a problem for us. And I hoped, that tearing some of the tents for the canvas to make bags for some of the rations, lightened the load also. When we emerge from the swamp we'll begin to see if it pays off. But that took all night for some of us. I just hoped that the four brass three-pounders and the Coehorn we kept were sufficient to overwhelm the large Seneca town at the foot of Seneca Lake.

Since we still had far to go and our rations were not likely to last, General Sullivan announced that he would like the army to agree to going on half-rations, figuring that the troops could survive handsomely on the fresh corn and vegetables as they were destroying the Indian's food supply. He coaxed them with flattery and said that they should freely vote on it; he would have the army reimburse them for the rations they didn't receive. All four divisions voted in favor of it without any dissent. They even gave three cheers for the assenting vote and for the general.

Sullivan also thought the army should send the sick and wounded back to Wyoming for their better care and to lighten the load on the pack horses that were not doing well on the lack of hay. They went down the Chemung before we left that waterway and at dark to insure their safety.

The routine destruction of Shequaga homes and crops began and was finished before the day was over. I cringed at girdling the fruit trees as they were loaded with apples and plums that would ripen soon. They had probably been sold as saplings by English traders between wars. Of course, it being early September, some of the apples supplemented our diets. We were able to rest for the balance of the fatiguing day and we went to sleep early to get a good start in the morning for the long trek up the east shore of Seneca Lake.

At the foot of the lake was Kanadasaga, a principal Seneca town, and we expected resistance there or at the lake's northeastern corner while crossing the outlet. At least, the Indian trail up the east bank of the lake was more apparent than what we had just been used to.

After slogging through thick forests, miring in swamps and leading our stumbling horses, it was a pleasant relief to follow the trail which rose on a bank of the lake and enabled us to be wafted with a mild breeze. The lake was thirty-six miles long, and we expected the easier path through the open country with random clusters of trees, and we were no more than a half mile from the shore.

Within five miles there were three small towns, perhaps three miles apart: Condahaw, Peach Orchard, and Appletree. I don't know whether we assigned those names or they were original but Anglicized, Indian names, but they were appropriate. I hate to say it, but we burned the few cabins, a longhouse at each one, and destroyed the small fields.

One of the particulars of all the lakes was their deep ravines with small brooks emptying into the lake. Some of them had large deltas, as if a large river had washed away the dirt in the ravines to fan out into the water. It made a perfect spot for the squaws to fashion a field of melons, pumpkins, squash, peas, and corn. They were as large as Olivia's in the garden she made at Tredyffrin. Alas, we had to ruin all these homes and fields that any of the soldiers would have loved to own. I know that it inspired many to think about coming here after the war.

One of the largest ravines had a town at its base and was so steep that we called the ravine Breakneck. It slowed us going down and coming up, but the whole fetch of the shoreline was a pleasure, just the same. On the flat at the bottom, Kendaia was the last and largest town on this side of the lake, but like all the others, we destroyed it.

A thin white boy was wandering around the town, probably because he was too weak, or didn't know where to go. Captain Machin asked his name, the name of his parents and where he was from, but none of these questions brought an answer. Then he asked for permission to adopt the child which was granted by a sympathetic Sullivan. I never knew whether the boy survived or how the relationship turned out. They were part of a group of other ill people, this time sent back to Fort Sullivan.

As we approached the northeast corner of the lake, we became anxious about fording the outlet which was about twenty yards wide and had a swift current. If the Indians were going to show any pluck and resistance, this was the strategic place to do it, but with all our training and directions for just such occurrences, no Indians appeared, and we crossed with no trouble.

We were still in peril because our path was due west along a sand bar and a wide marsh, with tall reeds, which could have been just right for another ambush, but again, nothing happened. It was so surprising that many thought the reason was that the enemy was gathering for a showdown at their major town of Kanadasaga, only a few miles away. As we moved to the northwestern corner of the lake, where there was a small creek, we passed some fine houses, the largest of which belonged to Chief Grahta. It was along more firm shoreline with a beautiful view down the lake and made a nice summer home for him. So said my friend, Chief Honeoye.

At last, we arrived at Kanadasaga, the principal town, or one of the principal towns of the Senecas, who for centuries were noted for their wide range and ferocious fighting ability. Surely, we expected that they would be waiting here to resist our terrible destruction of their dominion, but like all the towns, except for Newtown, it had been abandoned.

The whole complex was surrounded by a large circular field of corn, and the more central part was in orchards and smaller fields of the usual vegetables. At the very center was a large longhouse, which served as the town council house, and well-made homes which probably belonged to the town leaders. Some had glass windows, chimneys, and puncheons for floors. They were as fine as houses in any flourishing city on the coast.

Honeoye said that the blockhouse and stockade was one that Sir William had built during the French War. It shared the center of the town with the longhouse.

This had to be the finest soil I've ever seen; the corn was tall, the ears were almost two feet long, and all the rest of the fields were bountiful, enough to be the envy of any farmer in the campaign. I'm sure that some were making mental notes of exactly where the cleared land was so they could claim it after the war. The packhorses were attracted to the grassy sward in the town's center and we were glad to let them graze while we contemplated the whole.

But our orders were to destroy most of what we saw. It took all day to cut the corn stalks, sharpen our sabers and bayonets for further corn mayhem, and to trample, with horses and men, the rest of the astonishing agriculture. I felt as guilty afterwards as if I had violated all the tenets of the Bible. So did everyone I talked to.

Chief Honeoye said that he had talked with some of the townspeople a few years before and he had congratulated them on their industry and care. The Senecas answered that they planted and cared for the produce, but the clearing of trees had been done by the "ancient" ones, who preceded them. Imagine how difficult it must have been to clear away venerable and large trees over such an extensive area with primitive tools—there must have been over ten-thousand acres.

It was the end of the first week in September and the weather was turning crisp, and even frost occurred in the valleys. We still had at least two more weeks of work or war before we completed our mission, and, rather than rest from our labors, we had to be on the march early the next day. But our rations were disturbingly low and Chenussio, Little Beard's Town, was still about forty miles somewhere to the west. Our guides said it was even larger than Kanadasaga, and so it had to be destroyed. And then our mission would be completed.

Even so, General Sullivan called a council to vote on what to do: on the one hand, the military season was coming to an end and our supplies were dwindling, and our horses were starving and overly fatigued; on the other hand, our commissary said that if we cut back to meat every three days, and bread every five, we could sustain ourselves on the vegetables and fruit along the way. Our men voted to go on since we had accomplished most of what we'd been charged to do.

Before we left the area, Sullivan sent Major James Parr, Lieutenant Thomas Boyd, and two-hundred riflemen to destroy Kashong, a town seven miles down the west shore of the lake we had seen across from the eastern side. And Colonel John Harper was sent to Skoyase, a Cayuga community seven miles east on the Seneca River. The Indians had cleverly created several ponds to trap and raise fish for food at the latter town, but all was destroyed by fire and force before we could move west the next day.

Another detachment of fifty men under Captain John Reed was sent back to Fort Sullivan at Tioga to escort the sick, including Machin and the sick boy, as well as a number of jaded horses that had no value until they had decent forage. The men were ordered to build and supply a depot back at Kanawaholla on their return so that the division wouldn't have to be on short rations as we conclude the campaign.

We marched to the next lake west, Canandaigua, and the Seneca town of the same name. Compared to Kanadasaga it was a small community but with very fine homes that had chimneys and were solidly built. We sacked it like the others. Every day was practically the same as the rest as we were constantly destroying any structure in sight, and it was dull work since many of us would prefer to build rather than destroy. We then headed southwest to a cluster of small, separate lakes.

After a fourteen mile march, which was slightly downhill and gave us equally slight ease, we arrived at Honeoye Lake from which Dan Rettenhaus had made up his business name. We were not far from where the chief obtained his magic elixir, but he said nothing about it because he was afraid someone might steal the stuff and put him out of business. He said he thought there was only one source.

Honeoye had twenty homes with no Indians in them, of course, and Sullivan decided to divide his force into two divisions; one detachment to stay here and fortify the strongest and best located house, and the other to continue to Chenussio which he thought was about twenty-five miles to go. He could leave much impedimenta, such as rations for the forth and back remaining miles, baggage, extra ammunition, and carry only enough to satisfy a four day mission since Chenussio could be sacked and returned from in that period. The fortified house detachment was commanded by a Captain Cummings, and so it became Fort Cummings. The next day, the other detachment, ours, burnt the other nineteen homes and continued to the village of Conesus near the inlet of one of the small lakes.

Crispin had been busy drawing maps since we were deeply into little-known territory. He had measured distances, calculated heights of mountains, and lengths and widths of lakes, and noted jigs and jags of rivers and their tributaries, and, conscientiously, put all this information on paper. His hardest foray for this purpose was about to begin, for the maps that were available were useless and confusing, and Sullivan wanted his charts up-to-date. It was beautiful country, untouched by the hand of civilized men, and Trevor and I wanted to see it.

We approached Thomas Boyd, who had again been appointed by General Sullivan to lead a small detachment to search a way to Chenussio clear of ambush possibilities, to see if we could join him and Crispin, his impromptu cartographer. Boyd was receptive and raring to go since he was ambitious and wanted to make his mark in the army, but heavy rain had kept him inactive for several days. In view of what happened, I shall never forget that day. It was September twelfth.

That evening, Boyd had us muster. Instead of four or five volunteers there were about twenty-five, and enough light left in the day so that I could see that one of them was Al Arcularious! After Boyd had given us a pep talk and brief directions, I sauntered over to see our former legal savior at Monmouth the year before.

"What are you doing here? You were headed for the big city to build an-other law practice. I don't think the Seneca's want your legalese, just your scalp."

I called Crispin and Trevor over.

Al seemed surprised to see us. "You fellows get around. Last year you were carousing at the beach. Now you're summering in the mountains! You're still together? Where's Chief Honeoye?"

"He's one of our scouts and, at the moment, works for the main army. Are you part of Boyd's volunteers?"

"Yeah. After I left you and Englishtown, I went to Philadelphia to join any law firm that would have me, but they weren't interested. I decided I might as well show my true colors and join the rebel army through the influence of a few friends—and here I am—a private at Conesus Lake in upper New York!"

Just then, Lieutenant Boyd stopped briefly to say, "There you are, Al. Glad to see you've met these fellows—you're in good hands. Remember, since this is an all-night operation, we're leaving at eleven. See you at the inlet then" and he disappeared in the twilight.

Many of our missions didn't take a brief nap before leaving, but joined others around the campfires. Crispin, Trevor, Al, and I sat by the river away from fires so that our eyes wouldn't become smoky and could adjust to the dark, even though there was a rising moon. We found from Al that the reason he couldn't join a law firm was that prices had increased so high, and currency was so low, that no one could afford a lawyer any more. It was a bad time for the firm to take on another. We thought it strange since lawyers always seemed financially invincible.

Finally, Boyd's collection of volunteers crossed the inlet where a bridge was being rebuilt and went up a steep rise with only ten miles to Chenussio. He was about to continue going west when Hannyerry stopped him, and pointed northwest, saying that Chenuussio had moved five years ago, but the map hadn't been changed. We followed

Hannyerry's directions, and in a few hours, we were on the crest of a hill overlooking the Chenussio River and the town of Chenussio on a large flat on the other side. A few Seneca were there winding up the abandonment of the largest Indian town we'd seen.

Boyd expressed his disappointment by a hearty "damn." He had looked forward to leading a charge on a defended Seneca town, particularly the largest, but the humdrum of previous abandonments seemed to be our lot. After an hour of observation, we began to retrace our trail to Conesus. On the way, we saw four Indians. Tim Murphy, the sharpshooter who had shot General Fraser at Saratoga, shot and killed one and another private wounded another. The remaining three fled, probably to report this to Brant or Chief Little Beard, the war chief at Chenussio.

We continued our way back to the main army but soon caught up to the surviving three Indians plus a few others. Boyd should have known better; he had seen the dire effects of this common Indian strategy, but tossed the safety of himself and us to the winds, and followed the weak party of Indians, only to fall into an assemblage of a large ambush waiting for us. They fired their muskets with enough effect that Boyd led us to a patch of trees in a clearing. We had good cover there, but the Indians didn't. Even so, they were shooting more of us than we were of them.

I wasn't going to stay there and end up dead, so I bullied Trevor, Crispin, and Al to make a dash for thicker woods only a stone's throw down the hill. We ran like hell and Crispin took a bullet in the arm but he could still keep up with the rest of us, so we made it to where we all could sneak back to the main army, only a half-mile away. At first, I was worried that Arcularious wouldn't make it because of his chronic inactivity. I had forgotten that he'd been in the army for a year, and probably was in better shape, and had lost weight.

We were grateful for relief, but we worried for those who didn't run.

It turned out that this had been the place where Brant and Butler planned to ambush the main army, but the main army had proceeded another way, and it was too late for Brant to change his plans, so the Indian's ambush was wasted on us. The next day the remains of our men were found. All were shot dead and then mutilated in the usual Indian manner. Lieutenant Boyd and Sergeant Michael Parker were tortured more than usual, I'm told. The damage was horrible, and beyond the worst description; so bad, I can't write about it without having to puke. Hannyerry was brutally killed and hacked to pieces for being a traitor.

CHAPTER TWENTY-FIVE

THE DESTRUCTION OF Chenussio was anti-climax. The ambush of Boyd's detachment was worrisome enough, and we marveled that we got back to Sullivan's main army without serious injury. Crispin could flex his arm alright; the ball was easily extracted by Sullivan's doctor without much loss of blood, and he was happy that he could hand his accurate, up-to-date maps to General Sullivan.

Al Arcularious thought his year of army training had saved his life. His physical condition a year ago wouldn't have enabled him to run fast enough, he said. After seeing Boyd's remains and the gristly tortures he must have suffered, I preferred to stay with the main army. Looking for "adventure" had taken on an entirely new meaning, and I was content with cutting corn stalks and girdling apple trees, beginning the following day..

Chenussio was even larger than Kanadasaga and covered most of the flat valley of the Chenussio River. In the center of the complex was an enormous two-story Longhouse, largely made of cedar and painted red. Flanking that were a hundred and twenty-eight well constructed homes, with glass-like windows, and dirt floors, but no chimneys. The smoke of cooking and heating fires went out a hole in the roof, but left the elegant houses smoky-smelling and sooty.

The Chenussio valley was declared "one of the most beautiful areas of the country" by General Sullivan, and what I just described and the orchards and extensive cornfields justified his remarks. A white woman with an eight-month old baby were the only ones present when we explored the place. Both looked very malnourished and the baby looked so sick that it wasn't expected to live. They were from Nanticoke and had been captured last November when their town was raided. They were put in the care of Doctor Campfield.

Each house had been carefully searched for Indians in case they planned to lash out in close hand-to-hand fighting. All kinds of Indian artifacts had been left, including snow shoes, scalps and willow rings for mounting more expected scalps, heavy furniture, traps, skins, and furs. Some homes had been converted to food storehouses, with corn husks and husked corn piled to the eves. We found no braves hiding in the homes, but some of our guys snatched the furs and stuffed their backpacks.

Of course, all this and the fields were put to the torch, and the apple and peach trees were girdled. What we started at six in the morning, we near finished at two in the afternoon. It was ghastly, and despite the savagery that had been dealt Boyd and Parker, one couldn't help sympathize with the Indians, at least the women and children. Future generations of both Indians and whites would likely remember and perpetuate such horror on the frontier.

That morning was when two of our men discovered the remains of Boyd and Parker. The general was called over and he, too, had to restrain an urge to throw up. Many of the expedition saw the effects of this prolonged torture and wished they hadn't because the image would last in their memory. That's why I didn't want to see any of it. General Sullivan ordered that the remains be buried with full military honors, which was done next to a growth of wild plum trees bordering Little Beard Creek.

Afterwards, General Sullivan made another statement declaring that our mission had gone as far as practical and had been accomplished. We weren't going to Niagara but we'd soon be on our way to return to Tioga and Fort Sullivan. He thanked us for a good mission, gave a brief benediction for peace on the frontier, and everyone relaxed for the rest of the day, except the pickets and those whose duties still had to be performed.

The plan was to retrace our passage back the same way we came; we could then eat the vegetables from the remaining gardens and have no concern about making our way home. At Kanadasaga Sullivan appointed two large detachments; one under the command of Lieutenant Colonel Henry Dearborn to go up the west side of Cayuga Lake to make sure we'd destroyed all the Cayuga villages, and the other detachment was commanded by Lieutenant William Butler to do the same on the east side. Lieutenant Colonel William Smith was sent to take a detachment seven miles up the west side of Seneca Lake to finish the destruction of Kashong which was Seneca.

Colonel Peter Gansevoort, our former commander at Fort Stanwix, was sent along the major east-west trail through Iroquoia, to Fort Stanwix, and then to Teantontalago, the lower castle on the Mohawk, to arrest male Mohawks for imprisonment at Albany.

The main part of Sullivan's army was to return the way we came, up the east shore of Seneca Lake to Shequaga where we were to rendezvous with Dearborn and Butler at the site of former Kanawaholla where Captain Reed had been ordered to build a small fort, which of course he named Fort Reed.

Reed had brought fresh supplies from Tioga to his post, which he was supposed to do, and this and the other sorties were cause for celebration since Sullivan now declared that there was no longer a limit to the amount of meat and whiskey for the officers and men. With the army restored to its full complement, Sullivan sent two detachments up the Chemung River to destroy the Seneca village of Painted Post. The same abandonment there occurred as in all the other encounters, except for the Newtown ambush, and everyone was relieved that the dreadful job was finally done.

Good news had also arrived; Spain had finally joined the alliance with the United States and France and of more interest to us, army officers and men had been given a raise in pay. Now, all that was necessary was for the Congress to send it.

General Sullivan was so excited by the success of his expedition and the other good news that he decided to have a feu de joie, an arrangement wherein the soldiers lined up in a long line and he rode full tilt the length and back. As he did this, each soldier fired his musket sequentially in a lengthy fusillade.

The first feu were poorly done; it wouldn't do and he had them do it again and, this time, he cheered them.

The night's dinner was extraordinary. Aside from the pleasure of eating fresh food, a toast was raised to the success of the campaign. Successive toasts were made to Congress, then to Washington, and in a half hour or so, a total of thirteen toasts were made. The last was made by General Hand who, in his cups, was careful to pronounce each word just so. It went something like this: "to the enemies of this country, may they end up as packhorses." It got a huge laugh and everyone thought it was the most original toast of all. It referred to our poor packhorses that began to fail in large numbers due to little forage. We had to shoot many to rid them of their misery.

Before we left Fort Reed, Chief Blue Back of the Oneidas had a request to make of General Sullivan about the Cayugas. He asked that their villages be spared because, he said they hadn't participated in the frontier raids. He pleaded that if they were attacked as the Senecas had been that the Oneidas would be damaged because they would have to support the destitute Cayugas, many of whom were related by marriage and clans.

I heard that it was a moving and sincere-sounding request. But the general refused by saying that the Cayugas were as bad as the rest of the Iroquois and deserved no better treatment, and he could prove this. He was sorry for Hannyery being killed but his death had no bearing on the situation, he said, and that ended the plea. Blue Back had to go back to the Cayugas empty-handed.

Later, General Sullivan's contention was proved by fresh scalps that were found by Colonel Butler in Cayuga longhouses.

There was no practical reason for meeting up with Colonel Brodhead and going to Niagara. Rations were low and men and horses were exhausted beyond further effort. We were told later that Brodhead had left Fort Pitt with six hundred soldiers the same day we first reached Tioga and demolished ten Seneca and Mingo villages and their food stores, and returned with no casualties.

CHAPTER TWENTY-SIX

CRISPIN'S ARM WOUND healed better than his leg wound at Saratoga. He didn't have Annie or Jeanette to nurse him but he did have a bottle, and this was beginning to become worrisome. He had a sharp mind, was good at conversation, a good friend, and I hated to see him rely on alcohol so much. I hoped I could at least get him home to Annie where drink would be only a casual pleasure and not a recurring necessity.

He began to call me disloyal to my comrades because we ran to save our lives and the others, who were afraid to run, had a terrible fate. But Crispin had had erratic episodes before and got over them. And he was one who survived because of running the same time as I did.

We destroyed Fort Reed along with food we couldn't carry and made our way to Tioga in one day. From Fort Reed back to Tioga seemed much shorter than traveling in the dark the other way, and we were happy to be embraced by our fellows at Fort Sullivan with its tinge of civilization and ample and varied provisions. Using the bow to hunt was no longer prohibited because, as far as we could tell, no Indians were left or lurking to waylay lingerers. Archers were again sought after as friends, and as providers of venison.

As for the Indians, they had to go to Fort Niagara to keep from starving and for shelter. We had destroyed all their food and their means of hunting had been used up by warring against us. They had long since stopped hunting with bows and arrows in favor of muskets. In short they were in a bind—they had to accept the support of John Butler and British authority or starve. We believe that many did. As beautiful as their realm was, we soldiers were glad to leave it for a civilized regimen.

When we reached Fort Sullivan, we were greeted with cannonades, band music, and happy repetitious celebrations, and had the satisfaction of knowing that our war-weary feet could rest since we'd travel to Wyoming by boat, compliments of the Susquehanna. It was September 30th, a timely ending because of the fall season coming on quickly. Our expedition was considered a success and with no more than a total of forty casualties, some of which had nothing to do with combat, such as accidents, camp fever, and, in the last few days, a private of Butler's detachment who had an apparent heart attack.

General Sullivan wrote a report to send to Congress outlining the campaign. In addition to what I've written in this journal, he complained about the rough terrain, its narrow trails, mountains to surmount, defiles, and swamps, obsolete or otherwise bad maps, ignorant or faulty guides, having to widen the trails for the artillery, and the poor provisioning which delayed the campaign's start. We did have all those problems, but the way he complained, you'd think the campaign was a failure.

I think that the delay due to sloppy commissary work was providential despite its seemingly ruination of our efforts at the start because of several results that ensued: the delay meant that we wouldn't reach the Indian towns until their crops were about to ripen, so the destruction was thorough; it also meant that there wasn't enough time left in the season for them to replant, leaving them at the mercy of the British, who they were beginning to resent for inadequate protection; we shouldn't overlook the bounty of having fresh food from their gardens so that our rations didn't run out; and our artillery paid off, which at first, seemed to be too many and an overburden, especially over poor ground, but it panicked the ambushers at Newtown and almost made it possible to round up their leaders, and Newtown was the only full-fledged battle. And finally the rivers which simplified both Clinton's and Sullivan's arrival on the scene of operations. So what doomed in the beginning was a boon at the end. The total tag was estimated to be:

- Almost fifty towns destroyed
- Destruction of two hundred thousand bushels of corn and other grain

- Destruction of fifty thousand bushels of vegetables and fruit
- Ten thousand fruit trees burnt or girdled
- And many graves of their ancestors plundered

This last I thought was repugnant and not necessary

Sullivan's report included his suggestion to the Oneida sachems that they petition Congress for the right to hunt the now vacant lands of the Iroquois. He had to refuse them as he didn't think he had the necessary authority. He recommended that Congress approve the petition because of the Oneida's contribution to the success of the campaign.

Sullivan was with the troops when they reached Easton and went with the army on to Morristown for the winter. He then resigned his commission and ran for Congress.

CHAPTER TWENTY-SEVEN

AS YOU KNOW, Olivia, Annie Johnson, Natalie Latterlea, and Doctor Iverson's wife all made their home in the same place. Even though it was a little crowded, it was a nice location, close to stores, with a fine garden and a brook. It was also economical for them to share the rent. But Crispin and I were now garrisoned in Morristown and it was impossible to see them for any length of time, even during weekends.

We had to wait for the lease to run out or find someone to sublet who was satisfactory to our landlord and to Natalie Latterlea. Annie and Olivia were able to find a suitable replacement at Tredyffren and leased the Chatham place which pleased all of us, including the owner.

After General Henry Clinton abandoned the city, Philadelphia reverted to the hands of our government, and Washington appointed Benedict Arnold as administrator of the city. While it was an honorary position because Arnold's leg had been wounded a second time and he couldn't manage as a field officer, Arnold tried to exploit his position in various ways that bordered on villainy. This put him in trouble with the other local leaders who brought him to court. The case hasn't been settled as of this writing.

One would think that the continuous string of battles, intrigues, murders, and scandals would never cease but the newspapers needed fodder for their patrons and every incident was published.

The British under General Henry Clinton had shot away the monstrous iron chain which we had stretched across the Hudson at great expense. This action enabled him to attack Forts Montgomery and Clinton during the Burgoyne invasion. West Point, where the

Hudson makes a sharp turn among the Hudson Highlands, was finally considered a perfect place for a fort to prevent any more British ships from going upriver. Ships would lose headway as they made the necessary tack, thus making them easy targets for cannon on the bluffs there. Engineers were designing and constructing a stone fortification on the river's west side and had also considered building a small fort across the river on Constitution Island.

Polish Thaddeus Kosciuszko was the officer who had the credentials to oversee the job after his success for building the fortifications at Saratoga. Because of the British intention to rectify the Burgoyne fiasco, the fort was meant to guard against them and endure as one of the main bastions of the country; hence even greater expense was lavished.

Because of Arnold's unpopularity in Philadelphia, Washington appointed him commandant at West Point, a position for which Arnold had angled and Washington thought he was now best suited. To me, it seemed like a mild slap on the wrist for an active general like Arnold who had one of the best records for military achievement. But he was lame and seemed happy with semi-retirement. Besides, military action in the north had cooled down. The British were now trying to stir the Loyalists in the south.

Somehow, the Indians knew that the coming season would be severe. It was the coldest and snowiest winter that anyone could recall; so cold that cannon could be sledged across the Hudson from Staten Island to Manhattan, a feat that up to now was considered impossible. Of course Morristown suffered too, and cordwood sold at a premium. Currency had dropped even more in value and troops in Jersey were on the brink of mutiny. Despite our successes of the last few years, it was a difficult time.

In the spring, the Indians, after being maintained and supplied by the British at Niagara, began raiding again. This was as bad as before and they even broke into General Schuyler's mansion in Albany, caused some damage and ran off with one of the help. Cobleskill, Warrensbush, Schoharie, Fonda, Cherry Valley again, Johnstown and other Mohawk valley towns were attacked and burned.

Brant had taken over Oswego and made raids from there and the British made them from Wolf's Island in the St. Lawrence. Colonel John Brown, the verbal thorn in Benedict Arnold's side, was killed near Klock's Field in the fall of '80. As much as he could be severe, he was an able officer.

What shocked the nation was Benedict Arnold's attempt to sell West Point and the garrison to the British. By pure luck, three guards near Tarrytown detained a man who claimed to be John Anderson, but turned out to be John André, an aide de camp to General Clinton, who was the middle-man in Arnold's negotiations with Clinton. Also, General Washington was due to have breakfast with Arnold and view the construction at West Point on his return from Connecticut where he had been conferring with the French. Arnold tried to make a run for his British ship, curiously named the Vulture, but it had dropped downstream from its planned rendezvous with the traitor when it was shelled by American artillery. Even so, Arnold escaped.

Within the same day, Arnold's notorious plan was figured out by Washington and the authorities. Arnold had escaped, but John André was held and convicted as a spy. He was well liked and even our officers were charmed by him. He was one of the designers of the Mischianza to honor the retiring Howe, but despite André's request to be shot, he was hanged. The whole mess took only two weeks from intercepting André to hanging him.

Several attempts were made to capture Arnold but he seemed to be watched over by a guardian angel, and later made devastating raids on Virginia and Connecticut. If he had died at Saratoga, he would have been a hero, but he made a fool's choice and was doomed to die a traitor to his native country.

I had been musing about the last year and a half when, one day, Chief Honeoye and Crispin came back from Headquarters.

Crispin was ecstatic. "We have good news. They're only going to use militia against the Indians this time. We can relax. We may have to restrain some mutineers, though. We'll see."

My response seemed to surprise him. "I was just thinking about the Indians. All the work we went to subdue them, and here they're getting back at us. For what we call savages, that's a tribute to their organization and resolve to endure. A commander couldn't ask for anything more than that."

Crispin bristled. "You're sticking up for those bastards that tortured Boyd and Parker? What kind of a guy are you?"

199

I didn't answer him right away. I thought Crispin had more broadminded compassion than to make such a statement and to call me out as a molly-coddle. After all, I'd been his friend since boyhood and we'd had many conversations on different races and nationalities. He was usually on the side of brotherhood and goodwill rather than treating those with whom he disagreed as ignorant boobs, or savages. He had a short fuse and called me out for taking a position which he himself had once adopted.

The chief joined in the conversation with his usual level-headed observations.

"You're judging the whole Iroquois nation as monsters, Crispin. Remember, the people we came in contact with were their army, not their cooks, pharmacists, or diplomats. Do you think our military personnel are better behaved than the rest of us? Look at those white troops who scalped those they called savages, even skinned them to make a pair of boots, guys from New Jersey who ought to know better. Many are drunk most of the time. They may be good at fighting, but as hosts or diplomats of goodwill, they fail miserably."

"We weren't on a tour of diplomacy!"

"No, but we probably should have been. I was educated and grown up by, and to be, an Indian by the Onondagas. My adopted father was one of the kindest of men, but he would have smashed your head with a tomahawk if he thought you would attack his family or cheat them out of their garden patch.

"Now, the stories of our overreaching inhumanity will be discussed around their campfires for generations, and those future sons will insist on avenging what we did the few months we were let loose to destroy the Confederacy. I'm ashamed of my part in it."

Honeoye said in a few words what we should have known before we started the campaign.

However surprised he might have been, Crispin was not really listening, and insisted that we had to kill and destroy all they had to put down raids on the frontier.

I sided with the chief. "Crispin, imagine if you were an Indian, remember you had nothing to do or say whether you would be white or not. But imagine you are in a vast country where you are master, or at least the reigning contender of your domain and someone comes with an army from overseas with modern weapons and overwhelming numbers to use the weapons if they don't get what they want. What would you do if one of them takes your wigwam and food garden, or wants Annie as his girlfriend?" I hoped I'd built a story in which he could picture himself.

"I'd kill the bastard!"

"Why? He had just as much right to the land and your girl as you. Why not share them with him?"

"You must think I'm nuts! I bought the place fair and square. And Annie wants to be with me and no one else!"

"And you would kill to preserve this serenity?"

"Of course I would."

"Then, there's your answer."

"To what?"

"To why you, as an Indian, would act like a savage."

"Yeah, but this would be different! I'm not an Indian."

"You make my point, I hope you think about it, and realize that little is accomplished by violence in the long run. Peace is always better and cheaper no matter how you slice it."

The chief looked at me and winked. In time we would bring Crispin around to our way of thinking. But the chief wanted to convince Crispin of this maxim now.

"Some of my childhood friends are Onondagas, and I still see them and like them. One of them, Blacksnake, builds canoes for the tribe, but he isn't a ferocious warrior. Sometimes he doesn't even go with the war parties. He's generally peaceful and a good family man, he's revered in his village. You could equate him with a cabinet maker, or such, in any white community. Does that mean we should kill him and his family?"

Crispin recognized the situation but hesitated before he answered. "If we have to, to make his fellow villagers stop attacking us, the answer is "yes." He's like a rattlesnake: even if he doesn't bite, his friends do and so we kill him and his friends wherever we find them. Even Indians know that."

"What I'm trying to say is that, like any place, some people are cruel but most aren't. We can weed out and punish the villains and favor the others who have much to add to the benefit of all of us. This is just common sense, Crispin. We don't have to go to war and kill a whole society."

Crispin just pouted as he usually did when he was confused, angry, or wrong.

Since we were talking about villains, I wondered how the experiment with Wencesles Mochter was working. Was he still trying to filch funds where ever he could, or had he become an honest citizen and an agent for our country? I'll have to ask Annie if she's heard anything about him. The prospect of going back to Simsbury Mines must give him nightmares. Maybe, he's even gone back to England. That would be an easy out for him, unless he's wanted by the law there, as well. It could be.

Some other news happened to come to my attention. Chief Logan was killed in 1779 in a drunken brawl in a backwoods tavern. You might say "so what?," but he was the son of a French prisoner of the Indians who was adopted by the Oneidas and worked his way to become an important diplomat for the Iroquois. As such, his father was on the same level as Conrad Weiser, Pennsylvania's diplomat to the Indians. His father named him Logan because he admired William Penn's secretary and successor, Governor James Logan.

It's appropriate to remember Logan because he was a Mingo chief in the upper Ohio Valley who was known on the frontier for helping whites if they needed it. This friendship terminated when some Indian-hating renegades butchered his entire family. He thought it was Michael Cressap, a frontiersman, but it was some others whom other Indians gave a frightful death.

Anyway, Logan went on a vengeance spree and allegedly killed thirteen people before he was killed himself. Some people thought the killings were evidence of an Indian uprising and that it triggered Dunmore's War. Logan was an example of what we had been discussing with Crispin.

I told Crispin about him, but it will take a lot of similar stories and persuasion to change his mind.

The war with the Indians continued not just in New York, but in the Ohio country as well. Beside the Iroquois, other tribes such as the Shawnee, Delaware, Sauk and Fox, Chippewa, and Miami fought white immigrants invading their hunting grounds, or what we now call the Northwest Territory.

One of the Iroquois final forays in the Mohawk Valley was Tory Rangers, regulars, and Indians headed by a Major Ross of the British army, who started from Wolf Island in the St Lawrence. They swooped south and attacked Johnstown which attracted Marinus Willett who was now a full Colonel and head of the local militia.

They surged back and forth with musket volleys, but it was late October and winter was almost upon them.

This made the British column decide they'd had enough and started for home by going up West Canada Creek when Willett's force caught up with them. They had a skirmish and an Oneida warrior shot and killed Walter Butler, Colonel Butler's son, and the scourge of the Cherry Valley massacre. I thought that that ended the warfare on the frontier. But I was wrong.

An attack on Fort Oswego was attempted by our side under Willett. They skated up the Oswego River until the ice became dangerous, then they left the river and relied on an Oneida scout to get them there in time for a surprise attack at dawn, but he managed to get them lost in a snowstorm. This caused such a delay that their "surprise" attack was no longer valid so they aborted the mission.

Brant made one more attempt to raid, where we don't know, from Oswego. A runner from the fort caught up with them bearing news that a tentative treaty of peace had been signed which made him turn back to the fort.

This time, I was sure the raids were over. And this time I was right. Both Britain and the United States were tired of war and military operations lagged. Our delegation had been negotiating with France and Britain about peace and finally narrowed the points of major concern for all parties.

The treaty had been negotiated with the British largely by Benjamin Franklin, John Adams, and John Jay in Paris, and it enlarged the country all the way to the Mississippi River, by reason of the military success of George Rogers Clarke in the Ohio country.

But the British did not act as advocates for the Iroquois. They were entirely left out of the proceedings or the content of the treaty—left "hanging in the wind" is the colloquial phrase. The 1784 Treaty at Fort Stanwix was between the Federal government and New York and Pennsylvania, and finally the Indians. It carved up the land unoccupied and governed by the whites and left the Iroquois little of their former territory.

They had chosen the side they thought would win and they lost big. Red Jacket, a sachem and lively orator of the Senecas and Chief Big Tree, both thought the Indians should stay neutral because of the American's increasing numbers, but Brant and other chiefs defied this position because they knew their warriors could outfight the

"Bostonians." That was true in "hit and run" skirmishes: real war required perseverance and was different.

At the Fort Stanwix Treaty of 1768, the Iroquois had sold the British government a large tract of land south of the Ohio, called Kaintuck, for ten thousand pounds to deter western migration to the south of their realm, and this turned out to be an unsuccessful decision as well.

As a Confederacy, the Iroquois were doomed. They had devised a system of governance some say was a model for ours but their diplomacy was flawed, and history was unfavorable to them. Leaders in Europe were reigning badly and forcing their citizens to be malcontents so that they left the country and came here, forcing the westward migrations. The Indians' downfall may have been such a problem as drinking whiskey which the Indians craved although they lost all reason because of it.

What glory we could attain if our people abstained from the stuff.

As military action had decreased in the north, the British concentrated their forces in the south. General Clinton stayed in New York but the ministry under Lord Germain expected him to command Cornwallis and his forces six or seven hundred miles away. They were still arrogant enough to think that large numbers of Loyalists were anxious to rise and wrack their anger on rebel authorities. Some did, but, as usual, the British were over-optimistic. Washington sent his next best tactician, General Nathanael Greene, to deal with the mischief. That was after General Lincoln, the general we worked under at Ticonderoga, lost the second battle of Charleston.

General Clinton failed at the first attempt on Charleston in 1776, but he was determined to include the city as part of the British theater of operations to gain favor with the Loyalists in the South. It was a siege, plagued with storms and administrative problems, so that it took the better part of February and all of March, April, and half of May to subdue the poorly defended fortifications. Loss of Charleston was a foregone conclusion since Clinton had a substantial part of the British army in America there at the siege.

Reporting the day-to-day events kept the papers busy. Chief Honeoye couldn't understand how they could possibly hold out since the British had over seventeen thousand regulars and Hessians compared to a little more than two thousand rebels, and only a third of them were estimated to have been local or from South Carolina.

There were many military conflicts in the South; one of the first was the battle of Kings Mountain where Colonel Patrick Ferguson, the inventor of the breech-loading rifle, commanded some Tories against the "Over Mountain" men, who had a reputation of mean and ferocious fighting. Ferguson was on the crest of a hill and our patriots surrounded him, fought their way up the incline, and prevailed. The action killed Ferguson and captured many Tories, many of whom were slaughtered after they became prisoners. Between shameless events like this and Colonel Banastre Tarleton's cruelties, it was a hate war as well as one for territory.

A humiliation occurred when General Horatio Gates, who prevailed at Saratoga, was confronted by the British at Camden and ran a hundred miles to escape ignominious defeat. Of course this resulted in the general losing his hero prestige.

A more gratifying event occurred when Colonel Dan Morgan, expecting to be assaulted by Tarleton and his dragoons, interspersed militia with veterans in a defensive line to be able to withstand the rush of cavalry. The men were spaced behind low natural berms and ordered to fire only three shots, but at specific times. This confused Tarleton's men who were expecting the usual rout of American militia, in which the dragoons often killed many. "Tarleton's quarter" meant death even for those who surrendered.

As a result, Tarleton's unit was decimated and morale for the patriots increased and few Tories joined with General Cornwallis. This was the battle of the Cowpens, easy to confuse with the battle of Camden until one is aware of the different results.

General Greene showed his competence against Cornwallis by chasing him, or being chased like a fox, all over the Carolinas until Cornwallis retreated to a small undefended supply depot on the edge of Chesapeake Bay called Yorktown. At that moment, George Washington was conferring in Connecticut with French General Rochambeau on cooperating in an attack on New York City where the British had been supreme for five years.

When on August fourteenth, he heard that the French fleet was to be near at hand, Washington scrapped New York plans and mustered his troops to make a long march to Yorktown, where Cornwallis could be trapped between Admiral De Grass, his twenty-nine warships, three thousand French troops, and our own forces blocking the peninsular path of escape.

French Admiral De Barras was off New Foundland and might, by special fast cutter, be persuaded to come south to block British ships from New York from interfering. He was persuaded, and he did.

To make General Clinton, still concerned that Americans were going to attack New York, Washington ordered local bakers to fire ovens and start making bread as if the city was about to be besieged. This and other deceptions were for the benefit of spies (Washington was a master at seeding misinformation) but the commander in chief was already on the road to Yorktown and passing through Philadelphia. At the same time, the French fleet was instructed to block the entrance to the Chesapeake so that Cornwallis could neither flee or be reinforced.

General Heath at Peekskill was to remain in place to make Clinton think that nothing was amiss and that he was safe. This was the late summer of 1781 when no one thought the war was going to end soon.

My friends and I thought we were certain to be included in this grand scheme to capture even a second army of the vaunted British Empire, but we were kept at Morristown for what purpose, we weren't certain. Washington's immediate army camped overnight on August twenty-eighth near Chatham and Springfield, but our regiment wasn't included in the resolute corps or given orders to march.

I'd like to think our mission was to box in Clinton so he couldn't send additional troops to Cornwallis but Clinton made no such efforts until it was too late, just like he did with Burgoyne four years ago. British ineptitude was our main strength.

Crispin and Trevor thought we were acting as a rear unit to guard against another attack at Springfield to broach Hobart's Gap as General Knyphausen did in June of last year. Then, the German general was glory hunting in the absence of General Clinton, who was still at Charleston where he defeated the small rebel garrison.

Knyphausen thought the gap was defended by only militia and would be an easy prize. We surprised both him and General Greene with whom together we sent the Hessians running back to Staten Island. Within a few weeks, Knyphausen tried again and burned the town of Springfield but failed just as badly—the locals fought them off and saved Morristown. By then, General Clinton had come back from Charleston and recalled the Hessian General. But all of that was more than a year ago.

Every big name in our army was at Yorktown: Colonel Alexander Hamilton, General Nathanael Greene, Washington's cousin, Col. William Washington, General Lincoln, Lafayette, General "Mad Anthony" Wayne, General James Clinton, of Indian expedition fame, Goose van Schaik, who raided the Onondagas, Colonel Elias Dayton who rebuilt Fort Dayton, General Henry Knox and his artillery, James Gilliland from Willsboro, New York, who led fifty sappers and miners, and Stephen Moylan, the head of dragoons from Pennsylvania. There were others and most were famous but I didn't know, or know of them.

I almost forgot to mention Henry Dearborn, Timothy Pickering, and Edward Hand, all of whom had been high-level officers on the Sullivan expedition and now made up part of Washington's staff.

General Cornwallis commanded famous veteran officers and men, too:

General Charles O'Hara, Lt. Col. Banastre Tarleton, Lt. Col. James Simcoe, Lt. Col. John Hamilton, a Maj. O'Reilly, General William Phillips, and, I'm told, British General Benedict Arnold. Their commands were made up of crack veteran units such as the Black Watch, the Coldstream Guards, and the Queens Rangers.

The French contingent amounted to almost nine thousand men, including sailors and marines on shipboard; we couldn't have won without them.

Tracing Washington's progress south was made easy by the Pennsylvania Gazette. The day after camping at Chatham, the light infantry moved southeast, as if to envelop New York from Sandy Hook, (to deceive Clinton) but then they quickly shifted their path to Philadelphia where they marched down Broad Street under Washington and Rochambeau on September second. Four days later, they were at Head of Elk at the head of Chesapeake Bay.

On the way they insisted that Congress distribute their monthly pay, and in cash. Congress said they were so cash-poor that they had to consult Robert Morris again and he had to borrow from Rochambeau's war chest to make the payment. The French followed them a few days later through Philadelphia, and dazzled the onlookers with their fine uniforms, band music, and precise marching order.

Washington even stopped for three days at Mount Vernon, where he hadn't been for six years, but he arrived near Yorktown on September 14th. He had to be sure the French fleets arrived in time to close the net.

The engagement with the British started the day Washington arrived at Williamsburg, September twenty-seventh.

CHAPTER TWENTY-EIGHT

FROM OUR PLACE in Morristown, we read of the arrival and coordination of the two French fleets of Admirals De Grass and De Barras; all our infantry, artillerymen and heavy equipment, including units from the south, meeting at Yorktown, was a stroke of luck. But Chief Honeoye said it was a masterful bit of timing, with only a particle of luck that the French at sea could reach their destinations without storms or British interference. There was a severe naval clash off the Cape but the British bowed out after their ships were badly damaged and returned to New York for repairs.

The few remaining troops at Morristown were intrigued with the movement of troops of all the parties. To avoid confusion, Crispin took over part of the mess hall to draw on a slate a simple enlarged map of the area from an atlas, and positioned them according to the most recent newspaper reports. He mounted the map on an easel and people came into the mess hall from time to time, to check on the progress of this battle which could decide defeat or continuation of the war. We four were almost always there and others gravitated in and remained for hours.

More residents started to buy the New York papers to follow the continuing movements and actions, especially of our troops who had started digging what's known as a parallel to safely get closer to the enemy's positions.

Our French comrades approached the riverside fortifications from the northwest, forcing British pickets back towards the York River, and ours were digging in south east of Cornwallis's headquarters, which was three hundred yards from the waterfront. It wasn't a fort but of course the British used the sturdiest homes of residents to give them cover, and they built gun emplacements in ten redoubts, the most important of which were named redoubts nine and ten.

The British knew that their position denied them access to food and other supplies so they planned to scour the countryside across the river for forage. They sent two of their divisions across the York to Gloucester Point under the command of Tarleton and Lieutenant Thomas Dundas, and this fortification was opposed by General George Weedon's Virginia militia and Lauzun's Legion. On October first, General de Choisy took overall command at the point, just in time to push back a breakout a few days later.

All of this preparation for attack and defense took about a week. At this point, the French and we were about two miles from the center of the small town where their headquarters were.

The French moved forward little by little by digging entrenchments towards the British works and twelve hundred men of our forces were digging the two-thousand yard first parallel in our sector from the southeast. Most of this work was initially done at night to be out of sight of British marksmen, and enemy artillery fire was minimal. The sandy soil was easy to shovel and the nighttime cool air was appreciated so that dawn revealed that four redoubts with batteries were completed. In the meantime, twelve hundred other workers searched the woods nearby for material to make fascines, gabions, and other military structures for defense.

It took several days for this to be known to reporters so the papers Crispin was referring to were behind almost as much as a week. Most people didn't know the difference so no one complained or was affected. On their October ninth (the sixteenth by our calendar), the artillery batteries were ready to begin cannonading and formalities were such that Washington gave General St. Simon the honor of the French firing their guns first. Other batteries of the French and ours came into play so that by the next morning, the British batteries were bombarded so badly that they were firing off only six rounds an hour. Their headquarters were also in ruins and we heard that Cornwallis had to abandon it. He was cooped in with no place to go.

After several hours of watching Crispin explain and redraw the map, as well as having several cups of coffee, I had to relieve myself. However, there were men standing in several lines to the outhouses and I couldn't wait, so I went the short distance home. Afterwards, I decided to eat lunch since I was in my own house.

A soldier I'd known briefly at Monmouth, came to the house with a Ferguson rifle that he'd bought from another who found it at the Brandywine, and now he wanted to sell it.

Trevor had told me that these rifles were made and tested at Woolwich by British gun makers and that they only made a hundred of them. He didn't know why the high command didn't put them in service, because they had features that would have given their infantry the advantage over our flint-locks: they were accurate rifles in the hands of marksmen at three hundred yards and could be depended on firing even in wet weather; they were lighter by five pounds, and most important, they were loaded at the breech, not the muzzle; a man could load it even when lying on the ground.

The gun was in good condition and had the initials of P.F. carved in the stock—maybe it had been issued to Colonel Patrick Ferguson, the inventor—What a find!

I asked the fellow what he wanted for it. He said three pounds. I had that much hidden in a recess in my workbench, but I hesitated, mainly to see what he would say, just in case. When he dropped the price to two and a half pounds, I said, "sold," shook hands on the deal, poured him a mug of coffee, and quickly got the money from the workbench.

Thank goodness I had hard money: he may have refused currency. But the transaction was completed and I was the happy owner of one of only a hundred rifles known to be made.

The problem was where to put it. I didn't want to put it in plain sight, like over the fireplace—it was too valuable and I didn't like to have guns in the house. I finally took it outside to my tool shed to stash it with shovels and rakes. I thought that it would be safe enough there, for now, and I'd think of a better place tonight before I went to bed. Later, I covered the gun with a gunny sack and carried it out as if it was a pickaxe, and placed it under the roof beams of the shed on top of some old boards, out of site.

The whole business of buying the piece and hiding it took no longer that ten minutes but I wanted to finish my coffee and get back to Crispin's running dissertation, for he now managed his talk like an expert on Washington and the beginnings of the battle of Yorktown. I'll give him this, though: he explained what was going on in simple language and didn't try to impress people with words like enfilade, envelope, first parallel, and so on. As I listened to him, I fell asleep, and didn't wake up until Olivia and Annie came to get us.

The next day, we went back to the mess hall to resume passing on the second-hand, day-by-day news, and found that Cornwallis had already sent a flag of truce and a drummer to announce it. The cannonading had to stop so our people could hear the drummer, the paper said. Actually, the flag was not to talk of surrender, but to enable an older citizen of the town, Thomas Nelson, to cross into our lines; he was sixty-five and the uncle of the then governor, and merited this compliment. He is the one who told the paper that Cornwallis's headquarters had been demolished, as was his own home. It was expected as both places were in the better part of the town.

He also passed the word that news had arrived by boat that reinforcements were due Cornwallis within the week.

Crispin allowed as how he wished it was Clinton who was the rescuer. This was sarcastic reference to Clinton's tardy support for Burgoyne. But I doubted that many in Crispin's audience understood the real gist of his comment.

The British ship Charon, with forty-four guns, and three or four other ships were fired on by St. Simon's hot shot. They burst into flames and burned to the waterline before they sank in the channel. All of the enemy's redoubts were now firing, and before we could advance farther, we had to reduce or overcome their number nine and ten redoubt batteries.

Crispin noted that, by this time, we had five redoubts set with batteries which were cannonading in rapid order so that work could start on a second parallel five-hundred yards closer to the enemy's works. This was at dusk on October eleventh. One of our main objectives then was to concentrate on an attack on their number nine and ten redoubts, which were on the far right and near the end of the second parallel. To do this, a sloping shelf had to be dug so that our attack parties could quickly leave the cover of the parallel and minimize their exposure to enemy fire. Remember this was to be purely a bayonet operation—muskets were carried only to be able to use the fixed bayonets so that our action wouldn't be heard by their headquarters. Of course, the bayonet was a terrifying weapon as many of our men could testify.

People outside the mess hall must have gotten the word that our side was gearing for an important action because more came into the hall which caused Crispin to be flustered, but he prevailed. A silence came over the crowd as they listened to him read the paper that told the story, presumably from the battlefield.

Possibly the whole report was written by a reporter in the Raleigh Tavern in Williamsburg over several mugs of rum.

With the exit from the parallel finished, the leaders of the two assault parties had to be selected. Washington had Lafayette choose one of his men as a courtesy to honor the French, but Alexander Hamilton insisted that he should be a leader because he had seniority over the French candidate. So Hamilton was the commander for the enemy redoubt number ten, the one closer to the river. He had four hundred troops, and half of them were French.

The other assault party was all Frenchmen and led by a high French officer, a Colonel Deux-Ponts. Artilley had purposely been trained on nine and ten to soften them up before moving out, but it was later used in an attack on the enemy's Gloucester works across the York River as a diversion for the redoubt sortie.

The plan was for a signal gun to fire six times in a row at six-thirty in the evening as an alert. By prearrangement the sorties began exactly a half-hour later, and very quietly. The French legions had gone only about a hundred and twenty yards when some sharp-eyed redcoat cried out that they were on the move, and the British artillery belched fire causing severe losses and horrible wounds.

Crispin read this well and put emphasis on the words, "redcoats, losses," and "wounds."

At the time I wondered if he was hoping for a professional job as a reader. But he was more likely wishing that he was there on the battlefield sketching the battle as it happened.

After this, the French sortie came to a ditch, shortly followed by a palisade which delayed them even more. They had to have their axmen clear gaps in the wall so the survivors could get through and continue. From that point, it was a clear field to run at the defenders with their bayonets thrust forward in a dare-devil final climax. The few survivors at the British batteries threw down their arms and surrendered. That was the all-French assault on number nine, Crispin said, and his audience applauded. The British then feared that they were in a position to be enfiladed.

The assault on number ten by Alexander Hamilton's troops took place simultaneously and was very similar to the French except they didn't have axmen cut away the palisade: they just climbed it and suffered less delay and wounds as a result.

Both of the most dangerous redoubts were in our hands now, and Cornwallis blasted them with artillery. But it was still nighttime and our forces dug a ditch through the sandy soil to connect the captured redoubts to our system of parallels. Cornwallis was now in an impossible position and we expected a flag of truce to appear any time. But that didn't happen. Not yet.

Crispin's audience was on the edge of their seats.

After zeroing in on the batteries we'd just captured, the British sent a select group of about three-hundred and fifty men to overrun the place and spike the cannon which they were afraid were in a position that we could enfilade their troops. This was in the early morning of October 16th. Two of the batteries were in the process of being finished but the workmen were sleeping and some of them were French (This was on the border of the French and our sector) which surprised the attacking party.

The Count de Noailles (Lafayette's wife's relation) had been snoozing but was roused and realized that they were being infiltrated. His troops then challenged the invaders, captured five and killed or wounded seven. A few guns had been spiked with bayonets but were easily reamed out and brought back into action.

That night, General Cornwallis made an attempt to cross over to Gloucester Point with a detachment or two to fight his way out of his predicament and to open farmland and forage with the help of the relatively untouched units there, but a severe storm came up as they were half way across in the few boats they could collect. They had no choice but to return.

The next day was the fourth anniversary of Burgoyne's surrender at Saratoga, an unpleasant reminder of what might be in store now, and everyone was grim. (This is what the paper said and it was probably true, or should have been). As if to have his final say at this grand encounter, Cornwallis ordered every gun to fire a cannonade that expert veterans said was so loud, that a hundred pieces must have been firing at the same time.

In mid-morning when the bombardment had ceased, a drummer appeared beating the drum to signify that a parley was desired by

Cornwallis, and a British officer appeared to represent him. One of ours ran out, saluted and tied the customary handkerchief around the man's head to temporarily blind him, and led him to our lines.

The British requested a time to meet and discuss terms of surrender and asked for a twenty-four hour truce to work out a proposal. Washington insisted that they have this completed in only two hours, and at four-thirty that afternoon, it was done. Cornwallis' representative was Major Alexander Ross and Washington's were John Laurens and Noailles.

They met at the Moore House the following morning to work out the precise terms of surrender. The first of these were that "The same honors will be granted to the surrendering army as were granted to the garrison at Charles Town" a painful reminder to use at beginning bargaining, and they heatedly wrangled away the rest of the morning. By the end of the day they hadn't accomplished much and Washington had to enumerate his ideas in draft form, get his representatives to agree, and make a copy to submit the final form to be signed by Cornwallis. This was accomplished with the signatures of both Cornwallis and their Captain Thomas Simmons. Washington, Rochambeau, and Barras of the French Navy signed for the allies.

General Lord Cornwallis didn't appear, possibly due to humiliation, but his second in command was appointed to represent him at the surrender formalities and the deed was done. They were quite similar to those performed at Saratoga, and just as embarrassing, making it a more glorious victory.

This meant that the troops, the war chest, including artillery, materials and supplies under the command of Cornwallis, were out of the war, but the war was not over. Provisions regarding the officers paroles, keeping side arms, retention of the colors, of course the incarceration of the men and where, and such details were part of the deal, and the countries could still fight and be aggressive in other ways. But peace was just over the horizon though all the contenders and their people were tired of the drain of the war, which had dragged on since Lexington and Concord.

Crispin was not done at the easel until the last day of October. He was more knowledgeable about the war he'd been in for more than five years. Like everyone, he wanted to get out and get back to his painting and his Annie. I wasn't sure what I was going to do so far as earning a living was concerned. But Olivia and I would work it out. When I get all of my back pay, we'd be rich!

Towards the end, Crispin was getting so good at reporting the doings that his artistic vision came into play and he orally portrayed the surrender ceremony as if he'd personally been present. According to Crispin, every officer, in their best regimentals, was arrayed in line according to rank, and swords and horses, with fine accoutrements, radiated the importance of the occasion.

Not wishing to give up this opportunity to make money, Crispin wrote out the words he used as well as he could remember, drew important scenes of the redoubt sorties and the Gloucester Point episode, as well as the surrender, and had the volume printed. I don't know how well he did financially, but he dressed like macaroni during the rest of the war.

CHAPTER TWENTY-NINE

ONE OF THE first things I did after Yorktown was talk to Squire Lamsden about resigning my commission and getting out of the service. He offered me a chair and had his adjutant serve us coffee before he replied after some chit-chat about the weather and the war.

"From what I can tell from reading the papers and listening to veterans of the southern war, the British are tired of fighting us. It's costing them too much, and that's what the fighting was all about in the first place. With the French involved, the war has moved to the Caribbean and the Continent, and we can relax.

"I don't think your taking a long leave would harm the cause or bring blame to either of us. So keep your commission, but keep in touch. And good luck!" On my way out, I thanked God that Lamsden was my superior rather than someone like Cheyne.

The next thing I did was to write both the Brown Belt and Transmission Company and the Hibernia Ironworks plant on how my stock was doing and what the balance in my dividend account was. I had no other reason to go to Philadelphia so I stayed home and waited for an answer by the post.

When he found out that I was on leave, Crispin approached Lamsden and got the same answer as I did, so he and Annie, and I and Olivia, shared the house in Morristown. Our first dinner with all four of us enabled us to converse about what we would do for the foreseeable future and Wencesles Mochter and his whereabouts came up first.

We looked to Annie to tell us: "The last I heard, he was making a decent living selling house and property insurance. It's his own company and he has only one other to help him and share the profits. Of course, he's happy that he no longer has to worry about being in the mines at Simsbury—our carrot and stick policy is working."

I added to Mochter's trail. "The last time I saw him was at Saratoga: he and Captain Cheyne were scheming to rob the British war chest, and then, after that failed, digging up soldiers for whatever watches and rings they were buried with. Is his partner Cheyne?"

"I think it may be—it's some officer that he's known for some time and done business with before."

"Where does he do this? Around here?"

"He has an office in Newark, but he knocks on doors and comes out this far. I don't know that I'd buy any insurance from him, though. Who knows if his policies pay off if you have a loss?"

There was silence for about five seconds, as everyone chewed on his dinner and the prospect of Mochter meddling now that the war seemed to be over. So he hasn't gone back to England and we're likely to have him show up one of these days. God! Maybe Cheyne'll come here, too. I couldn't stand the son of a bitch.

Then Olivia asked if we needed property insurance which I thought was a peculiar question since we had very little property and we rented this place. We could hardly stay here if it weren't for Crispin and Annie to share the rent. But, instead of showing my impatience (for having little to show for more than five years). I kept my mouth shut and changed the subject. But I sure as hell wouldn't buy insurance from Mochter.

With all this time on my hands I wanted to get an anvil and tools to get back to smithing. Working with my hands was pleasing and I might even make some money by making special springs to mount on coaches and wagons to give sensitive rears more comfortable rides.

Henry Pierson was likely to know where I could get some tools. I ought to go see if he's back from the wars and still being helped by his sons and also, if he started making springs like mine. He kind of fancied them, but I hope he doesn't compete with me. I'm starting off fresh, with no patrons or even anyone knowing I'm in the blacksmith business. I should learn to call it a profession.

As I rode up to Pierson's old hut, I noticed no sounds of hammers banging metal—what if he got killed? Not Hank, he was a veteran of the French War, a survivor. Just then, I heard him yell,

"Elkanah, bring your tongs!" I had to smile when I shook hands with my old comrade.

He smiled back, but put me off because he had a red hot horseshoe ready to be hammered into its final form. His son held it with the tongs, he rasped it a few licks and quenched it before he could greet me back. But he offered me his left hand instead of his right because the right was missing! I tried to avoid gawking at what wasn't there.

"This taught me a whole new way of blacksmithing, Jamie. Are you out of the army now? Tell me where you've been since we saw each other." Hank wanted to avoid either of us being awkward or embarrassed.

I was still staring at his missing hand as I brought him up-to-date on my duty at Fort Stanwix, Saratoga, and Monmouth. Of course, I mentioned missing the excitement of Yorktown and then my prolonged leave at Morristown.

Hank volunteered, "don't worry about my hand. I got it, or lost it, at Paoli. Like most, you probably want to know how it happened. Am I right?"

I confessed that I was curious, but wouldn't press if it offended him.

Without further ado, he began. "I was with one of Mad Anthony's regiments at Paoli Tavern where several of us had had a drink after harassing Howe's troops who were thwarting Washington. That was our mission just before Philadelphia was taken. It was the end of September and nights were cooling off, with dew covering everything.

"The next day, we were to annoy Howe's baggage train on the north side of the Schuykill. But someone, probably a Tory, blew our cover. Word leaked out about this and where our encampment was. God knows we were vulnerable. In the middle of the night, their Major General Grey attacked us as we were sleeping with a small fire going. Our pickets fired shots to warn us of the attack but it was too late. They were on us and used nothing but bayonets, so it was quiet and bloody.

"Some kid corporal with the Black Watch was about to stick me with his piece and I grabbed it, thinking it was better to hurt my hand than my gut. It damned near cut my fingers off, but what lost the hand was infection and the threat of gangrene. I guess the surgeon saved my life by amputating it.

"Wayne managed to save our cannon and send the redcoats packing but we lost about a hundred and fifty overall. It could have been a hundred fifty-one if it weren't for the doctor."

I thought of what it must have been like if I were in a similar situation, and was more able to sympathize because of this. But Hank said he didn't want sympathy—"just recognition that he had done his part in fighting the redcoats."

I asked him where I might buy an anvil to get back into business. He thought I must be intuitive, since his older son no longer wanted to be a blacksmith; he sold me the anvil he was going to give him.

Several months later, Hank told me that several homes nearby had been robbed of their sterling silver service. Olivia and I liked the people in Morristown, and it had a good reputation for few crimes. One result was that our sheriff blamed himself for not patrolling as much as he should. He then inspected every angle and aspect of the robberies, including questioning the neighbors, and found a factor common to the homes victimized.

The area residents had been solicited for home and property insurance, a new business enterprise in, not just Morristown, but along the seaboard. The salesman carried plaques which, when mounted on the street side of the house, showed the fire company that the house was insured and a fire should be put out rather than ignored. He also carried stock certificates that the company was astute enough to provide in the event that the salesman could convince them to be shareowners, if not policyholders. The sheriff suspected that part of the sales program was for the salesmen to rob nearby resident's homes who didn't subscribe to their blandishments. Needless to say, patrons were safe and so was the premium money.

The salesman in this case sounded very much to me that he was none other than Wencesles Mochter. With the war in abeyance, he had chosen this "reputable" way to make a living.

I don't know whether he had a list of resident's names to be introduced to, or just made cold calls, but I expected me, or my house were on the roster or I would have the "pleasure" of his call before long. He preferred to be allowed in the house so he could size up the contents to determine if the place should be robbed.

One day, when I was rearranging and throwing away junk in the tool shed, he came into the back yard and began his pitch. He didn't recognize me because I had been wearing a beard for several years, ever since Saratoga, for that matter. I had to tend to it only once a week instead of daily. But Mochter was unmistakable with his skin-tight bald head, van Dyke beard, and his ever-present ivory-headed, blackthorn cane. And the non-sensible manner he had in trying to gain a point of argument. Yes, instead of making the insurance service attractive, he launched into an argument about it at the very beginning of his sales talk. It almost seemed like we would come to blows.

He showed me the plaque first, as if it was an attractive feature that any proud owner would desire. When I showed no interest, he went into a frenzy about the perils of fires, the number dying in the extremity of pain because of the flames, the cost to rebuild, and the ruination of neighborhoods where burned homes weren't restored.

His last resort was to throw himself on my mercy to help him win a sales contest. He said the prize was a week in New York! Then he went on about what good fellows the Tories in New York were. What a jerk!

It was all I could do to keep from laughing at this adolescent pitch, so centered on what he wanted than on what would be appealing to me, the prospect. He was able to finally see that I had no interest in his program, but this is when he insisted on a "gentleman's" argument about the benefits of insurance.

He talked as if I wanted my house to burn to defy him. Of course, as a renter, it wasn't my house, but he didn't bother to ascertain that. He could have made a more productive call on someone else if he had. After half the morning, he finally left. I covertly timed him to test his durability and he'd used forty-five minutes of my time..

I had occasion to meet my neighbors when they met after another robbery. We compared notes on calls Mochter made on most of them and the same line was used wherever he went. He had made no sale at the burned neighbors, or anyplace else, so we expected arson to happen to at least one of us. Knowing this, the group had asked Sheriff Mcginty to talk to us about what we could do to protect ourselves and what the sheriff's department might suggest as their official help for taxpayers.

He suggested that we keep an around-the-clock vigil, retain a barrel of water at the downspout, have half a dozen water buckets, and pray to God. He suggested that we also number our houses for ease of locating us. This was a great idea that, fire or not, would simplify other problems.

I told them the culprit's name and suggested that if he made a call on them, that they send a kid to the sheriff to tell him what we've been talking about—the connection between the attempted policy sale, robberies, and the fire. Most important was that the kid asked the sheriff to come to the victim's aid right then, right away.

This set of circumstances and suggestions didn't inspire anyone, but fires were reduced during the winter.

By this time the Treaty between the British Empire and the United States had been signed in Paris. The main feature was that we had gained our independence from Great Britain.

Our boundaries were set along the St. Croix River on the southern edge of Nova Scotia north to the forty-fifth latitude and extending to and along the St. Lawrence River to the middle line of the Great Lakes, then to the Lake of the Woods south to the source of the Mississippi River (no one knew for certain where that was) to the thirty-first latitude and east to the Apalachicola and St, Mary's rivers and the Atlantic. This excerpts the city of New Orleans, which came under Spanish control for their part in the Seven Years War.

Other features of the treaty were that the citizens had the right to fish off of New Foundland, Nova Scotia, and some small islands there, and to cure their catch on the uninhabited shores of Nova Scotia and Labrador. Creditors of both countries were to have their accounts honored, and Congress was to recommend that the states return confiscated property to Loyalists. We also had the free navigation of the Mississippi River to its mouth. No one was to be later penalized for actions during the war, and Britain was to evacuate American territory with "convenient speed."

Life would be different with redcoats and Tories off our back.

We had more than doubled our territory and gained a measure of prestige in the world at a minimal cost. That is, unless you or your family, were one of the casualties.

The Indians came out on the losing side: Because the Iroquois claimed the area from New York west to the Mississippi by right of conquest, and they sided with the British, all this was forfeit.

Subsequent treaties at Fort Stanwix specified the reservations the Indians had to live in, in New York. Take it or leave it, the Confederacy had no say in the matter. We certainly knew how to infuriate our Native Americans.

A good chunk of land in the Finger Lakes region was set aside for Revolutionary War veterans who had met the requirements for land bounties, but that's a long story that would be fitting for another chronicle.

The denouement of this chronicle, however, requires that the story of Wencesles Mochter to be completed.

Mochter thought that Annie McLauren was my wife since he saw her living in our house. He evidently thought that she was the cause of his stay at Simsbury and wanted to use threats to her as leverage to get me in a favorable position where he could harm both of us. I let him think so and told both of the girls about Mochter's most recent contribution to the crimes of Morris County.

I was afraid of this wild man, who once tried to silence me with a hoisted log when I was in a rowboat on the Schuykill. That sounds made-up but Dan Reitenhaus, alias Chief Honeoye, was there and would vouch for my story. The girls were excited to think that some adventure would enter their lives. They wanted to plan a way of finally putting Mochter away so he wouldn't bother anyone. At first, I didn't want to kill him, but as the weeks passed, I thought, why not? Getting rid of him would be best for everybody.

We schemed a plan to lock him in the house, but, ironically, we had no property insurance, and the house wasn't ours.

Next, I thought to make him curious about the Ferguson rifle. It was worth a lot more than I paid for it, and he might want me to insure it. I could irritate him so much that he'd want to kill me and use the rifle to do it. But, just in time, we would have McGinty step out and arrest him on about three or four witnessed charges.

Annie, who had experience in police work, said that all this was fantasy and it wouldn't work. But there was another step in the plan which slipped my mind, I didn't want to admit this, so I dropped the idea and asked the girls what other ideas they had.

I still wanted to recall the final act of my plan and wracked my brain to bring it out of the deep and unresponsive recesses of my brain—it had been a stunning idea and nothing to tie me, or the girls, to the "accident." It had to do with the Ferguson rifle.

I went over and over the times I had contact with Mochter: the first was the night I met Olivia at the Guy Fawkes Day dance. He had forced Olivia to a dance with him and when that dance was over he forced her again, not crudely, but it was still coercion and I and Olivia resented it because we knew the chemistry between us was right. That's right; he later accused me of stealing her from him. She had known him before as a source of landscape clients, but that was as far as it went.

The next time I saw him was truly an encounter: The old sycamore had blown over in a heavy storm which brought the roots of the tipped-over tree to about nine feet above the ground. I had been fishing the month before and hooked on to a large trout which broke the leader on the roots of the sycamore. The main thing was that I stumbled on a yellow-colored rock, which proved to be a gold ingot, entwined in the roots of the tree, and that's what I was really trying to reach when Mochter chanced on the scene.

He never saw the gold, but his knowledge of the history of a rich monastery which had been confiscated by the Tudors, made him think I had taken something of value. He complained several times but never went to the law for legal assistance.

The next time was on the Schuykill, as I've already described. That's when I met Honeoye, and Olivia and I finally met the Bartrams at his Gardens. I think the final experience was when we were fishing in the Kittatinny Mountains and we shot it out with him and his disgruntled unpaid workers. We turned him over to Annie McLauren, who since married Crispin, and worked for the American government, such as it was, for catching counterfeiters. That's when Mochter was sent to Simsbury Mines.

If I were him, I would be infuriated for some young nobody giving me so much trouble over fake currency. After all, Benjamin Franklin made some of his estate printing the stuff. But that's irrelevant. Put this all together and there must be some way I can snare Mochter into a trap. That's what I said in an effort to scheme his capture.

Oh! I forgot the first thing we did to annoy him when we were boys: Crispin rebuilt faulty seat supports in Mochter's outhouse; and we were on watch to warn him of Mochter coming near. What a fall in the crap for the deserving! If I remind him of all that, perhaps he'll get so angry as to get at us and his demise. I still think the rifle has a part to play.

After a period of re-thinking, we all came to the conclusion that we were making Mochter's capture too complicated. We could simply wait for him to make his call, let him in and tie him up, and inform sheriff McGinty. The problem would be waiting for him and later, for McGinty. We waited now with apprehension.

One other item was to make sure I had powder and ball to fit the barrel of the Ferguson, and put both within sight of the rifle inside the tool shed. I had finally remembered the part to be played by the rifle! But how was I to kill him? Since the war, I couldn't pull the trigger on anybody.

About two weeks later, a neighbor's kid ran over to our house saying that Mochter was in the neighborhood and we should be on the alert. We gave the kid some cookies, thanked him, and sent him back to his home. Both Annie and Olivia stood back of the windows to watch for him and his horse. It had taken about an hour for two neighbors to listen and send him on his way, but our house was next.

When he knocked on the door, I called for him to come around back, I had planned to be at the tool shed when he called; it was part of my scheme.

This time he had a leather portfolio containing printed leaflets on his insurance which he handed to me and began to browbeat me with its virtues. I disagreed with him enough to get him extremely angry so that he picked up the rifle and butted me in the gut so that he knocked the wind out of me and I fell. I was dizzy and not sure what then happened, but when I was able to stand, he was busy loading the rifle.

Now, what I had forgotten (and finally recalled) came into play. The Ferguson rifle was breach loading rather than loaded from the muzzle, but he didn't know that, and was loading it the usual way, as one would load a flintlock, so that it now had two loads, instead of one. As a double-shotted rifle, it would explode when he pulled the trigger.

I turned to run and noticed the girls had come to the back windows and had seen all; his knocking my wind out, loading the gun, and aiming it at my head. They screamed and I ducked away from an expected explosion that I thought would kill both of us. Mochter lowered the gun, I assume because he smelled a trap with the girls watching and neighbors staring from their yards. But he brought the piece back up and squeezed the trigger.

I was all right and out of harm's way. But Mochter was bloody all over and had fallen on top of the tools. His last words were, "Why'd you do that? I was just trying to sell insurance!"

McGinty arrived on a scene he wasn't expecting. He shook my hand and said there was a reward from the North American Insurance Company for apprehending a man who was tarnishing their business by misrepresentation. The next day, I received an answer to my quest of Brown Belt: we had a dividend account with nine hundred pounds, and our shares had doubled!

Olivia and I sent a note to our friends about our good luck and invited them to a party on Guy Fawkes Day, November fifth. This was Olivia's and my eighth anniversary of meeting each other. There were twenty present, but our best friends were Crispin, Annie, Trevor Shaw, Chief Honeoye, and Bill Farrell, my old book-store friend and his witty wife from Peekskill. What a party that was!

BIBLIOGRAPHY

BOATNER, Mark Mayo III. *Encyclopedia of the American Revolution.* Bicentennial Edition. David McKay Company Inc. New York p.1290

ECKERT, Allan W. *Wilderness War.* Bantam Books. New York, 1982 p.564

FISCHER, David Hackett. *Washington's Crossing.* Oxford University Press. Oxford, 2004 p.564

FORBES, Esther. *Paul Revere & The World He Lived In.* Houghton Mifflin Company. Boston, 1942 p.510

FORD, Howard S. *Sure Signs: Stories Behind the Historical Markers of Central New York.* 1stBooks. Bloomington, Indiana, 2002 p.394

LUNDIN, Leonard. *Cockpit of the Revolution: The War for Independence in New Jersey.* Princeton University Press. Princeton, 1940 p.463

NICKERSON, Hoffman. *The Turning Point Of The Revolution or Burgoyne In America.* Scholar's Workshop. New Jersey, 1928 p.500

ABOUT THE AUTHOR

AFTER WRITING SURE Signs: Stories Behind the Historical Markers of Central New York, Howard Ford wrote Some Call it Treason, a novel about a young English couple and their friend who, together, visited the American colonies and joined the rebels just before the Revolution. The second book in the series, In All Cases Whatsoever, released in 2012, reflects the unwavering arrogance of the English government, an attitude largely responsible for the war. Those who fought the Revolution, whether soldier or spy, were not only brave, but cunning and resourceful, and worthy of our attention for their fortitude. A Just Cause is the third and final book in this exciting historical fiction trilogy.

Ford is retired from the financial services industry. He and his wife, Ann, live in upstate New York.

www.ingramcontent.com/pod-product-compliance
Lightning Source LLC
Chambersburg PA
CBHW021436020726
47499CB00006BA/2023